THE RIVER

By Beverly Lewis

HOME TO HICKORY HOLLOW
The Fiddler
The Bridesmaid
The Guardian
The Secret Keeper
The Last Bride

THE ROSE TRILOGY
The Thorn • *The Judgment* • *The Mercy*

ABRAM'S DAUGHTERS
The Covenant • *The Betrayal* • *The Sacrifice*
The Prodigal • *The Revelation*

THE HERITAGE OF LANCASTER COUNTY
The Shunning • *The Confession* • *The Reckoning*

ANNIE'S PEOPLE
The Preacher's Daughter • *The Englisher* • *The Brethren*

THE COURTSHIP OF NELLIE FISHER
The Parting • *The Forbidden* • *The Longing*

SEASONS OF GRACE
The Secret • *The Missing* • *The Telling*

The Postcard • *The Crossroad*
The Redemption of Sarah Cain
October Song • *Sanctuary* (with David Lewis) • *The Sunroom*
Child of Mine (with David Lewis) • *The River*
The Love Letters • *The Photograph*

Amish Prayers
The Beverly Lewis Amish Heritage Cookbook

www.beverlylewis.com

BEVERLY LEWIS

THE RIVER

BETHANYHOUSE
a division of Baker Publishing Group
Minneapolis, Minnesota

© 2014 by Beverly M. Lewis, Inc.

Published by Bethany House Publishers
11400 Hampshire Avenue South
Bloomington, Minnesota 55438
www.bethanyhouse.com

Bethany House Publishers is a division of
Baker Publishing Group, Grand Rapids, Michigan

Printed in the United States of America

Library of Congress Cataloging-in-Publication Data
Lewis, Beverly.
    The River / Beverly Lewis.
        pages cm
        Summary: "When two sisters return home for a visit after leaving the Amish world, both are troubled by the secrets—and the people—they left behind"— Provided by publisher.
        ISBN 978-0-7642-1273-4 (cloth : alk. paper) — ISBN 978-0-7642-1245-1 (pbk. : alk. paper) — ISBN 978-0-7642-1274-1 (large-print pbk. : alk. paper)
        1. Amish—Fiction. 2. Sisters—Fiction. 3. Lancaster County (Pa.)—Fiction. 4. Christian fiction. I. Title.
    PS3562.E9383R58 2014
    813'.54—dc23   2014012199

Scripture quotations are from the King James Version of the Bible.

Cover design by Dan Thornberg, Design Source Creative Services
Art direction by Paul Higdon

16 17 18 19 20 21 22   9 8 7 6 5 4 3

To
Loretta Steiger,
with love and gratitude
for all the years of our friendship.

Give unto them beauty for ashes,
the oil of joy for mourning,
the garment of praise for the spirit of heaviness. . . .

—Isaiah 61:3 KJV

PROLOGUE

AUTUMN 1977

My Amish family would be shocked to lay eyes on me now, considering my chin-length hair, makeup, and jeans. They'd be just as dismayed by my home's modern appliances—the freezer, the microwave, the dishwasher, all miraculously fueled by electricity. And they'd be stunned at how easily I've taken to driving a car, a *red* car, no less, as if I'd been born an Englisher.

So, needless to say, I'm digging in my heels about returning home for my parents' anniversary gathering at the farmhouse where I managed to grow up without any of the conveniences I now take for granted.

Honestly, I figure there's no need to add salt to an open wound. Besides, I've never known anyone to celebrate such things in Eden Valley. Not amongst the Plain folk I was raised around.

Even so, my oldest brother, Melvin, wrote urging me to come, adding: *And please bring Ruthie. It's ever so important. Everyone else will be there!*

Everyone? It seems like decades since I stepped off the screened-in back porch and waved good-bye to poor worried *Mamm* and Lancaster County. But it's only been eight years, to be exact.

Despite how quickly I acclimated to the fancy world, my Amish roots are planted deep within me. My Englisher husband confirms that fact frequently as he witnesses my devotion to hard work and my continuing appreciation for gardening, sewing, and cooking from scratch. And I know he values my efforts to inspire a love of the simple gifts—biblical characteristics essential for a happy life—in our four-year-old twin daughters. After all, it's both a blessing and a challenge to grow up in the world of the English.

Dawdi Mast, my mother's *Daed*, would turn in his grave if he knew I'd embraced the fancy life. But believe me, I never abandoned *das Alt Gebrauch*—the Old Ways—to cause anyone ill. Some probably suspect I fled to escape the enduring strain between my tetchy father and me, and two of my older brothers—Chester, as well as Joseph, one of the twins. Goodness, but Daed and I never saw eye to eye, always feuding about one thing or another, neither of us giving in a speck.

Mainly, though, I had to leave because of little Anna. *Precious Anna, never forgotten, forever missed.* The memories of my sister's accident are still so raw and real. *Ach,* those bitter years following that dreadful day . . . forever impressed on my heart.

Some of the People thought it was the enticing draw of the Conestoga River—the sweep of its power—that lured my five-year-old sister to its blustery banks that mid-July day. Others spoke *vorwitzich*—boldly—of God's sovereign will, saying that it was sweet Anna's time to depart this old world.

But I knew the truth. My little sister drowned because of me.

I glanced again at Melvin's handwritten note and wondered just how hard it would be to step back into the muddle of my Plain family—six married brothers and our aging parents. Melvin had hinted that our father was no longer his vigorous self at fifty-eight.

"Will I regret *not* going?" I wondered aloud.

I turned toward the kitchen window as Kris's brand-new apple-red 1977 Buick Skylark pulled into the driveway. He'd taken our girls to run a few "secret errands" after working at Rockport Hardware, where he was now manager.

Promptly, I stuffed the invitation into the nearest drawer, reluctant to broach the topic with my husband as he made plans for my thirty-first birthday, a little more than a week away.

From my vantage point, I watched our identical golden-haired darlings get out of the car, all smiles and giggles, so similar in likeness to little Anna when she was their age. How remarkable that the Lord had seen fit to give me two constant reminders of my youngest sister. Some days, it was almost haunting.

Naturally, Kris had never seen pictures of Anna, because according to the church ordinance, they were forbidden. The second commandment was ever my family's guide on that subject, yet I'd known Amish couples to stray from the bishop's strict rule, snapping furtive photos of their newborns.

My twins, Jenya and Tavani, their birthday purchases in hand, scampered toward the front door, eyes bright. All the while, my brain noodled Melvin's invitation. *Can I bring myself to do this?* I wondered. *Will Daed and Mamm even welcome me?*

One thing was sure: I would *not* return to Amish country without my only living sister as a kind of buffer. And since the chances of Ruth agreeing to go at all, even with me, were slim to none, I finally dismissed the notion and opened my arms to our daughters.

Kris waited patiently for his own hug and inquired about supper, beaming his contagious smile at me as the twins hurried off to their rooms, jabbering to each other.

"Did you find everything you went for?" I teased, going to the fridge.

"The birthday girl's not supposed to ask questions." Kris winked. "Isn't that what you always tell *us*?"

Lost in thought, I removed the defrosted chicken, recalling the days I gutted Daed's chickens and turkeys. Ruthie was the plucker. Oh, the long, tiresome days pulling innards out of those dead birds.

"Hon?"

I turned, dazed, caught between two worlds. "Oh . . . right." I paused, raising my palms. "No, really, I have everything I want right here," I said to Kris. "You, the girls, and our life together."

A quizzical expression crossed my husband's handsome face, and his dark eyes penetrated mine. "You all right, hon?"

My husband always knew. He just did. But I wasn't ready to talk about my brother's note. Not yet. Not until I phoned Ruthie to see how quickly she, too, might dismiss the idea.

I gave Kris a half-hearted shrug, and he touched my arm. "We'll talk when you're ready," he said softly. "Okay?"

"Sure." I smiled faintly.

Kris nodded and reached for the newspaper on the counter.

He headed down the few steps to the family room while I washed my hands to prepare supper.

Truth be told, there was no way Ruth would think of returning to the scene of her own private heartache. *"Nix kumm raus*—Nothin' doing!" she would say. She'd demonstrated real dignity when Wilmer Kauffman ditched her for the Jamborees. And while we both had been taught to forgive, I doubted Ruthie would ever quite forget. In fact, her wrenching disappointment had played right into the joy of having her join me in the English world, five years after my own hasty exit from our secluded Amish valley—yet another reason for our parents' frustration with me.

I stole her from them. Occasionally, I felt some remorse over that. But now we were both reasonably settled in Rockport, Massachusetts, like two fugitives from the Amish world, living our fancy lives within walking distance of the harbor.

No, pondering Ruth's painful past and my own unsettled issues, the answer was clear to me. Our Amish siblings would just have to carry on without us at the November celebration. And that's all there was to it.

CHAPTER 1

Eden Valley.

Someone perceptive had chosen the name for the verdant area where Melvin Lantz and his five married brothers resided. Although empty nesters, their parents, Lester and Sylvia, continued to work the farm at the old homestead just west of Melvin's, near the turnoff to Stone Road.

Back when that section of God's green earth was first organized into a rural community of acreage and roads, someone had also decided the narrow road running past Melvin's big farm should be called Eden Road. It was true that the surrounding farmland and woodlots, corncribs, and lines of fields were often described as almost heavenly by the good folk who lived and worked there, including Melvin himself.

No, there was absolutely no doubt in Melvin's mind that the Lord God above had reached His mighty hand down and placed a second Eden-like garden right in the midst of them. And as strongly as he felt about it, Melvin couldn't help but wonder why his sisters hadn't managed to stay put there with the People.

From the doorway of his harness and tack shop, the thirty-eight-year-old Amishman watched his younger brother Joseph lift the reins and head out of the lane with his horse and open wagon.

Don't be too antsy, Melvin told himself, recalling the uneasy conversation with Joseph just now. After all, it had been only a week since he figured his Plain-turned-fancy sisters had received his invitation by mail. But to think Joseph was already pushing his nose in to see if there'd been a response.

Tilly and Ruth, Melvin thought, buttoning his black work coat. *Such an impudent pair!*

It wasn't the first time he'd considered them in such a light. Even now, it still unnerved him when he thought of Tilly's gall in persuading their more mild-mannered sibling, just twenty at the time, to leave behind her upbringing. The whole thing had stumped him and his wife, Susannah. But then, you just never knew what people were thinking deep in their heart of hearts.

The Good Lord knew, though, and Melvin had tried not to let his sisters' leaving get the best of him. All the same, his father believed it was a blemish upon their family, even though Tilly and Ruth had never surrendered their lives in holy baptism, joining church. And with Tilly married and solidly settled in the English world, her return was near impossible. But that didn't stop Melvin from hoping and praying that *Gott* might lead Ruth back to where she belonged.

Somehow . . .

Shielding his eyes, Melvin watched a crow spread its black wings wide and coast easily across the gray sky. He wondered if Tilly, especially, was ever sorry she'd spread her own restless wings. That kind of freedom was what his wife and two of his brothers assumed Tilly had sought in stepping away from the church. As for Ruthie, however, none of them really understood why she had followed in her older sister's footsteps. Not when she'd always before made her own decisions.

Melvin forced out a breath, knowing it was time to get back to work. It was a mild October day with scarcely a breeze. *The air sure could use a good clearing out*, he thought, recalling his wife saying the same thing that very morning as she eyed the dreary sky. *"All the poor folk round the valley suffering here lately with sore throats and runny noses could certainly benefit."* Recently, she'd seemed more eager for the arrival of cold weather than other autumns. She was even busy sewing two coats—one for herself, the other for a sister. It dawned on him that she might be wishing Tilly and Ruth were around to make coats for, too. But no, they'd been gone too long for her to think that.

My dear Susannah, he thought. *The girls' leaving tore her heart up, same as Mamm's. . . .*

Down near the front of the house, not far from Eden Road, Melvin spotted his next younger brother shuffling up the lane. Though just thirty-six, Chester had lost his easy stride after his oldest son, Curly Pete, left the People with plans to join the army as soon as possible.

Melvin carried a soft spot in his heart for poor Chester, who'd been through rough waters with his boy. "Hullo, *Bruder*!" called Melvin, moving away from the shop just yards from the back door of his house. He walked toward Chester. "What brings ya?"

"Ain't gonna be but a minute." Chester offered nary a smile. Something was up.

"Just killin' time, then?"

"*Nee*. Not a'tall." Chester removed his black felt hat, then motioned for Melvin to go inside the harness shop and followed in step right behind. The familiar smell of oil and cleaners filled the air. Chester glanced about the place, as if checking to see if they were alone. "Might I speak bluntly, Melvin?"

"Why should today be different than any other?"

Chester's gray eyes narrowed. "Have ya heard anything back from Tilly and Ruth?"

"Not a word."

"Well now, that wonders me."

Melvin drew a slow breath before saying what was on his mind. "I doubt they'll come at all."

Shaking his head, Chester muttered, "Probably embarrassed after turnin' away from Plain life like they did." He turned to sit himself down on the three-legged stool by one of the wooden worktables. Behind him a wall of shelving was bursting with bridles and lines, essential equipment to help driving horses pull buggies with ease. Chester leaned his elbow on the table and glanced at the ceiling, then at Melvin. "Best be contacting them again in a week or so, if ya don't hear back right soon."

"Why's that?" Melvin asked, not wanting to push the issue with either Tilly or Ruth. After all, other than an occasional letter to Mamm or one of the womenfolk from Ruth, they hardly had contact with them.

"Not to worry ya, but . . ."

"What is it?" Melvin frowned.

Chester picked up a nearly finished bridle from the worktable as if to inspect it. "Wasn't gonna say anything, but maybe I oughta." He paused and made eye contact again. "I just came from visiting Daed and Mamm. To tell the truth, our father's lookin' awful pale. Whiter than fresh milk."

18

Melvin didn't like hearing this. "He's been complaining 'bout his heart racing and sometimes skipping beats, Mamm says. But I didn't think it was that bad."

Chester nodded slowly. "Heard that, too."

"Has he seen a doctor?"

"A few days ago, *jah*." Chester looked down at his hat. Then, slowly, he raised his eyes to meet Melvin's. "Doc says he might need a pacemaker if he wants to live much longer."

Daed won't hear of it, Melvin knew full well, and the knowledge settled uneasily into his gut.

The two of them were mighty quiet, and the sound of Melvin's hunting dog filled his ears just now. The old hound was barking himself nearly hoarse, down by the road.

At last Melvin said quietly, "How long can Daed manage . . . without it?"

"Optimistically? A few months, according to the doctor." Chester's face was grim. "Like I said, better try and call our sisters. I 'spect if one comes, the other will follow."

Melvin doubted it. Although he'd sent Tilly an invitation, he couldn't imagine her showing up, with or without Ruth.

Besides, Melvin disliked using their father's poor ticker to get the two of them home for the anniversary. Just didn't seem right.

Nee . . . *better they come on their own, without anyone pushin'.*

Melvin's wife served his favorite meal at noon—buttered noodles and hot porcupine meatballs with onions and ground black pepper. It was one of Susannah's best-ever dishes.

Later, after a dessert of chocolate fudge pudding, he lingered at the head of the table—his designated spot. It was a rare moment when he was alone with his wife there in the kitchen. Their teenage sons, Caleb and Benny, had made themselves scarce this afternoon and hurried back out to the barn, and then who knew where. His boys were in the midst of their *Rumschpringe*—the running-around years—and Melvin, though he'd raised them to be God-fearing young men, found himself frequently giving them up to the Lord God's protection and grace.

Susannah kept studying him, like she sensed he was procrastinating on something. And she was right, even though he'd never been one to put off important things before. His father had disciplined that character flaw clean out of him.

Truth be told, he wasn't the best choice to phone Tilly. Not in the least. He sat there, trying to relax. Susannah's eyes twinkled as she mentioned a wedding quilt for one of their many nieces.

"I want to help stitch it up a few days from now," she said.

He gave a nod, soaking in her presence. Like him, she was creeping up on forty, but Susannah was still attractive, without a speck of gray in her hair.

"You're awful quiet, dear." She reached for his hand. "Everything all right?"

He hemmed and hawed, then finally revealed what Chester had told him about Daed's weak heart. "Ya know, I really hate havin' to tell my sisters this," he admitted. "Bad enough having to tell it to you."

"Even so, they oughta know, *jah*?" Susannah pursed her lips, her gentle eyes on him.

He nodded, grateful for her cool hand in his.

Her shoulders rose and fell. "Well, and if Chester knows what he's talking 'bout, it might just be the last time the whole family gathers for—"

"Now, now, Susannah, we don't know anything of the kind. We'll leave that with the Lord, all right?"

With a bob of her head, she slid her hand away and rose to carry the dessert dishes to the sink.

He sat still, recalling the last time the family had been together, all of them. Back before Tilly left. Daed and Tilly had butted heads, enough to keep Tilly away for such a long time. It seemed that very little ever got past Daed when it came to that sister. He was her brick wall, so to speak, and looking back, Melvin realized she'd regularly pounded her head against that wall. And for the hundredth time, he wondered why Daed and Tilly had been at odds. *From her early childhood . . .*

Without saying more, Melvin stood and made his way out to the back room, where he pulled on his work coat, still thinking about his ailing father. Always such a strong man . . . till now.

The door squeaked when he opened it, and he decided to turn right around and go back inside, where he found the WD-40 and sprayed the hinges. Then, once he'd returned the spray back to its shelf, Melvin finally headed outdoors and picked his way over the acreage, fertile land farmed for two hundred years and counting. Aware of the hush that afternoon, he squinted into the sun and thanked God for this peaceful place just south of Strasburg, hidden away from the world and its temptations.

Lord, grant me the right words tonight, he prayed. *And if it be Thy will, soften Tilly and Ruth's hearts to the family . . . and our need of them at this time.*

CHAPTER 2

*R*uth Lantz sat on the tall wooden stool rewriting her grocery list in what her Mamm would not consider a real kitchen, it was that small. "A *gut* thing she won't ever see it," muttered Ruth, fretting over which of many Amish recipes to make tomorrow evening for supper. She had been planning the get-together with three of her friends from church, craving some good fellowship. On such occasions, she was ever so thankful for the recipes she'd stored away in her head. Amish recipes, passed down through the generations as if by osmosis—merely by watching her mother gather the ingredients and mix them together. Mamm had never spoken to her about any of the ingredients or instructions as Ruth worked alongside her, even when Ruth was but a child. Yet somehow she'd managed to absorb them simply by doing, just as her sister had.

Goodness, must I think back to all that? Ruth checked on the amount of milk and orange juice in her fridge, and chuckled at the memories. It wasn't often she allowed her thoughts to creep back to those days, but there were times when she felt more connected to her childhood than others. This afternoon was one of them.

Eyeing her checkbook, she considered reconciling it against her bank statement, then dismissed the idea, putting it off. *It's been a long and tiresome week*, she thought, stretching. In spite of feeling tired, she was glad for her job as a medical records assistant—within walking distance of her house, even though she owned a car, purchased shortly after leaving Eden Valley.

When the phone rang, Ruth hesitated to answer. Even after three years, she would readily admit to being startled by its shrill sound. Lately, though, she had been getting calls from James Montgomery, a very nice young man who'd taken her out for coffee, then a lovely dinner at a restaurant near the Rockport harbor. She was becoming fond of him and liked the fact that he was active in her church as an usher and a Sunday school teacher for junior-high boys. *I think he's sweet on me*, she thought, wondering if Jim might be calling again.

At the thought, she slid off the stool and took the receiver out of its cradle on the wall. "Hullo, Ruth Lantz speaking."

"Ruthie . . . it's your brother Melvin."

She managed to find her voice. "Melvin? Such a long time since we've talked."

He agreed and went on somewhat hesitantly to ask if she'd received his invitation.

"I did, but . . ." She was afraid he'd hang up if she said right away that she couldn't go.

"Ain't a party, really," he said now. "And prob'ly not anything you're used to anymore. Just the whole family getting together under the same roof . . . again. To mark the day, ya know."

"It's nice to be included, but honestly, it's such short notice."

She decided not to string him along. "I can't go without taking time off work."

"*Jah*, expected that." He sighed. "Have ya heard at all from Tilly 'bout this?"

"Not just yet," she replied, knowing Tilly wouldn't think of going back for anything.

He was quiet for a moment. "Well, I was hopin' you two would consider comin' together, maybe." There was something in Melvin's tone, something that made her tense.

"I just don't know."

"I planned to call Tilly but decided at the last minute to dial you up first."

At least he's frank, she thought, a swell of memories rushing back.

"Well, if ya can't come, I understand," he said flatly.

Ruth almost said, *"No, you don't,"* but knew better than to speak up to her eldest brother. She wondered what to say.

"But, Ruthie, ya need to know . . . our father's in an awful bad way. It's his heart. The doctor's saying he's only got a few months unless he gets a pacemaker. And you know Daed."

Tears sprang to her eyes. "Such terrible news." She sighed audibly. "Tilly needs to be told. She really does."

"Would ya mind callin' her, then?"

"I'll fill her in, sure."

"Right away?" Melvin's words seemed to catch in his throat. She promised she would.

How very odd to think their own brother couldn't bring himself to contact Tilly, yet he didn't seem to mind calling her. This was, after all, the first time Ruth had spoken to anyone in the family but Mamm since she embraced the English life.

She thanked Melvin for calling and said good-bye. After

she hung up, Ruth held her breath, then slowly let herself slide down the wall, devastated by the news. She sat on the linoleum, crossing her legs and rubbing her knees, suddenly aware of the soft denim of her worldly jeans.

In all truth, hearing her brother's voice in her ear was like saying good-bye to Eden Valley all over again. But even now Ruth refused to let herself think too much about the conclusion of her former life. Or Will Kauffman.

"I don't really want to go," Ruth told Tilly by phone a few minutes later. "And I know *you* don't, either." She'd kept her promise to Melvin by calling their sister, and it was clear that Tilly was on the same page with her. "So it's settled, then," Ruth stated.

"Absolutely." Tilly sounded as certain as ever. Ruth could just imagine her sister's tight expression. "I might consider going in ten years, for their fiftieth," Tilly said, laughing a little.

"If Daed's still alive."

Tilly was quiet for a moment. "So he *is* ailing, then?"

"Evidently so." Then, realizing she was soft-pedaling, she told her, "Melvin sounded worried."

Tilly's silence then surely meant she was considering all of that, but in the end she dug in her heels, even after Ruth explained about Daed's heart trouble. And surprisingly, Tilly quickly turned the conversation around to their small city's harvest festival and the annual Scarecrow Stroll. "Rockport's the place to be this time of year, Ruthie. It'll be fun . . . remember last October?"

Ruth recalled walking her feet off, visiting every last one of the little shops that backed up to the harbor and voting for

26

their favorite scarecrows with Tilly and her twins, Jenya and Tavani. "Let's take the girls along again," said Ruth.

"It'd be great to see you," Tilly said. "How about stopping by tomorrow night, too? Besides church, it's been a couple weeks. We don't live neighbors, of course, but we're not that far away, dear sister."

"It *has* been too long," Ruth agreed, remembering how often they'd gotten together at each other's homes when she first moved to the area. *After Tilly helped me leave Eden Valley.*

"The twins are growin' so fast," Tilly said, her tone more thoughtful. Ruth guessed she might still be pondering Melvin's urging them to come. The news of their father's health must be weighing on her, too, just as it was on Ruth. Tilly would never admit that, however.

Ruth begged off politely, saying she had dinner plans. "Some friends from church are coming over."

"Another time, then?"

"Next week?" Ruth could hear the twins in the background, clamoring for their mother's attention. "Well, I'd better let you go . . . sounds like you're busy."

"The girls send their love to *Aendi* Ruth," Tilly added. "Take care now."

Aendi . . .

"Talk to ya later."

Tilly said good-bye, too, then hung up.

Ruth turned to look at the sky, that sliver of blue she could just see from her small brownstone on the edge of town. She pondered her older sister's reaction to the invitation and seeming disinterest in their father's health. Why was Tilly so closed to their Amish family?

Moving to the other end of the small kitchen, Ruth stopped

to reach up and straighten her hand-stitched wall sampler. She had sewn it the same fall she'd turned sixteen, the fall she'd just started to attend Sunday-night Singings and other youth gatherings. *When Wilmer first began courting me.*

She ran her pointer finger over the smooth satin stitching, a pictorial representation of Eden Valley, complete with the one-room schoolhouse she and Tilly both had attended. "Before things fell apart."

Glancing outside at the sky again, she wondered how she'd feel if their father passed away before she had the chance to see him again.

Ruth checked her wristwatch and put on her belted navy blue all-weather coat. Then, after grabbing her grocery list and shoulder bag, she made her way out the back door. "Time's a-wastin'," she said, once again dismissing the invitation.

Just isn't meant to be.

"What'd Tilly say?" Susannah asked after Melvin trudged in the back door. Thankfully, she'd waited long enough for him to sit down and get comfortable near her shiny black cookstove. Stretching out his stocking feet, he was glad for the warmth of the dying embers.

"Well, I put in the call to Ruthie instead," he admitted.

Susannah was *schmaert* enough to sense when he was upset. A good thing, too, since he didn't have it in him to repeat the phone conversation word for word. "So, are they comin'?" she asked.

Melvin shook his head. "There's no getting Tilly back here. And whether or not Ruth will come, I'd hate to say." He drew a breath. "Not sure we'll ever see those two again."

"I'm so sorry, dear." She studied him. "I hope ya know, you're a very caring brother."

Despite his gloomy outlook, he did harbor a small fraction of hope for Ruth to come, now that she knew of their father's struggle, health-wise. As for Tilly . . . well, her reluctance didn't mean she was a heartless person—to the contrary. *She's sensitive like nobody's business.*

Melvin pressed his thumb and pointer finger around the metal band he wore on his right hand and twisted it repeatedly. Far as he knew, he was the youngest Amishman round Eden Valley who suffered with arthritis. The bishop didn't mind that he and a few others wore the healing rings to help alleviate pain.

Bishop doesn't mind, but Daed does, he thought. *How's that right?*

By now, Tilly had likely turned Ruth against their father, and maybe all of them. Why else was Ruth so adamant about not coming?

People can get off work if they really need to. . . .

Susannah's face looked soft in the golden hue of the old gas lamp hanging over the kitchen table. "If Tilly stays away, maybe it's 'cause she's still angry. Could that be?" she asked.

"It wonders me."

Susannah continued. "Some months ago, your mother told me privately that she thinks it was best that Tilly left."

He was surprised his mother would tell his wife such a thing, though the womenfolk did have ample time to talk—*or is it gossip?*—at canning bees and applesauce making.

"Some things are better left unsaid," Susannah said real quiet-like.

So his wife did sense something amiss, but since he wasn't

one to press, Melvin let it be. "I'm thinkin' we'll just go ahead then and plan things as is," he decided. "Unless we hear otherwise."

"You've done what you could, Melvin."

He wasn't so sure. After all, he could've said more to get Ruthie to budge a little. *Plenty more.*

CHAPTER 3

*R*uth set the small kitchen table with her yellow-and-white-checkered place mats the following afternoon, wanting things as pretty as possible for her friends. She'd made a pot of delicious cabbage patch stew, which she'd always loved as a girl, hoping Cathy, Jeannie, and Lorna would enjoy it, too. Ruth had also planned for a pan of homemade corn bread and some red beet eggs, as well as the dill pickles she'd put up last summer with Tilly. After the cozy eating nook was to her liking, she hurried to fry up the apple fritters. *Mamm's favorite.*

Jeannie Marshall, whom Ruth had known the longest of the three young women, had phoned earlier to ask if they might play Dutch Blitz, a game she'd heard of from a friend of a friend in Lancaster County. Ruth wasn't especially keen on revisiting that particular game—one she and Will had played frequently with other couples—yet she'd agreed to play tonight. After all, Jeannie was her guest. *"It'll be so interesting to have this glimpse into your former life,"* the brunette with a penchant for drama had told her.

Interesting was the hallmark of the entire meal, as it turned out. Cathy Donaldson, whom Ruth had met a few weeks ago and now hoped to introduce to Jeannie and Lorna, brought along a black photo album she'd organized over the years, and after dessert plates were cleared away, she shared the history behind a number of pictures of her older brother, Richard.

"I always called him Ricky because I couldn't address him by such a formal name. Richard just did not fit," said Cathy, her brown eyes alight. "Ricky was the kind of person who attracted others without really trying. Ever know anyone like that?"

Ruth had, but she wouldn't open that door. She rarely divulged much about her former Plain life. *Plain as custard . . .*

Lorna Musser nodded her head and bit her lip. "What do you think made Ricky such a magnetic personality?"

"We'd *all* like to know," Jeannie said, glancing at Ruth and leaning closer to the table to see the page of pictures in Cathy's album.

Cathy described his friendly, caring manner. "And, as you can see, he had good looks. But there was something about the way he talked to you; a person knew he really wanted to listen."

"He was fond of people," Ruth said. *Like Will Kauffman,* she caught herself thinking.

"Was he ever!" Cathy turned the page to reveal a sequence of birthday photos where Richard was squeezing his eyes shut and supposedly making a wish, then blowing out the birthday candles, accepting a piece of chocolate cake from someone's hand, and taking his first bite. "Ricky was also the most confident and optimistic person I've ever known," Cathy added.

Ruth wondered why Cathy was intent on talking in the past tense about her brother. "Was this birthday an extra-special one, maybe?" she asked.

Cathy covered the magnetic pages with her hands and

looked away for a long moment. "Yes, it was. You see, Ricky died three months after this birthday. Just seventeen."

Lorna gasped, and the mood in the kitchen grew solemn.

"I cherish these pictures because of that," she said more quietly.

Jeannie was the first to speak. "Oh, honey . . . we're so sorry."

So awful sad, thought Ruth, unable to say anything. She felt herself closing up suddenly, pushing the sadness away and wishing Cathy hadn't brought the photos.

Lorna sighed and asked to see the album more closely. She turned the page back to the first photo of Ricky.

Cathy stared down at the table. "This weekend's the eighth anniversary of Ricky's death," she told them. "I miss him terribly."

They sat there, visibly subdued. Jeannie was sympathetic yet somehow managed to steer the conversation in a new direction, to her sister's engagement and forthcoming wedding next spring.

Later, after an amusing game of Dutch Blitz, Cathy looked somehow different to Ruth, as if her intimate sharing had altered her. As much as Ruth wanted the evening to go well, she wasn't sure Cathy had enjoyed herself after the pictures and all the talk about Ricky.

Ruth and her friends lingered in the front room, relaxing and chatting about upcoming church events.

After a time, when they were putting on their coats, Cathy thanked Ruth for the Amish-style meal. "I really hope I didn't put a damper on things," she added more softly.

"No, no. I'm glad you felt comfortable sharing," she replied, trying to be gracious.

"You're very kind, Ruth. Thank you."

The four of them exchanged good-byes, and Ruth's friends headed outdoors to their individual cars.

Felt comfortable sharing . . . The irony of Ruth's own words wasn't lost on her as she returned to the kitchen to wash dishes by hand. Ruth was comfortable sharing her recipes, but her darkest days in Eden Valley . . . those were something she only talked about with Tilly.

Later, once Ruth had finished drying the dishes, she went to sit in the chair where Cathy had sat at supper, staring over at the colorful handmade sampler on the wall, which presently hung perfectly straight. Her gaze fell on the weatherworn phone shanty she'd embroidered years before; she wished now she'd never included it. *"Be careful who you love,"* Uncle Abner Mast had once stated.

He wasn't kidding. Ruth thought again of her first beau.

Uncle Abner was her mother's oldest brother and, because of his years, quite level-headed.

"Why wasn't I more careful?" Ruth whispered, getting up out of habit to sweep the floor. But no, she wouldn't let herself think on that, not on top of everything else tonight.

In many ways, the supper had been a success, yet she wondered why Cathy Donaldson had felt the need to tell them about her brother's death, and why hearing about it had nagged Ruth so.

Ruth shrugged it off and finished sweeping the floor, getting into all the corners beneath the cupboards. When that was done, she moseyed into the cozy living room, where she turned on her small radio. It was one of her few worldly pleasures, besides her car. She did not yet own a television, nor did she care to, and she permitted herself only wholesome books, especially devotionals.

She reached for the newspaper and flipped through it, but

her heart wasn't in it. Restless, she pushed one of the sofa pillows behind her head and reclined, thinking ahead to seeing her friend Jim Montgomery tomorrow at the small community church up the street. It was nothing at all like the house-church gatherings of her Amish upbringing. No bishop and no dress code. There was a world missions program she found intriguing, as did Jim, who talked of someday traveling overseas to some of these church-related projects.

A pitter-patter of critter feet scampered across the roof at that moment, and she visualized a long-tailed red squirrel. She'd heard stories of her older brother Chester's son Curly Pete leaving food out for the squirrels as part of his daily chores, particularly during the late fall months . . . when he was little.

Unable to relax, Ruth got up and went to draw her bathwater. All the while, she felt plagued by the thought of her father's failing health. She knew she must talk to Tilly again . . . soon.

Tonight, she decided, after a good, long soak.

Tilly immediately sensed something was wrong when Ruthie called. Her sister certainly didn't sound her cheerful self and may have even been crying. No, Tilly realized she *was* crying, and the more they talked, the raspier Ruth's voice became.

"Why *shouldn't* we reconsider the trip?" Ruthie was saying, calming down a bit now. "I mean, because of Daed's heart."

Tilly was puzzled. "I thought we'd agreed not to go. What's changed your mind?"

"A couple of things." Ruth sounded more sad than upset. "But I can't see my way clear without you along."

"Look, I know this has to be enormous to come full circle like this, sister, but—"

35

"Please understand, it's not that I *want* to go. But I think we *ought* to." Ruthie sniffled into the phone.

Tilly felt a sudden sense of dread. "Have you thought about . . . going alone?"

"I can't, Tilly. Not without you."

Tilly didn't appreciate being pushed into a corner. "I don't know. I'll have to think about it some. I never really imagined myself going back, you know . . . even for a few days."

"I understand." Ruth was quiet for a beat. "But I couldn't bear it by myself."

The idea of returning to spend time with their family—to see Daed and Mamm face-to-face without anyone to support her—was too much for Tilly, too, but there was no need to tell Ruth what she surely already knew.

"Oh, and have a happy birthday tomorrow," Ruth said just then.

"Thanks. And we'll see you at church."

"That's right, but I can't bend your ear there, can I?"

Tilly laughed. "You'd better not. But you're welcome to join us at the house, of course."

"I will if I can," Ruth said. "I volunteered to help out with the women's luncheon afterward and don't know how long it'll last." She paused. "But I'd like to treat you to a birthday lunch sometime soon."

Tilly laughed. "A chance to celebrate my birthday twice? How can I refuse!"

They exchanged good-byes and hung up.

Tilly remained seated at the window and stared out at the inky sky. *How can I possibly survive a weekend in Lancaster County?*

36

CHAPTER 4

*F*ollowing early worship the next day, before Kris thoughtfully fired up the grill for the birthday steaks, Tilly hurried upstairs and threw open the cedar chest under the window. "I *know* it's in here somewhere," she fretted as she lifted layer upon layer of handmade quilts and linens.

Then, seeing the small plastic bag, she lovingly removed it. How many years had it been since she'd set eyes on little Anna's white organdy head covering? Not thinking it wrong at the time, Tilly had taken it from her mother's room without saying anything when she moved to Massachusetts. But the Scripture reading in this morning's sermon had stirred things in her mind and heart.

She studied the delicate *Kapp*, which she'd sewn for Anna, and carefully lifted it from its wrapping. Even now, her little sister's death seemed a stab to Tilly's awareness. *So very final.* Holding it against her face, she thought, *Oh, Anna, I miss you so.* Her petite baby sister had shadowed Tilly from the time she was a toddler.

Tilly pondered Ruth's sudden insistence that they return to Eden Valley, and for the first time, gave it serious thought.

Ruth wants to go, she mused as she turned the little cap over in her hands, eyes filling with tears. *If for no other reason, I should go and give this back to Mamm.*

She knelt there and wiped her eyes, trying her best to envision a setting where she and her mother could sit quietly together and actually have a conversation. At the end of her days there, they'd scarcely had more than a few words to say to each other, although her mother wrote occasionally, keeping Tilly updated when new babies were born and about family doings.

"Tilly, are you up there?" her husband called from the foot of the stairs.

"I'll be right down, hon." She put the head covering back into its safe spot and wondered if returning it was a good enough reason to put herself through the agony of facing her family, a family that had all but disowned her.

No, but I should do it for Ruthie.

"You'll miss the harvest festival here," Kris mentioned later, while Tilly cleared the cake plates from her birthday celebration.

"I know," she admitted, "but with my father's health so poor, it seems like the right decision."

He reluctantly agreed. "I could take the girls downtown next Saturday to choose their favorite scarecrow, but I can't afford to miss work on Monday."

She explained that Ruth was really the one pressing to go—at least for the anniversary. "She doesn't want to wait around."

Nodding thoughtfully, her husband caught Tilly's eye. "Maybe your sister has unfinished business there."

38

"Oh, Ruthie closed that door, believe me."

Kris slipped his arm around her waist. "It's not like you, or Ruthie, to want to go back, hon."

"Right." She nodded. "*This* is my home now." Tilly met his lips as he leaned down to kiss her.

Kris murmured, not arguing for or against any longer.

She moved from his embrace and turned on the hot water, then began to rinse and scrape the dishes. "Do you think your mother might agree to come and help with the girls?" Tilly asked.

"Move in, you mean?" Kris smirked.

"I'd only be gone from Friday morning till we get back the following Monday afternoon." She looked over her shoulder at him. "If your mom can't help out, I'll drop the whole idea."

They tossed it around further, and Kris surprised her by saying, "I think it's you who wants to go." He reached for the phone on the built-in desk across the kitchen. "Let's just find out if it suits Mom and be done with it," he suggested.

Tilly thanked him and loaded the dishwasher, happy every day of her modern life for such timesaving conveniences, recalling the hours she'd spent in Mamm's kitchen washing oodles of dishes. Pots and pans, too. From the age of six on, the chore had seemed daunting.

While she worked, Kris talked with his mother on the phone. Tilly knew how blessed she was with her helpful husband. He was thoughtful, too, and she believed unreservedly that their first meeting had been intended by God—the Wednesday evening she'd walked into their church and was warmly welcomed by handsome Kris Barrows. They'd dated eight months before becoming engaged, his parents accepting her as their own. *Despite my Plain background,* she thought gratefully.

Hearing Kris describe the possible scenario for his mother just now, Tilly prayed silently, *Please, Lord, give us a stop sign if this is a mistake.*

∞

For the first couple of years after Tilly left, Melvin Lantz did what siblings do when someone in the family does a strange and hurtful thing. He prayed, determined never to give up hope, thinking surely Tilly would grow up and realize her contrariness.

"Hurry and come to your senses," he had sometimes found himself saying aloud as he worked in the stable or drove the market wagon over back roads . . . whenever his thoughts wandered to the sister who'd never seemed to mesh well with the rest of the family. That was before he'd heard that she had married, discarding the Amish life for good. After that, Melvin knew there was no chance of real reconciliation.

As the years merged into more, there was only news about Tilly via Ruth. At the time Tilly left, fifteen-year-old Ruth was the only one in the family who even knew where Tilly had gone . . . and later, that she'd married and given birth to twin daughters.

Melvin had always assumed Tilly would have preferred to correspond with her childhood best friend, Josie Riehl, who'd married Melvin and Tilly's younger brother Sam. But, oddly enough, it was *Ruthie* whom Tilly'd chosen to share her thoughts with. This still struck Melvin as surprising, since, with eight years between them, the two sisters hadn't been all that close before.

Walking along Eden Road toward his parents' old farmhouse now, Melvin was anxious to get the anniversary plans under way. Thus far, he and his brothers had kept it quiet from Daed and Mamm, but today he felt it was time to tell them something about the gathering next Saturday noon for dessert. "Sure wouldn't want to surprise them *too* much," he whispered to himself, uneasy about his father's heart.

Ruth stayed after the ladies' luncheon in the church basement, helping with cleanup in the kitchen. When she dried her hands and left for the stairs, she heard Jim Montgomery's voice and noticed he and two other men had just finished tearing down the folding tables and chairs.

"Ruth," he called to her, looking especially smart in his tan suit. His light brown hair was swept to one side and waved gently over his forehead and, like most young men his age, Jim's sideburns were wide and long. "It's nice to see you."

"You too, Jim." She mentioned her part in the luncheon, pleased by his seeking her out this soon after their dinner date last week. His interest was conveyed in his glance and the way he walked quickly toward her. It was obvious he couldn't suppress how he felt about her.

"Are you going to church tonight?" He sported his usual engaging smile.

"I am."

"What if I picked you up? We could sit together," he said, his golden-brown eyes twinkling. "And . . . there's a great little pie place not far from here."

"Sounds wonderful." She smiled.

He nodded and pushed one hand into his trouser pocket.

"Terrific. I'll look forward to it." He walked her outside and to her car, then waved and headed off to his own vehicle.

This is a big step, Ruth thought, realizing how very public their friendship was becoming.

Ruth wondered if Tilly would approve of Jim, but since Tilly and her family didn't always attend Sunday evening services, Ruth decided she didn't need to reveal anything. *Not just yet.*

Sitting with Jim in church turned out to be less intimidating than Ruth might have expected. For one thing, not a single person looked twice at them during the brief fellowship time prior to the sermon. And afterward, Jim didn't want to linger, so they made a quick exit.

At the pie place, which looked almost like a Mennonite grandmother's breakfast room, complete with floral wallpaper and ruffled yellow curtains, Jim asked what she'd like to eat and politely ordered for her.

They'd chosen a comfy booth, away from the more occupied area where families were talking and enjoying dessert—everything from pies to cake and ice cream.

Jim mentioned how happy some of the families looked, in particular one family of six, where the mother beamed down at a new baby. Ruth wondered if it was a roundabout way to gauge her interest in children. "Having a large family can surely be a blessing," she said. "Though my own family hit some rather rough patches." She paused, not ready to tell him all about that, though he had to suspect as much, seeing as how she and Tilly were no longer Amish. "Sometimes it's hard for me to believe it's been three years since I've seen them. But my sister and I are planning a trip back—next weekend, in fact."

A slow smile spread across his clean-shaven face, and he leaned one arm on the table. "Well, I hope you don't forget about me with all those eligible farmers around," he quipped.

She appreciated his charming attempt to lighten her mood. It was almost as if he knew about her heartbreak over Will. *Long past.*

"I won't be gone for more than a few days," she added.

He was nodding. "Good to know."

Thoroughly enjoying their time together, Ruth found herself comparing Jim to Will—the two men were as unalike in manner as they were in appearance. *Jim seems to know his mind . . . and he's steadfast in the Lord, too. And what a gentleman!*

She found herself relieved yet again that she hadn't stayed in Eden Valley, waiting for Will Kauffman to get his life straightened out.

CHAPTER 5

*W*hat'll we do about attending church if Sunday's a Preaching service?" Ruthie broached the topic to Tilly as they headed southwest on I-95 around Boston the following Friday.

Tilly still couldn't believe they were actually going home, let alone talking of Amish house church. "Well, *I'm* not interested," she said, hands tight on the steering wheel.

"I'd rather not go, either, but since I'm staying with Mamm and Daed, I'll be expected to."

"Honestly, I think you'll be expected to do a lot of things if you stay at the house."

Ruth grimaced. "Well, it's better all around for me to stay with them."

She doesn't want to offend our parents, Tilly thought but said no more. In Tilly's opinion, Uncle Abner and Aunt Naomi were the much preferred company, followed by their brother Melvin and his wife, Susannah. Melvin's friendly, pleasant tone on the phone the other day when Tilly called him certainly demonstrated that. Aunt Naomi had sounded genuinely delighted when Tilly connected with her, too.

Despite her lingering misgivings about the trip, Tilly was happy for this special sister time—she and Ruth even managed to laugh from time to time. As always, they truly appreciated each other's company.

Eventually Ruth dozed off, her light blond hair falling loosely around her face. The color had a liveliness to it—like the flash of a match struck in the wind. Tilly remembered the first time she'd held newborn Ruth, an hour after her birth. To eight-year-old Tilly, tiny Ruth had been better than a new dolly.

⌒⌒

Hours later, as they were entering the state of Connecticut, Tilly mentioned, "No pressure, Ruthie, but Aunt Naomi was very nice about saying there would be room for both of us at their place. That is, if you change your mind before we arrive."

"I appreciate that."

"Just thought you should know . . . in case things get, well, prickly at Daed and Mamm's."

Ruth nodded. "It's only three short nights, and then we'll be heading home again."

Home. Tilly glanced at her pretty sister. In all truth, she was glad they were staying at separate locations, since then Ruth might not have to know Tilly's secret—Tilly could time her conversation with Mamm so Ruth was out in the barn or with her beloved horses in the stable at Daed's. And Ruth could be spared overhearing Mamm's tongue-lashing for Tilly making off with their little sister's *Kapp*. Mamm—Daed, too—wouldn't take Tilly's age into consideration. You were to respect your elders your whole life and follow the rules of their household.

Much later, they took a detour to pick up burgers and something to drink near Terre Hill, north of Lancaster. Unexpectedly, she saw a road sign for the old Weaverland Bridge, which crossed the Conestoga River just ahead. Tilly shivered as they approached the river, forever fixed in her mind and heart.

"Is it too late to turn back?" she murmured.

The sun shone bright against the windshield as Ruth listened to the radio. Her favorite love song was playing. The lyrics to "It Was Almost Like a Song" always gripped her, but today she had to look toward the window so Tilly wouldn't see the tears welling up as the singer crooned.

The first verse described her and Will's courtship exactly. As the song continued, Ruth felt the old angst again, remembering all that went wrong between her and Wilmer Kauffman. Their special love had ended so abruptly. *Out of necessity,* Ruth reminded herself.

Ruth had never understood why Will followed his friend Lloyd Blank to join the wild buddy group, the Jamborees. This had perplexed her, because she'd never known Will to be swayed by anyone. *So many unanswered questions.*

Ruth had continued to scratch her head over Will's choices, and she wondered now if he'd settled on a girl from that Amish "gang" for his bride. If he was already married, it was wrong for her to second-guess what had transpired between them. Or even to pine for him, if that's what she was feeling while hearing this sad love song.

To think she was going back home, where the risk of running into Will and any wife, and possibly a baby, was quite high. Oh, why hadn't Ruth thought this through before pleading with Tilly to return?

I must be a glutton for punishment, she thought, knowing her growing relationship with Jim should put Will far from her mind. Yet the feeling of melancholy lasted all the way to the turnoff to Strasburg and beyond.

———

It was Tilly's idea to drive directly to Uncle Abner's, bypassing their father's farmhouse. It made little sense, perhaps, but Tilly wasn't ready to see her parents without the emotional cushion of more siblings.

Ruth went along with the notion with some measure of uncertainty, ever concerned with good manners. "Hope this won't add more fuel to the fire," she told Tilly.

At the small historic square at the intersection of Route 896 and 741, Ruth's face lit up as she pointed out the creamery while they waited for the light to change. "I loved that old place, didn't you?"

"Plenty of happy memories there?" Tilly asked.

Ruth nodded dreamily.

Probably with Will Kauffman, Tilly surmised.

"They have the best ice cream—the most varieties I've ever seen in one place," Ruth said.

Tilly'd had her own pleasant experiences there, too, with a couple young beaus before she'd decided she couldn't live in Lancaster County any longer.

Another world ago . . .

The remaining portion of their trip was a short distance of only a few miles, and Tilly slowed as they approached White Oak Road where it intersected with May Post Office Road. It was still hard to believe that they were actually headed toward Eden Valley after all this time away from home. She was struck by the height of certain trees, as well as the additional homes that had been built in the last eight years. And the brilliance of the red sugar maples.

This was the road we took to the picnic that summertime morning. Tilly's thoughts flew back to the day that had begun with such promise. Their English neighbors, the Eshlemans, had taken them in their large van to visit Mamm's ailing aunt at Lancaster General Hospital early that morning. *An off-Sunday from Preaching,* Tilly recalled. After the hospital visit, they'd gone to Central Park in Lancaster around noon, having invited their neighbors to join them for a picnic—they wouldn't have considered stopping at a restaurant on the Lord's Day. The weather was warm and humid, and the hours following were filled with the sweet tastes of watermelon and other delicious treats—homemade root beer and nice cold meadow tea.

There were long swings at the lovely park, and if you pumped hard enough and leaned way back, it seemed you could nearly touch the clouds with your bare feet. And there were seesaws, too—everything a child could enjoy against the backdrop of the beautiful Conestoga River.

The river, thought Tilly, her shoulders tensing. *So much was lost in the space of one dreadful afternoon.*

CHAPTER 6

*R*uth was staring at Tilly. "I think we just missed our turn."

"Oh, you're right." She'd fallen into a rabbit hole, as Kris liked to say when she daydreamed. "Should've been watching more closely." Now Tilly was frustrated with herself; she'd have to drive another mile or more out of her way to make a safe U-turn.

"It's okay," Ruth offered. "We're not expected at Mamm's for at least an hour yet."

"Good thing." Tilly looked at her. "You'll want to freshen up before we head there, right?"

"Well, I didn't put on any makeup. Didn't you notice?"

Tilly smiled. "You wear very little anyway."

"I like the natural look. Always have."

"Probably for the better, 'specially around the home folk."

"Ain't that the truth," said Ruth.

They exchanged knowing glances.

Ruth touched her arm. "You all right, sister?"

"I *have* to be, don't I?"

"Are you sorry you came with me?" Ruth asked.

"Someone has to protect you."

She tried not to sigh as they drove past a large cornfield, then turned onto the familiar road, taking in its beauty. One picturesque memory after another competed for Tilly's attention as she scanned the rolling hills beyond. How could she not remember the glow of a thousand lightning bugs over the pastureland, the delicate way the sky looked at dawn in early spring, or the strident bawl of a newborn calf? She recalled, too, the easy ascent of Mamm's first yellow blooms up the tall arbor Daed had built in the rosy bower between the south side of the house and the potting shed.

Where Anna used to play, thought Tilly, her heart sinking anew, torn about returning here, memories agonizingly near.

"What's going through your mind?" Ruth asked suddenly.

Tilly shrugged. "Oh, you know."

"Well, it's not *that,* I hope."

Tilly fell silent. It was hard *not* to remember how things were before Anna drowned.

"Seems like just yesterday, doesn't it?"

"It does at times. I wonder if Mamm and Daed have managed to forget the worst of it," Tilly said softly.

Ruth frowned. "Go easy on yourself, hard as it is. You must think they're holding a grudge against you for leaving . . . and eventually taking me with you."

Clearly, Ruth had no idea what she'd meant.

Tilly spotted the mailbox for Abner Mast and slowly negotiated the turn into the treed lane, gathering her wits, reminding herself to breathe.

I can do this. . . .

"Just look at the size of those tree trunks," Ruth pointed out.

Tilly was also taken aback by the thick, spreading underbrush, as well. Clay pots of deep purple and gold mums highlighted the long front walkway, and two willow rockers looked lonesome on the wide porch. "Life goes on," she whispered.

Tilly recalled her aunt's gentle voice when, a few days ago, Aunt Naomi had received Tilly's call on her English neighbor's telephone. Tilly had arranged in advance for her aunt to go there to take the call. *"You and Ruthie must stay with us,"* Aunt Naomi had insisted.

Ruthie had declined hastily when Tilly relayed the kind invitation. *"I want to stay at our parents' farmhouse in my old bedroom, like before I left."*

Privately, Tilly wondered if that was really why Ruth wanted to sleep at the old home place.

What's she thinking? It seemed odd her sister wouldn't say when she was usually so forthcoming.

"Well, here we are," Tilly stated bravely, glancing at her sister.

Tilly knew Uncle Abner was staunchly Old Order Amish—no ifs, ands, or buts. From the moment he'd reverently bowed his knee on baptism day at nineteen, yielding himself wholly to the Lord and the People, Abner had never looked back. The large man had the tender heart of a child and especially enjoyed spending time with his nephews and nieces. He'd often declared that he fit in much better with the younger generation than with grown-ups, and Uncle Abner went out of his way to avoid folks who took life too seriously. He'd always paid special attention to Tilly, supposedly his favorite, or so Ruthie had pointed out years ago. Tilly had brushed it off, but she knew one thing was sure: Uncle Abner had a knack for making folks laugh right out loud. It was generally known that if he teased you, he was in reality very fond of you.

Tilly parked the car near the old icehouse, just down from the front yard, her thoughts turning to two of Abner's younger sons, Elmer and Henry, her close-in-age cousins. The boys were sleepwalkers who had once walked right out the back door and into the yard, jabbering all the while. Uncle Abner had decided that instead of allowing his sons' nighttime hours to be an obstacle to his own rest, he would occasionally tie their feet to their beds, making sure to unfasten them before the boys awakened. The boys might never have known, but after they were both married, Uncle Abner let it slip at a church gathering, as Tilly recalled now. She had to smile at the memory and wondered if Elmer's and Henry's wives had devised a way to keep their spouses from roaming about while they and their children slept.

These and other recollections flitted through Tilly's mind as she got out of the car and went to open the trunk. When she'd retrieved her suitcase, she motioned for Ruth to go inside with her, even though Ruth didn't intend to stay there.

The two young women headed up the well-manicured front footpath toward the white porch before Tilly remembered that none of the Plain folk they'd grown up around ever used their front doors, at least not as a rule. She laughed at her near mistake and turned to go around the side of the house. "What was I thinking?" she muttered, glancing at Ruth, who gave her a quick smile of encouragement.

In a quick minute, Uncle Abner's deep voice echoed across the driveway.

"*Willkumm* to ya, Tilly and Ruth." He lumbered over from the stable. "We've been expectin' yous." He wore a hospitable grin as he brushed his hands on his black work trousers. His gray shirt was highlighted by black suspenders, and there were dozens of grayish speckles in his long brown beard that hadn't been there before.

She felt sure she could count on her uncle not to comment on their fancy attire or how she'd influenced Ruthie to leave the People. Tilly knew him too well to think otherwise. Uncle Abner could be quite frank, but he was not ill-mannered. Besides, he'd talked privately with her before she'd ever left Eden Valley, his tone gentle. Momentarily, she wondered if their uncle had done the same with her sister when she decided to go. If so, Ruth had never shared that.

"*Hoscht du shunn gesse?*" He tugged on his beard and waved toward the house.

"*Denki,*" Ruth said, brightening. "But we stopped along the way to pick up hamburgers and ate in the car."

He raised his eyebrows at the outlandish notion of eating anywhere but with one's feet firmly planted beneath a dinner table. "Was that enough for a *gut* sound sleep tonight? Moreover, your aunt's been bakin' up a storm. You won't hurt her feelings, now, will ya?"

Tilly knew they ought to eat at least something here, as well as later at their parents' house, if invited. It was the courteous thing, after all.

Abner led them inside the farmhouse by way of the side door. Brightly colored rag rugs lay in a vertical row on the old linoleum—Aunt Naomi was a stickler for clean shoes, so no one dared track dirt in from the barn or anywhere else.

"Naomi, *kumm hiwwe,*" he called happily, and his wife came bustling toward them from the kitchen and opened her plump arms, a big smile on her round, rosy face.

"*Ach,* you're both here," she said, stepping back and looking at them fondly, her hands holding Tilly's. "And you, Ruthie.

Just look how you've grown up." She moved to embrace her, as well.

Tilly was pleased at the warm welcome, though she should have expected it.

"How long a drive did you have?" Aunt Naomi asked.

"Well, we were on the road by seven this morning," Ruthie said, "and we decided to drive straight through. It was a little less than eight hours with one stop for gasoline and another for . . . well, whatnot."

"We grabbed some cheeseburgers near Terre Hill," Tilly added. She could almost see the thoughts whirling in Uncle Abner's head as he calculated the vast difference between the miles a car could travel in such a short while versus a horse and buggy.

It wasn't long before Ruthie was settled at the kitchen table with Uncle Abner, where she poured hot coffee to go with the warm pumpkin pie Aunt Naomi had sliced for her. The inviting aroma of this particular kitchen stirred Tilly's senses.

Eventually Tilly left with Aunt Naomi, going to the main floor guest bedroom adjacent to the front room. "*Denki* for asking me to stay here," Tilly said, stepping into the spacious yet sparsely furnished room, just as she remembered it. *So like Mamm's bedrooms at home.*

"Are ya sure your sister won't join ya?"

"Ruth's got her sights set on her old room. But she appreciates your offer."

"Whatever's best, then." The demure woman opened the heavy pine blanket chest at the foot of the bed and pulled out two extra quilts. "It gets chilly at night round here this time of year."

Bet she thinks my blood's gotten thin, living with central heat, Tilly thought. *And she's probably right.*

Tilly reached for her aunt's hand, thankful for the considerate welcome. "Not sure where I would've stayed without your invitation," she said quietly, not wanting to ponder it.

"Well, your Mamma will surely want to spend some time with you *and* Ruthie before ya head back home. She's been missin' ya, Tilly."

Tilly guessed Daed and Naomi had talked at length about her and Ruthie's coming, being siblings themselves. "We're looking forward to the reunion tomorrow noon," Tilly said.

"Sylvia's talked of nothing else since she heard the news."

Tilly gave a smile. "Their wedding anniversary will be *wunnerbaar-gut, jah?*"

"Such a special time for the whole family," Naomi agreed. "Be sure and have some pie and coffee when you're ready." She waved and left the room.

The whole family won't be present, Tilly thought with a shiver and wandered to the tall window to peer out at the verdant farmland and grazing land. *Especially pretty in winter, under a fresh coating of snow.* She found herself sighing. No matter where a person lived, newly fallen snow all too soon took on a gray tinge. "Nothing stays new for very long," she whispered sadly.

For the umpteenth time, she wished she'd stayed back with Kris and their girls. Feeling overwhelmed, Tilly let herself sink onto the bed and leaned her head into her hands.

CHAPTER 7

*H*ow old did ya say you are now?" Uncle Abner teased as he and Ruth sat at the kitchen table.

"I *didn't* say." Ruth smiled, enjoying the lighthearted encounter with one of her favorite relatives.

Abner guffawed heartily. "I daresay you've got yourself a beau somewhere, though, ain't?" He dramatically folded his arms and beamed at her.

Ruth shook her head before she thought better of it. *Jim's a real possibility.*

"Ain't holdin' the fellas at arm's length, are ya?" her uncle pressed.

"Why do you ask?"

He pointed toward her left hand. "Might've thought by now you'd have yourself a diamond ring."

Like the English, he means.

"That would require a very serious young man, though," she replied, playing along.

He nodded slowly. "You're right 'bout that."

Ruth dismissed his remark and looked around the kitchen, with its sturdy oak shelf and day clock near the double sink. It was the same clock she'd stared at while having dinner here with her parents following Tilly's unexplained and sudden exit. As Ruth recalled, the meal had been meant as a time to console her parents in particular, although Ruth had received solace, too, simply by listening to Uncle Abner talk at the table. The man had a kindly way of expressing himself.

"He seems to care about everyone, no matter," her mother had always said of him.

Presently, he reached to pour more coffee into his cup. "I 'spect your mother's holdin' her breath till she lays eyes on ya again."

This pleased Ruth. "And . . . she'll be happy to see Tilly, too," she said, not certain it was true.

Her uncle took his time responding, eyeing her carefully. *"Jah,* the *both* of you," he said at last.

This took her by surprise, since she'd wondered if her parents might still be upset about Tilly's leaving. *And encouraging me to leave, too . . .*

She heard a knock at the back door, and Abner rose to answer it. Ruth could hear muffled talking, the low sound of another man's voice. Younger, and one she thought she recognized.

When her uncle was delayed, Ruth spooned up some more sugar and stirred it into her remaining half cup of coffee. *Seems strange, being here. Strange but good.*

After a short time, the men's talking ceased. Then, lo and behold, Will Kauffman's best buddy, Lloyd Blank, came walking in with Uncle Abner and sat down at the table like it was the only thing to do. He nodded in her direction but didn't say a word at first, as if unable to find any words to speak. It was downright awkward.

Ruth clenched her jaw. The dark-haired fellow with narrow brown eyes was the very reason Wilmer had chosen to join the rowdiest buddy bunch in all of Lancaster County. Seeing Lloyd again made Ruth want to run right out the back door and never look back.

Instead, she picked up her coffee and took small sips—all she could manage. Her hands were terribly unsteady.

Finally, Lloyd leaned forward. "Heard you were comin' home, Ruthie." He frowned slightly. "You wouldn't look any different if it weren't for those fancy clothes."

She could scarcely swallow. Back when she and Lloyd were in school together, Ruth had thought of him as foolish and, at times, even *lidderlich*—despicable.

Uncle Abner intervened. "Ruth and her sister are just visiting."

Lloyd nodded slowly, locking eyes with Ruth. "Well, if ya don't mind, there's someone who'd like to see ya." Ruth's heart dropped, and she felt as if all the air had been sucked from the room. "If you can spare the time," Lloyd added.

Ruth looked away, steeling her will.

"'Tis Wilmer," Lloyd said more softly. "*He's* asking 'bout ya."

She winced, and Lloyd's eyebrows wavered as if he'd noticed.

Ruth glanced at her uncle, hoping for support. "What does Will want?" she asked Lloyd.

"Oh, just to talk."

Ruth spotted Tilly coming into the kitchen with Aunt Naomi and was relieved when she didn't have a chance to accept or decline. She pushed back her coffee cup and saucer as gently as possible, fingers trembling. That quick, she got up to join her sister.

Goodness, but she found it curious that Uncle Abner hadn't offered to introduce Lloyd to Tilly.

She could hear Aunt Naomi chattering about getting Tilly a bite to eat and maybe getting Ruth something more, too, but Ruth hurried to the opposite side of her sister, flanking her all the way to the back door.

Aunt Naomi's face registered bewilderment.

"*Denki* for your hospitality, Aunt Naomi," Tilly said, her voice low. "But we really should get Ruth to Mamm and Daed's soon." She glanced furtively toward the kitchen, and Ruth guessed she wondered what Lloyd was up to that made Ruth so anxious to depart.

Aunt Naomi seemed reluctant to let them go but wished them well as they hastened to put on their coats, then left just as quickly.

"*Schlofschtermich*—nightmarish," Ruth admitted to Tilly as they drove away. "That's exactly what it was."

Tilly didn't reply at first, not knowing what to say. She had, however, recognized the Blank boy immediately.

"Lloyd, of all people," Ruthie declared, shaking her head. "Will sent *him*?"

By the rancor in Ruthie's voice and the change in her demeanor, Tilly assumed her sister still held a grudge from years past. "I told you it was a mistake to come here," Tilly said, eyeing Ruthie, who was dabbing her blue eyes with a tissue.

"We're here now—we can't just leave."

We could, if we dared, Tilly thought. "So now we're headed to see Daed and Mamm . . . some escape plan, *jah*?" Tilly's remark had the desired effect on Ruth, who offered a small smile.

"How do you think it will go?" Ruth asked.

"Truthfully, my being with you will probably cause a ruckus." Tilly gave a shrug. "Maybe I should just stay in the car and hold off on seeing them till tomorrow at the anniversary gathering."

Ruth shook her head. "Oh no, Tilly. That'll just make things worse. I'm sure of it."

Tilly knew her sister was likely right. "So then I'll paste on a smile and accompany you inside—get it over with."

Ruth turned and stared at her, eyebrows arched. "I'm sure they don't hate you."

Whether they did or not wasn't important anymore. "Daed and Mamm have every reason to be disappointed in me, I'm sure." Tilly spotted the tall farmhouse where they'd grown up, a quarter of a mile ahead. "Look, there's our childhood home." She paused, taking in the view. She felt numb.

"Do you have any happy memories at all?" Ruth asked softly.

"A few." Tilly glanced at her sister. "How about you?"

"If you don't mind my saying so . . . I have a-plenty, *jah*." She looked at Tilly and suddenly smiled. Both of them did.

"Well, you sounded just like you used to," Tilly said, chuckling.

"Wonder if we'll be talking *Deitsch* again soon. Will it all come flying back?" Ruth asked, looking out the window as Tilly pulled into the long, lonely lane.

"I'm sure it'll slip into our conversations." Tilly breathed a sigh. "Hey, there's no sign of a welcoming committee here."

"Looks that way."

"And all for the better."

Ruth was the first to reach to open her door, and Tilly followed her out to lift the trunk. While she tried not to look about her too much, Tilly *did* notice the old tire swing in the backyard, hanging from the stately oak by its well-worn rope. And the tall windmill out back, and the well pump, too. Some of the trappings of childhood.

A strange sensation swelled up in her, and she felt panicked. She had to physically will herself not to run. *My father has a feeble heart*, she reminded herself as she trudged up the back steps.

Will he get help from a doctor, or suffer and die too soon?

❧

Melvin happened to see a car with a Massachusetts license plate make the curve and creep past his house. There was no mistaking Tilly and Ruth—he'd caught Tilly's grim expression from where he stood in the yard. She seemed to be gripping the steering wheel, her jaw set.

He'd heard from Uncle Abner that only Ruth was staying at their parents'. *So Tilly's with our aunt and uncle.* Probably a *schmaert* idea when too much stress put their father at high risk for trouble. Melvin would hate to think of Tilly, especially, coming home only to trigger a massive stroke or something in their father. Melvin would never forgive himself for inviting her.

Carrying his old rake, its handle smooth in his hand, Melvin ambled around the side of the house to the barn, second-guessing his resolve to bring the family together.

Am I really such a Grautkopp?

CHAPTER 8

When Mamm came to the door, Tilly was taken aback by her appearance. After so many years, her mother looked as shapeless as a collapsed loaf of bread, though she brightened a bit when she spotted Ruth standing there, too. "*Ach*, here you are. You girls must be tired from your trip," Mamm said softly. It wasn't the jovial greeting they'd received at Uncle Abner's, but there wasn't an edge to her voice, either.

"Not too bad, really, but I guess I shouldn't say, since Tilly was the one driving," Ruth said, opening her arms for a quick hug. "Nice to see you, Mamm."

Their mother stepped back, looking them over. Then she stretched her hand out to gently cup Tilly's chin. She smiled almost shyly at both of them as she slipped her arm around Ruth and led her inside, Tilly following behind.

The house smelled of pot roast and carrots. And if Tilly wasn't mistaken, she detected a cake in the enticing meld of aromas, too. Her father was nowhere to be seen, which was a relief. She thought of simply going up the back stairs with Ruthie to help her get nicely settled. Then she could slip outdoors again and sit in the car. Or take a walk.

Yet even as she planned to do that, she saw the place where she'd always sat at the far end of the table, over on her mother's side. This table where Tilly had felt like a duck in a flock of chickens as Daed went around the table, interacting with all of her siblings. *Rarely me,* she thought. *Memories I'd rather forget.*

"Hope yous haven't eaten supper," Mamm said to Ruth, who beckoned Tilly toward the stairs with them, her eyes questioning when Tilly remained in the kitchen.

Tilly wondered if Ruth would reveal they'd spoiled their appetite with first cheeseburgers and then the pumpkin pie and coffee Ruth had enjoyed earlier at Aunt Naomi's table. But Ruth said nothing of the sort as she and Mamm ascended the staircase together.

Will some of our brothers come for tonight's meal? Tilly wondered, hoping so. While she'd yearned to be singled out by Daed as a youngster, she simply could not bear the thought of it now, having to answer one question after another—if he were to even acknowledge her presence. In fact, the anxiety over that possibility made her feel downright nauseous.

After a few minutes standing out on the back steps, breathing in the cool autumn air, Tilly decided against waiting around for Ruth and Mamm. So she made herself scarce and hurried to the car.

Shielding her eyes, she looked toward the nearby pasture-land, where a phone shanty stood not far away. She'd used it occasionally during her teen years to call for their neighbors, or to get a ride somewhere too far to take their horse and carriage. Eager now to phone her husband, Tilly started the car and backed out of the lane, hoping Ruth would forgive her for leaving without a word. After all, Kris would surely wonder if Tilly had arrived safely, and now was an ideal time to talk.

It didn't take long to reach the shanty by car. When she had somewhat regained her bearings, Tilly parked on the dirt shoulder and got out to pick her way across the newly plowed field toward the familiar phone shack. Sheltered by a thicket of trees and brush, it was concealed just the way the bishop preferred—over the years, the undergrowth had nearly consumed the rustic little shed.

She pushed open the wooden door and heard it scrape, remembering how, one summer night, she'd startled her older twin brothers, Jacob and Joseph, while they'd fussed inside, hollering at each other. Not knowing what to make of it, she'd guessed they were squabbling over the same girl. *"You didn't see us here,* jah?" Jacob had hissed in *Deitsch,* and she'd been good and never told on them.

Making her way into the cramped, stuffy space, Tilly looked about her. She blinked to see Ruth's initials etched into the wood near the receiver. *Ruthie was determined to carve out her place in the world. . . .* Tilly recalled how certain her sister had once been that Will Kauffman was a part of that world, until Will chose a buddy group clear out on the fringes.

Die Youngie in the Jamborees seemed to go out of their way to emulate the English life by pushing all the boundaries of the Amish church—owning cars, wearing stylish clothing, attending movie theatres and rock concerts. Some of its members even played competitive sports like baseball—another no-no under the *Ordnung* of the People here. *The reputation of a young person is marked by the group they choose during* Rumschpringe, Tilly thought, remembering. She puffed out her cheeks.

Suddenly drained of energy, she picked up the receiver and dialed home.

"I'm here safely, hon . . . in Eden Valley," she told Kris when he answered on the second ring.

"How was the trip?"

"Really pretty this time of year," she said, sighing. "The drive was just fine."

"You sound tired."

"Yes, well." She paused. "Actually, everyone has been okay so far, but I really don't belong here. . . . I feel it in my bones."

"Sorry to hear it, hon."

She nodded absently. "Thank goodness I'll only be here a few days."

Kris was silent for a moment. "The girls miss you already. And so do I." He said how happy his mother seemed to be, tending to everything. "She really enjoys grandmothering."

Tilly didn't know why, but hearing this made her yearn for home even more. "The girls must be enjoying her."

"They are."

"Good, then. That's what counts."

"So . . . you'll be all right for the duration?"

"I'll make the best of it somehow."

He said he loved her.

"I love you and the girls, too, Kris. I'll see you Monday afternoon—can't wait."

Tilly hung up and leaned against the rough wall. She felt the past close in like an unstoppable wave. She was a little girl all over again—petite Tilly Lantz, and a mischief, for sure. In her mind, she was sneaking to the laundry chute in her parents' house after everyone had gone to bed and sliding down its narrow black burrow, landing in a pile of bedsheets.

She had been caught off guard when her father was waiting for her in the dank, cold cellar—how had he known what monkey business she'd intended?

She could never do anything right, it seemed, at least where her father was concerned. The knowledge had been ingrained in her as surely as Ruth's initials on the wall there.

"I was always in trouble . . . always wrong." She let the words fall from her lips, reaching for the shanty door to yank it open.

On the return drive to her parents', Tilly slowed when she saw a young woman strolling along the left side of the road, walking a large German shepherd. Tilly felt a rush of anticipation as she realized that this was her former best friend, Josie Riehl, now wife to Tilly's brother Sam.

Honking and waving, Tilly quickly pulled over to the shoulder and stopped the car. Jumping out, she called to her. "Josie . . . it's me, Tilly!"

The blond, blue-eyed young woman turned and offered the barest hint of a smile. "I heard you might be home for the celebration tomorrow."

"I brought Ruthie along, too."

"*Des gut*, really 'tis."

Tilly wasn't sure if she should cross the road or not. It was the oddest thing, Josie being so aloof. But then again, Tilly had snubbed her, leaving her dearest friend out in the cold when Tilly began corresponding only with Ruthie after Tilly's departure. Still, she wondered if she shouldn't at least attempt an apology for her years of silence, try to make amends. *Is it a good idea?*

Standing there on her side of the road, she felt the barrier—the invisible *Do not trespass* sign between them.

"How long will ya be around, Tilly?" A safe enough question.

"We leave early Monday morning," Tilly replied, her mouth like cardboard.

"S'pose you have to get back home right quick, *jah?*"

Tilly nodded and wondered what to do with her hands, wanting to fold them in prayer, in all truth. She shoved them into her coat pockets, noting the pain in Josie's eyes. "I guess we'll see you and Sam at the gathering tomorrow, then."

"*Jah*, over at the house." Josie waved so halfheartedly Tilly wasn't sure she meant it as a farewell.

"Would you like a lift, wherever you're headed?"

Josie glanced down at the dog. "That's all right. *Denki.* This one needs some *gut* exercise, I'm thinkin'." With that, Josie turned and headed up the road, the dog's leash wound around her right hand.

She's holding me at a distance . . . and with good reason.

"What else can I expect?" Tilly muttered as she moved back toward her car.

Ruth was astonished to see her former room kept precisely the way she'd left it. Never had she dreamed her mother would leave the bed positioned the same, with the headboard facing north and the matching quilt and decorative pillows set just so against the pillow shams Ruth had embroidered. Even her Amish clothing still hung where she'd left it—the for-good dresses on the wooden pegs in the far corner just across from the modest dresser. *Will they still fit?* she wondered.

Ruth didn't dare to look in the drawers, didn't want to see the remainder of her clothing neatly folded there . . . or the shoes under the bed. Surely, they were still on the far side.

But she tried not to reveal her astonishment as her mother

offered to help her hang up her clothes just now, not saying much.

Later, when Ruth's suitcase was emptied and put away for the time being, Mamm sat on the bed, seeming to want Ruth to sit with her.

"If you'd like to take some of the items from your hope chest back with you, that'd be all right." Mamm motioned toward the gleaming chest at the foot of the bed.

Ruth hadn't expected this. "Are you sure, Mamm?"

"Why do you ask?"

"It's just that . . ." Ruth couldn't say, *I feel unworthy.*

"You made most of what's in there. I want you to have it."

"Thanks, Mamm . . . er, *Denki.* I appreciate it."

Mamm turned and remarked on the exceptionally pretty quilt's Sunshine and Shadow pattern, and the small yet distinct flaw sewn in for good measure, as was their custom. *To avoid pride.*

"We made one like this for Anna, too," Ruth mentioned without thinking, then glanced across the hall at the closed door. "Remember?"

"Daed and I still keep Anna's room locked," Mamm was quick to say. "It's best that way."

Ruth was surprised. So, even that hadn't changed. Suddenly she yearned to step inside Anna's small room, to touch her things. "Do you ever visit her grave?" asked Ruth quietly.

"I go." Mamm bowed her head. "Every month on the date of Anna's accident."

"So often . . ."

"Well, *someone* must tend to—"

Ruth shivered involuntarily. "But Anna's not buried there. She was never found."

"Even so," Mamm said sadly. "'Tis a mother's duty of love."

It wasn't just strange hearing her mother talk like this; it was downright crushing. Mamm's hold on the past seemed as tight as ever. *Maybe more so*, Ruth thought, gritting her teeth.

CHAPTER 9

On her way back down Eden Road, Tilly noticed the lack of scarecrows and jack-o'-lanterns on the Amish and English neighbors' porches. Given her restless and discouraged state after only a couple hours back in her original neck of the woods, she was beginning to believe she was on a futile mission. And it wasn't as though Mamm would be keen to talk about Anna.

No one else will be, either. . . .

Taking her time, she drove around the area, passing several bank barns and a small sawmill, two greenhouses, and resplendent pastures dotted with brown Jersey cows. Most Amish farmers agreed that Jerseys produced milk with higher butterfat, making for creamier milk and especially rich ice cream. Her mouth watered at these thoughts.

Later, to the familiar strains of "You Light Up My Life," Tilly turned south onto Groff Road down near her brother Chester's redbrick house. Two men she did not recognize stood out talking near the large bench wagon parked in the lane. *So, there is church this Sunday,* Tilly thought at the sight of the familiar wagon. She wondered whose turn it was to host the meeting—not that she'd be going. Ruth, however, still seemed all right with the idea, despite Tilly's refusal.

"What do I care?" she murmured, recalling the last time she'd attended a Preaching service. *So long ago.*

A quarter mile up the road, old Bishop Isaac's place came into view. Tilly saw what looked like a carpentry shop built back behind the farmhouse. "When did *this* happen?" She found it interesting that the man of God had to supplement his farming income. Farming was certainly the preferred way to make a living, and anything else could be frowned on. Yet she surely wasn't one to judge, sitting there driving her fancy car.

Tilly pressed the accelerator and drove toward Josie's parents' sprawling acreage. She wished Josie hadn't been so distant to her earlier, as though she were afraid to talk to Tilly. Or worse, harboring resentment.

She has no idea what life was like for me when I left home, thought Tilly. *None at all.*

She recalled that Ruth had written to tell her when Josie's first child was born, six years ago. A son whom she and Sam had named Sammy. Then, two years later, a baby girl, Johanna.

Yawning, Tilly glanced in her rearview mirror. She couldn't let Josie's reaction to her spoil her time exploring Eden Valley. No, she must choose to think back on their friendlier days and years, when they'd always shared their thoughts with each other . . . and their secrets, too. It would do her no good to ponder the loss of such a good friend. That was the last thing Tilly needed this weekend.

Besides, a devout Amish girl like Josie might not have been too thrilled to receive my letters.

Tilly refused to let her emotions take over. She was killing time, nothing more, while Ruthie and Mamm were getting caught up on the years they'd missed. *Ruth sure doesn't need me breathing down her neck.*

She slowed the car to a crawl when she recognized her Lantz grandparents' homestead just ahead. She assumed that by now her widowed grandmother had moved into one of the *Dawdi Haus* additions at a son or daughter's farmhouse. Hadn't Ruth mentioned as much once? Tilly sighed. Her uncertainty about such things was the price she'd paid for not staying in touch.

Nonetheless, there stood the splendid white house with its black front door and trim, a matching white two-story barn off to the left. Her father's mother, *Mammi* Lantz, would sometimes have Tilly stay over, and she'd loved sleeping in the small spare bedroom, where an old feather mattress became her cozy nest for the night. Tilly's father insisted that Mammi Lantz went out of her way to spoil her; however, his saying it didn't faze her grandmother one iota. *"I wish I'd had a little girl to love,"* Mammi Lantz would whisper to Tilly as she tucked her in beneath handmade quilts that sometimes smelled of mothballs.

Her grandmother's remark had lingered in Tilly's mind all these years, though Tilly wondered now why Mammi Lantz, who was so well loved by her four sons, including Tilly's own father, felt such a loss. Was Mammi disappointed—even pained—by the absence of a daughter?

Back when she was a little girl, when Tilly was sad and feeling lonely and lying in her own bed at home, she sometimes soothed herself to sleep by imagining her grandmother's cool hand lightly on hers, or the wonderful-good feather bed not so far away.

But as Tilly grew older, times with Mammi Lantz grew less frequent—she had to be around *"to help out at her own home,"*

Daed often said. And so it was with many of the joys of Tilly's life as duty took precedence over all else . . . even people.

Maybe Daed never realized how fond I was of Mammi, Tilly thought now, though she wouldn't have believed it back then. With her return to her parents' home imminent, she was doing her best to think well of Daed, hoping a change in perspective might ease the coming reunion.

CHAPTER 10

*A*fter managing to navigate nearly every road in Eden Valley, Tilly had driven past the blacksmith's shop, Deacon Kauffman's farm, and the one-room schoolhouse where Amish and Mennonite children alike had attended alongside several English children, too, when Tilly was young.

Presently, she headed back to Daed's farm, lest Ruth become upset at her prolonged disappearance. She turned into the driveway and parked only a few dozen yards from where her brother Melvin was getting out of his gray enclosed carriage.

When he noticed her, he didn't waste a minute in coming and surprised her by opening her door and waiting good-naturedly until she got out. Then, closing it firmly, he kept his hand on the handle. "You *are* here," Melvin said with a smile. "*Gut* to see ya, *Schweschder.*"

"Safe and sound." She nodded toward the house. "Ruth's visiting with Mamm."

"I came to give Daed a hand in the stable." He touched the brim of his black hat. "Would ya want to help me water the animals?"

She turned to look again at the house, squinting to see

into the kitchen windows, but there was no sign of Ruthie or Mamm. "I'm not exactly dressed for barn chores, am I?"

"*Ach*, I'll fix you up." He motioned for her to follow him. "You can wear one of Daed's long work aprons."

Thoughtful. Tilly hurried to keep up. Now that she was back at the farm, she felt tense and kept looking over her shoulder for her father to appear.

The stable smelled of sweet alfalfa bales, humidity, and sweat from the animals. Tilly was surprised to discover she'd almost missed these surroundings. How many hours had she spent out here watering field mules or the driving horses? One of her favorite pastimes. The livestock had always been like family pets.

"How is it, comin' back home after all this time?" Melvin reached up for the brown apron he'd promised, took it down from its peg, and slipped it over her head. "If ya don't mind me askin'?"

"It's . . . real different, I'll admit."

"I'd 'spect so."

She tied on the apron while Melvin pulled two buckets off a small stack. "Still, it's mighty *gut* of you and Ruthie . . . showin' up for the anniversary an' all."

She nodded, trailing along with him, the brother she'd felt closest to back when, in spite of the difference in their ages. Melvin had always demonstrated a gentle side toward her, no matter Daed's mood. "Guess you never thought you'd see the likes of me again," she ventured.

"Well now, Tilly, ain't a *gut* time to be sarcastic." His tender gaze on her belied the seeming rebuke. "I'm *glad* to see ya again, sister!"

He still cares. The realization made her skin prickle.

They moved silently to the young colts' pen and filled the water trough, and then on to the ponies'. Tilly felt tongue-tied and was thankful when Melvin began to talk again, revealing the plans for tomorrow's gathering.

"All the boys and their families will be here," he said, referring to their brothers. "Chester and I'd thought of having the get-together out here in the barn, getting things all redded up, like for Preachin'. But Sam and the twins thought better of it. Besides, this late in October, ya just never know 'bout the weather."

She listened, curious if other Amish families were starting to have these kinds of celebrations, too. Was the English world closing in?

"Instead of a big doin's and a feast, there'll be a sheet cake Susannah and Josie are baking. Chocolate with buttercream frosting, is what I hear. We'll have us some fruit punch, too, and maybe a dish full of the creamy mints Mamm likes." He straightened, and she noticed he was much taller than she remembered, even taller than their father. "The adults can stand around in the kitchen since there'll be no gettin' everyone's feet under Mamm's table," he continued. "The little ones will need to sit there."

"Who will give the blessing?" Tilly asked without thinking.

Her brother cocked his head, frowning. "Daed will lead the silent prayer, like always."

She'd completely forgotten her family didn't verbalize their prayers like she and Kris and the girls.

"Did ya think Bishop Isaac and the other ministers might be present, then?" Melvin was still looking askance at her.

"Not really, no."

"What, then?"

She shrugged, not wanting to clarify her blunder.

Melvin let it drop. "Too bad your husband and daughters didn't come along," he said, moving toward the mules. "Would've liked to meet 'em."

"I didn't think—"

Melvin shook his head, catching her eye. "*Nee*—prob'ly not."

At that moment, their father's ear-piercing whistle caught them off guard. Their heads jerked in unison at the shrill sound. With two fingers between his lips, Daed could be heard for nearly a mile away.

"Is he signaling you?" Tilly asked quietly, clenching her jaw.

"Might just be." With that, Melvin left her there with a lone bucket and the dark-eyed stares of eight mules.

In her mother's spacious, sun-splashed kitchen, Ruth wiped her hands on the black apron she'd borrowed. "I assume you've asked Daed to consider getting a pacemaker, then?" Ruth said, continuing to chop raw vegetables for a tossed salad.

Mamm nodded and stopped to lean against the counter. Wearing one of her brown choring dresses and black aprons, she looked much as she always had on an ordinary weekday. "Ain't anyone gonna change his mind, neither."

"Wish he'd take his doctor's advice."

"It's no use." Mamm put her hand on her chest. "He's decided and that's all there is to it."

"Then Daed's days are numbered?" Ruth was aware of the lump in her throat.

"Daughter . . . must ya say it like that?" Mamm wiped her

brow on the back of her forearm. "It's hard enough seein' him fail like this. And ever so quickly, too."

"I'm sorry." Ruth blinked back tears. "Really, I am."

Her mother sighed and brushed past her to the head of the table, where she pulled out Daed's chair and sat. She looked tired all of a sudden, and her blue-gray eyes seemed darker as she stared back at Ruth. "We Amish live each day with God's will in mind, first and foremost." She kept her gaze fixed on her. "Maybe you've forgotten certain things, ain't so?"

To the contrary, Ruth wholeheartedly believed what her mother said. She also believed there were benefits to consulting a doctor.

But Mamm had more on her mind. "Don't be forgetting, the Lord God knows the day of our birth, and the very moment we'll die, too." Mamm's eyes welled up, and she pulled a hankie from under her long sleeve.

"Mamm, I didn't mean to—"

"Ain't worth troublin' yourself. Not a whit." Her mother rose and plodded to the icebox in the far corner. She opened it and reached for a pitcher and began to pour cold meadow tea into four green tumblers.

The ice in the glasses crackled, and Ruth realized then that only four would be present for supper—she, Tilly, Mamm, and Daed.

Poor Tilly! she thought, her heart sinking.

CHAPTER 11

*H*aving returned to the barn, Melvin watched in disbelief, although he should've known something like this might happen. Just having Tilly home again had been risky.

Ruth had come wandering out to the stable a few minutes before, making a beeline to the corner and whispering to Tilly, "It's just going to be us at supper with Daed and Mamm."

Next thing, and without so much as a good-bye to Melvin, Tilly turned tail and scurried to her car, then backed out of the driveway and promptly drove in the direction of Uncle Abner's.

Melvin now wished he and Susannah might have invited themselves over for the meal. Anything to ward off Tilly being uncomfortable on this, her first night home. *Why do Daed and Tilly have that effect on each other?* Melvin was baffled yet again.

It was then Ruth spotted him. She looked almost embarrassed for Tilly's dramatic behavior.

"Hullo, Melvin," she said. "It's nice to see you." She gave him a warm smile, and they talked for a moment as Melvin finished his chores, then got into his carriage and headed to his house for supper.

"Something's already up," his wife told him as she met him at the back door. "Tilly came flyin' past the house in that fancy car of hers like she was bein' chased."

Nodding at her expressive account, he stepped inside. He'd figured Susannah might have seen that.

"By now, poor Naomi's prob'ly had an earful."

"Well, maybe not. Tilly used to keep things inside till they blew," he reminded her.

A light went on in Susannah's eyes. Now she, too, was nodding. "Ain't always been Tilly's fault, though. Don't forget." She hung up Melvin's hat for him.

"No, but for whatever reason, that sister's never really fit in here," he said, remembering.

∞

"Kris, I'm not sure I can do this," Tilly said into the phone at the little shed. Here she'd only been in Eden Valley a few hours, and she'd retreated twice to make a call. "I'm sorry to bother you again like this. Just needed to hear your voice right now."

"Honey, please try to take a deep breath, okay? And you're never a bother."

"It's just that everything's coming back to me," Tilly continued. "I can't let my father break my heart again. I won't!"

Kris was silent for a moment. "It's not worth getting so upset. Maybe you should shorten your stay, hon."

"What about Ruthie? I can't just leave her."

"Maybe you could get a hotel somewhere, go into town, perhaps." His tone was calm and even, just what Tilly needed.

She hated to sound panicked. Nevertheless, everything around her was a miserable reminder of the past.

"Listen, Tilly, I'll come get you, and you can leave the car there for Ruth. Is that a possibility?"

She wasn't surprised he would offer this. Kris was not only sensible and kind, but from the very first, he'd somehow understood the pain of her growing-up years. Not because he could relate to them, but because he'd taken the time to really listen during the hours she'd spent sharing with him. How she welcomed his caring prayers!

"I could be there by early morning," Kris urged.

"But the girls . . ." As she calmed down some and began to think things through more logically, she was beginning to feel foolish.

"I'm willing, Tilly. Just say the word."

She brushed away her tears and sniffled. "I came with Ruthie for a reason," she told him. "And I also need to return something I took from my mother." Tilly revealed what she meant by that.

"But seriously, do you need a face-to-face encounter for that?"

She said she thought she ought to at least hand the *Kapp* to Mamm and apologize outright. "I won't involve my father, of course."

Kris said that was probably a wise idea. "Don't you think you could do that before I arrive tomorrow?"

She moaned. "Oh, Kris . . . I can't expect you to drive all that way. Besides, it's foreign territory for you here."

"No," he said. "It's your family *heritage*. Maybe it's time I saw God's green earth for myself."

Picturing her wonderful husband getting out of his car and

walking with her toward her father's house was the kind of awkward scenario she'd always dreaded. There was no need for Kris to do what he was offering, and she didn't want to put him in the middle of a brewing pot of old stew. "Thanks, hon," she said. "But I'm going to figure this out on my own."

After they'd said good-bye, Tilly drove past her father's house, feeling freer, knowing she wouldn't have to endure Daed's disapproval just yet. It might be better for Ruthie if Tilly wasn't at Mamm's table tonight—it would give her more time with Daed and Mamm, a chance to enjoy all the attention the first evening back.

And I'll be fine with Uncle Abner and Aunt Naomi . . . besides, Naomi baked up a storm. Tilly recalled her uncle's earlier remark and was heartened by the prospect of having supper with her kindly aunt and uncle instead.

"Only *one* person ever led a perfect life," Uncle Abner told Tilly as they sat around the table together later. It was just the three of them—Tilly and her aunt and uncle—though there was food enough for a feast. "You'll keep that in mind, *jah*, Tilly?"

She listened and believed, but her uncle couldn't possibly know how difficult it was for her to forgive herself. Not just for leaving Lancaster County, or for taking Ruthie away, but also for being thoughtless the week of Anna's drowning. No, she could never forget how she'd lost her patience with little Anna, and she had never breathed a word of it to anyone. Not even to Ruth.

"Would ya care for more potatoes or anything else?" Aunt Naomi asked, looking at Tilly.

"Everything's delicious, but no thanks."

Uncle Abner tilted his head. "You don't eat so heartily up in Rockport, do ya?" His grin was merry.

"I'm not as plump as I might've been had I stayed around here," she admitted.

He laughed. "Well, we Amishmen prefer our women nice and round." Here he winked at Naomi, who lightheartedly waved right back at him. "Mashed potatoes swimming in butter or topped with *gut*, thick gravy never hurt anyone."

Tilly wouldn't say what she was thinking. She'd read an article about the ill effects of an overly rich diet, especially on the heart. She wondered if her father was still a heavy eater but decided that, since she hadn't had the nerve to stay for supper over there, it wasn't right to ask.

"Well, and the farmers work off all those calories, don't forget," Naomi piped up, which brought another smile to Uncle Abner's sunburnt face. "They need to start the day with a big breakfast, too."

"Better be ready come mornin', Tilly," Uncle Abner said with another wink.

Having been on the opposite end of all that food, helping Mamm prepare the generous hot meal, Tilly remembered and smiled.

The sound of the day clock ticking broke the silent pause.

"So," her uncle said, "I s'pose if we'd known it was goin' to be just you and your sister over at your parents' tonight for supper, your aunt Naomi and I might've offered to show up and eat over there with yous."

"Oh, now, Abner," said Naomi. "You don't mean it."

"I certainly do."

Tilly had to keep her smile in check. These two had always been entertaining.

"You honestly would've burst into Sylvia's kitchen uninvited?" asked Naomi.

"*Puh!* And why not?"

"What purpose would *that* have served?"

Uncle Abner reached for his tumbler of water, his eyebrows twitching as he drank. When he'd finished, he wiped his mouth on the back of his long-sleeved shirt and said, "If it made Tilly more comfortable, I think we just might've."

It warmed Tilly's heart, and she wished for words to express her appreciation but felt weary. She thought of her drive around Eden Valley that afternoon and her unexpected encounter with Josie.

"Keep in mind tomorrow's a brand-new day," Uncle Abner said, looking at her. "His mercies are new every morning."

Tilly agreed. "Melvin says all of my remaining siblings will be present at the anniversary gathering."

Aunt Naomi patted her arm lightly. "That's what we've heard, too, my dear."

So maybe I'll be safe, thought Tilly, wondering how Ruthie was faring with their parents.

Rising, she helped clear the table before bringing over the big Dutch apple pie and placing it on the table. Naomi carried the homemade whipped cream and set it down smack-dab in front of Abner, who beamed.

"This'll fatten ya up, Tilly-girl," he said, reaching for the spoon and dipping into the whipped cream, a mischievous look on his round face. "Be sure an' put plenty on your pie." He glanced at Naomi. "Cut her a nice big piece, won't ya, dear?"

"Oh, all right," Tilly replied at last. "Anything to chase the heebie-jeebies away."

"A little pie with whipped cream is *gut* for what ails ya," Uncle Abner said with a grin.

But Tilly knew better, thinking again of her father's poor health.

CHAPTER 12

The sky had turned silvery white as dusk began to fall over the landscape, the sun a large pearled onion. It was as if the very countryside was Ruth's companion, familiar as it still was to her. *Familiar and foreboding.* While she dried dishes for her mother across from the windows, she noticed the trees were beginning to cast shadows in the waning light.

She stacked another white plate in the cupboard, and the little cow-shaped creamer caught her eye—its handle the tail. *Mamm's birthday gift from Tilly*, she recalled, startled to see Mamm had kept it, considering everything.

Ruth turned and let her gaze roam to her father's chair at the head of the table and recalled their conversation during the meal earlier. She assumed the unexpected pleasantness was due to Tilly's absence. Daed had been more relaxed than Ruth anticipated—he'd seemed pleased to see her. Talkative too. Presently, he'd gone out to check on two new calves even as Mamm scoured a large pan in the sink.

Nothing had been said about Tilly's disappearance prior to supper, though since her parents hadn't mentioned it, Ruth suspected they were relieved, which made her feel uneasy. Even sad.

Mamm broke the tranquility. "Besides the family get-together, is there another reason why you and Tilly wanted to visit after all this time away?" Her eyes probed Ruthie's.

"I felt the Lord nudging me."

"The *Lord?*" Mamm turned swiftly. "Oh, Ruthie, are ya thinkin' of changing your mind and—"

"No, Mamma. I didn't mean that."

Her mother's face drooped; she looked terribly disappointed. "*Ach*, I can still pray, ain't so?"

Ruth groaned inwardly. Mamm's remark had put Ruth's stomach in knots. She held her breath, and when her mother leaned down to rinse out the sink, Ruth closed her eyes. In the space of less than a minute, her mother's demeanor had changed to one of misery.

Tilly was especially lonesome for Kris and the twins as she unpacked in the main level guest room at her uncle and aunt's. The kitchen had been long since redded up, and she and her aunt and uncle had sat awhile at the table as Tilly got caught up on various folk, including Mammi Lantz. Mammi, it turned out, currently resided in the small *Dawdi Haus* attached to the main farmhouse where her oldest son, Tilly's uncle Hank, lived with his wife.

Uncle Abner urged Tilly to go over and pay a visit to her grandmother. *"How about before you head home Monday?"* he'd said with a serious look. *"At her age, ya never know . . ."*

Tilly closed the bedroom door but saw no way to lock it for complete privacy. Even so, she felt secure enough to remove

Anna's *Kapp* from its wrapping. After all, her aunt and uncle had retired to their room.

As she held her little sister's delicate white head covering, Tilly bowed her head and asked for divine guidance in approaching her mother. "Help me know the right way to do this—the best way to honor You, Lord," she prayed.

Later, when she had returned the *Kapp* to her suitcase and was ready for bed, Tilly felt she should be as forthright as possible. *As plainspoken as Mamm will allow me to be.* She reached over to extinguish the lantern on the small table next to the bed, but instead of settling into bed, she stepped to the window and raised the dark green shade to peer out in the direction of her parents' home. She could not see the farmhouse, but she imagined a golden flicker of light in one of the upstairs windows.

She prayed for her sister, asking God to give Ruthie a peaceful night of sleep.

Tilly's eyes roamed the moon-swept landscape to the hill beyond, where Anna's grave marker stood less than a mile away. But Tilly would leave that particular visit for Monday morning, before they drove back home. *If at all.*

There was another location she felt even more compelled to visit, a place she'd always thought she would never want to see again—Central Park in Lancaster City, where Anna had fallen into the river. No need to breathe a word to Ruth, or anyone, for that matter. Tilly would go alone and pay her respects before leaving for Rockport.

❧

Ruth had waited till the house was quiet before she crept down the back staircase to pour milk in a cup and then, just as silently, returned to her room. Now, as she sat on the bed, the small gas lantern illuminating the room, she stared at the locked door across the hallway. If Mamm hadn't reminded her it was locked, she might not feel so drawn to go over and peer into the keyhole. *Human nature*, she thought.

What if I jimmied the lock with a hairpin? She'd seen one of her twin brothers do this in the past at a cousin's. Jacob, she thought it was. *Always the prankster.*

She began to quietly sing a verse from a favorite hymn. "I will sing of my Redeemer, and His wondrous love to me; on the cruel cross He suffered from the curse to set me free." She continued to hum, knowing she would miss her church this Sunday. The comforting hymn brought her peace as she sat there, a guest in her parents' home.

Getting up, Ruth closed her door and lined up her slippers where her feet would land when she got out of bed in the morning. She put out the lantern and slipped into bed beneath the Sunshine and Shadows quilt.

Lying still, Ruth prayed her silent Amish rote prayers, in honor of the old days. And when she was finished, the thought crossed her mind that she might have been wrong to be put out earlier today by Wilmer's friend Lloyd Blank. *Was I, Lord?*

Sighing, she rolled over and slid deeper into the covers, hoping Tilly was as cozy tonight as she felt here in her old bed. Ruth also hoped with all of her heart for a happy day tomorrow, especially for her parents, then wished that her dreams might be sweet ones. And to encourage that, she slipped in a quick prayer for Jim Montgomery, thankful for their growing friendship.

∞

In the soft light of his lantern, Melvin noticed a bunch of old newspapers still scattered on the floor in one corner of the kitchen, where Susannah had churned butter today. He recalled helping her at one point, both of them taking turns churning. He'd grinned when the telltale yellow dots finally appeared, then slowly formed into a rich glob. Susannah had been the one to pour off the buttermilk right quick. His dear wife was a hardworking woman, and he thanked the Good Lord for her each and every day.

Making his way out to the utility room now, Melvin reached for his work jacket and pushed his arms into it. While Susannah slept soundly, he would check on his ailing mule, knowing he might need to call the vet first thing in the morning. *An inconvenience, considering the family plans,* he thought as he put on his old work boots and headed outdoors.

A big harvest moon shone starkly this night. Melvin glanced over yonder toward Daed's, wondering if Ruth had been treated cordially at supper. Up until recently, Daed had been known to make occasional asides about Tilly and her disloyalty, but he'd spared Ruth. He'd always preferred Ruth to Tilly, though it was Anna who'd been his favorite. *The baby of the family . . .*

In all truth, there had never been any child quite as favored as Anna, amongst her family, at least. Many had taken notice of it, but no one had ever said a word, knowing she was Daed and Mamm's youngest. As a toddler, Anna had been eager to please, but he and Susannah had seen another side of little Anna that had worried him at times. It nagged at him, even now.

Melvin had never been able to completely erase the memory of her screams that terrible afternoon. Right after Anna's fall, the wind had torn through the treetops along the river, punctuating the horror. He and Chester had leapt into the dark waters, along with other men, but Anna's thrashing took her life before they could swim out to her. His heart broke anew at the memory—so unnecessary, her death.

Three sisters lost to us—one to death, the others to English life.

Lifting his eyes to the night sky, Melvin watched the radiant moon's climb over the neighbors' tobacco shed. Tilly and Ruth's long-awaited return had definitely stirred up the excruciating past.

"You must move on, dear," Susannah had gently suggested so many times he'd lost count.

Not easy.

He slid open the stable door and heard the low moaning of his poor, sick mule.

CHAPTER 13

Tilly was indistinctly aware of the refrain of birds and a faint scent of flowers and beeswax. Was she dreaming? She reveled in the feeling, delightfully relaxed . . . thinking it was springtime and that she was a young girl again.

Slowly, she sat up in bed and began to realize she was not in her old room but rather in her Mast uncle and aunt's house. Absorbing her pleasant surroundings, she was thankful she'd left one of the window shades up, providing an appealing view of the landscape—the field visible even from her cozy perch. Late October in Lancaster County had always been splendid.

As she loved to do, Tilly offered a prayer of blessing for the day, then slipped out of bed to get her Bible from the dresser, where she'd left it last evening. Turning to the psalms, she located her bookmark. "'I will lift up mine eyes unto the hills, from whence cometh my help. My help cometh from the Lord, which made heaven and earth.'" She relished the inspiration. It was certainly a day that could well be laden with circumstances beyond her control; a day she must give wholly to the Lord, who'd never left or deserted her, in spite of the many mistakes she'd made.

Thinking now of her mother, Tilly decided to write a note instead of attempting a face-to-face apology—awkward at best, particularly on a day meant for celebration. This way, she could simply leave it with Anna's *Kapp* in her parents' bedroom and be done with it.

Dear Mamm,

I'm returning Anna's head covering, offering my apology for taking it when I left Eden Valley. I hope you can understand that it was all I had of my baby sister. That may sound like a poor excuse, I realize, and I know it probably holds special meaning for you, too. I am sorry if this has caused you further pain. Please forgive me?

Your daughter, Tilly

She struggled with conflicting emotions as she wrote. Truly, she felt that her parents, Daed especially, had consistently viewed her as always in the wrong, filled with naughtiness and a tendency to blunder. Perhaps they'd suspected all along that she'd taken the *Kapp*.

Locating Anna's *Kapp* in her suitcase, Tilly put it and the note into her purse and snapped it shut. She would give the timing of its return to God and trust that all would be well.

"Sometime before Tilly and I leave for home, would you mind opening up Anna's room?" Ruth asked Mamm while stirring eggs and milk for a breakfast of scrambled eggs and bacon. "I'd like to see it again."

"I'm sure you would, dear, but—"

"If it's too painful, I'd—"

"Well, *jah*, 'tis certainly that."

Ruth knew she must honor that, even though she didn't know why she couldn't be given the key, perhaps, and go in there on her own. But seeing her mother's eyes dim just now, she thought better of pressing the issue.

"When do ya think Tilly'll be over?" Mamm asked while separating the bacon strips before putting them into the black frying pan on the cookstove.

"She didn't say." Ruth really didn't know when to expect her sister. Truth was, Tilly was even more on edge than Ruth, evidenced by the way she'd exited so quickly prior to suppertime.

"Well, do you expect she'll come for the dessert today at noon?" Mamm asked, her face showing concern.

"That's why we're here," Ruth replied. "I'd be shocked if she didn't show up."

Mamma bobbed her head, still looking serious. "Since you won't be around for long, it'd be nice to see *both* of yous."

Ruth was happy to hear it, thinking at least Mamm was getting used to the idea that Tilly was back in Eden Valley.

"We'll have a bite to eat before everyone arrives," Mamm added. "I'm plannin' to make some tuna salad after breakfast."

"It'll be fun having all of us Lantz kids under the same roof, right?"

Mamm smiled and patted her shoulder. "So nice, *jah*."

Ruth prayed it would be not only nice . . . but wonderful.

Tilly counted four carriages parked in her parents' northeast yard when she arrived on foot—with all her brothers' families in attendance, she'd decided it wiser to leave her car behind.

She'd already enjoyed some delicious corn chowder and a toasted cheese sandwich at Aunt Naomi's table after helping her aunt make lunch. It brought back such good memories, a bright spot she sorely needed as she made her way up the driveway, then past the deeply colored mums along the side of the house. Tilly remembered all the times she and Ruthie had planted flowers for their mother. Ruth had always been the one with the green thumb, or so their father pointed out. Tilly, on the other hand, had been known to overwater plants—particularly a problem for the more finicky rosebushes, causing them to wither and die.

Seeing the buggies, Tilly wondered if everyone had already arrived. Aware of her pounding heart, she wished Ruth might spot her and come running outside so they could go in together, two sisters united.

Breathing a silent prayer for peace, she was glad she'd worn a modest-length skirt and had taken care to brush her hair back into a low ponytail. She made her feet move one in front of the other as she headed around to the back door, hearing the happy chatter inside. There was laughter, too.

She reached for the storm door and pressed the handle, wishing she could just sneak inside and avoid causing a scene.

The door swung open with a creak, and Tilly slipped inside and spotted Josie, wearing a royal blue dress with a white cape apron. She was helping Ruth cut the anniversary cake centered on the long table as other sisters-in-law passed around dessert plates.

From the way it looked, Tilly seemed to be late for the celebration and didn't know how that could've happened when she'd tried so hard to be on time. *This time*, she thought, remembering her childhood nickname: Too-late Tilly.

Allen saw her and nodded, then glanced at Daed. Did he fear tension between them?

Several others looked her way, as well, then quickly at Daed, as if expecting something to happen. Oh, Tilly could feel the pressure in the room—the undertow of the old expectations. She hung back a bit.

Soon Chester began to lead out in his clear baritone voice, and they all joined in, just like at church, minus the pitch pipe. "Happy anniversary to you, happy anniversary to you, happy anniversary dear Daed and Mamm . . . happy anniversary to you!"

Tilly sang, too, while standing beside her brother Sam, Josie's husband, who was behind most of the cluster of family. He was dressed in Sunday clothes—the black trousers, white shirt, and black frock coat worn by Lancaster Amishmen. When he glanced at her, Sam smiled amidst the commotion of so many crowded in the kitchen, large as it was.

"Hi," she said softly, grateful for his welcome.

"Well, looks like you *are* here," Sam said. "*Gut* for you, brave girl."

Brave? If only he knew, she thought, offering her own smile and stepping in next to him. "How's the cake?"

"It looks *wunnerbaar-gut*," Sam said. "Oh, here, take this piece." He offered his untouched plate and fork.

Glad for it, she thanked him and accepted the plate.

Meanwhile, Sam moved forward through the line, past thirty-four-year-old Jacob and Joseph and their respective wives, Becky and Rachel . . . and then Allen, two years older than Ruth, along with his brunette wife, Hannah. Allen's two little boys were sitting cross-legged on the floor over near the windowed wall. Except for Tilly and Ruth, everyone in the room looked like they were dressed for Preaching service.

Sam finally made his way to the table and asked Josie for another plate. "Sure, here's another piece," Josie told her husband. She glanced up, eyes twinkling, then noticed Tilly. "Thought for a minute you were already hopin' for seconds."

Standing on the perimeter as she was, Tilly wished she might not be seen by her parents. But in a few short minutes, Daed looked her way and seemed to study her, his head tilted. What was that look? But no, she knew better than to hope. He wasn't really acknowledging her presence so much as just noticing her there.

She made herself smile for him, and he nodded yet again. Maybe he *was* acknowledging her, his expression more pleasant than any she'd known all the years growing up. Because of that, Tilly felt brave enough to inch through the crowd to attempt to greet him.

Her father took a couple of bites of cake, then stopped, fork in hand, and grimaced as if in pain. He gave an odd glance at the ceiling before leaning to whisper something to Mamm. She looked up at him sweetly, then frowned—a look of concern, perhaps. And before Tilly could get to him, Daed excused himself and left the kitchen.

He made his way through the next room, where Mamm had always kept her china hutch and other nice dishes on display—especially her collection of teacups and saucers. He trudged to the front room sofa like a horse following furrowed ground. Daed sat gingerly for a moment before slowly reclining, his glasses sliding down his nose. His right hand rested on his chest.

A foreboding came over her, and Tilly realized how very much she wanted to speak to him, despite his apparent fatigue. Determined, she pressed onward and saw Mamm look over her shoulder at Daed before going to talk with Chester, her expression grave.

Keep going, Tilly told herself, unintentionally blocked again by more family members. *Follow him . . . offer a friendly greeting.*

But by the time she'd stopped to chat with a couple of her sisters-in-law, Tilly saw that Daed was sound asleep. Pausing in the doorway between the large kitchen and the wide hallway, she regretted all the years of absence. *I'm too late.*

CHAPTER 14

*R*emember all the turkeys we slaughtered that winter before you left?" Tilly's brother Allen asked while Sam stood nearby.

"How can you forget something like that?" Tilly said, queasy at the memory. "It was traumatic."

This brought a welcome laugh, and Tilly finally began to feel like she was blending in a little, despite her modern clothes and hair.

"I remember those birds hanging upside down, all stiff and plucked nearly bald," she said, grimacing.

Allen nodded. "So many leftover feathers . . . and those bloodied eyes, too."

"Ew . . . must we remember *that*?" Tilly shook her head, recalling the seemingly never-ending work to accomplish. She could still feel the gravel, as her father had always called the crop located between the gullet and windpipe. "It makes it a challenge to enjoy a slice of anniversary cake." She looked at her plate and noticed she'd eaten only half her piece. Too busy talking . . . reconnecting.

"You've been a city girl for too long, *jah*?" Allen joked.

Sam nodded in agreement.

"Well, you know," she said, "turkey season was never really my cup of tea."

As she inched around and visited with each of her brothers and wives, Tilly repeatedly glanced toward the front room. Mamm was there now, bending low, saying something to Daed, who opened his eyes and moved his lips in response.

Tilly gave a sigh of relief and turned her attention more fully to her small nieces and nephews, some she'd never met—born since her leaving.

Later, she also enjoyed visiting with Melvin's teenage sons, Caleb and Benny, who openly asked questions about her car. This made Tilly nervous, wondering who might overhear.

"Do ya know how to change the oil?" Benny was asking, blue eyes bright. His clean blond hair shone, bangs cut in a perfect line across his forehead.

"What about jacking up the car if a tire goes flat?" Caleb asked before she could answer Benny. "Can you do that, too?"

Looking around, she felt incredibly sheepish. "You two aren't thinking of trading in your courting buggies for cars, are you?"

"*Nee*, wouldn't think of it," Benny admitted.

"Daed would have our necks on a block," Caleb said.

Like all those turkeys, thought Tilly.

"Well then, why don't you stick with hitching up and taking good care of the harness and bridle?" she said for good measure.

"Well, *you* didn't stay," Benny shot back.

Tilly inhaled, feeling self-conscious. She'd caused enough trouble, helping Ruth leave Eden Valley—she wouldn't be seen as responsible for luring away these two, as well.

"So maybe Amish life ain't for everyone," Caleb concluded.

"Please don't pattern your lives after mine," she said earnestly. "I had issues . . . nothing to do with being Plain."

"If you say so," Benny said.

She wasn't sure they believed her, but Caleb changed the subject and said how nice it was to see her again. And Benny added he hoped she'd stay in touch.

"I'll do that," she promised, eager to get going, wishing Ruthie might walk her back to Uncle Abner's. Except now she spotted her sister talking animatedly with several of their sisters-in-law, over in the corner near Mamm, who'd returned to the kitchen, looking weary, her glance returning to the front room.

I need to say good-bye to Daed, thought Tilly, hoping it wouldn't be the last time.

Tilly's awful jumpy, Melvin thought as he mingled with his siblings and their spouses. Chester and Joseph were together in the corner, talking and drinking more coffee than eating cake, although everyone had been served at least one ample slice. He also saw as he went to the table for seconds that there was plenty of cake left over. Melvin couldn't resist licking off his fingers.

"I saw that," his wife said, creeping up behind him.

"And I suspect you're wantin' seconds, too." He winked at her.

She leaned close to whisper, "Do ya think Tilly and Ruth are havin' a nice time?"

"*Gut* as can be." He had been observing both of them, especially Tilly. "Daed's not doin' too well, though," he said.

"Mamm says he thinks he ate too much cake," Susannah

offered, her lips near his ear. "But honestly, he's never had any trouble with sweets before."

He nodded toward the front room. "Should one of us go and check on him?"

Susannah wrinkled her brow. "*Nee*, I think he just needs some quiet. And your Mamm gave him some hawthorn berry tea—the 'great heart healer,' some call it."

Melvin had read about the home remedy in *Die Botschaft* not long ago. That and cayenne pepper dissolved in hot water had reportedly saved many lives during a heart attack. Of course, he'd also read enough about arrhythmia to know that his father needed more drastic intervention.

He felt tugged in the direction of the front room, eager to know how Daed was doing. Yet he did not heed it, not wanting to single out his father. *"Don't make a fuss,"* Daed had drilled into them since they were little tykes. Though Daed was a man who did not wish to have attention drawn toward him, he must feel bad about missing much of the family's party for him and Mamm.

Across the room, Melvin saw Tilly showing pictures from her wallet to Josie and assumed they were of Tilly's husband and daughters. Sam and Josie's young son and daughter were standing near, too, on tiptoes to see the pictures. The sight warmed his heart, especially when Josie slipped her arm around Tilly's waist. *Love overlooks and forgives*, he thought, thankful he'd stuck out his neck and invited Tilly and Ruth.

Now if I could just get Daed to see the light about that pacemaker, he thought, forking up some more cake. *An uphill battle, for certain.*

Some time later, Tilly was standing at the back door window watching each family leave for home—there were chores to get to, including milking. Benny and Caleb lingered, however, and were standing partially hidden over near the old slanting corncrib, puffing on a shared cigar. *Are they wondering where I parked my car?*

She stepped away from the window and smiled at the tender sight of Ruth and Mamm sipping tea at the table. Sam and Josie and their two children were still there, too, Sam having more coffee at one corner of the table, talking quietly with Josie. Josie was expressing concern that Daed might need to see the doctor again, and Sam solemnly agreed.

With everyone occupied—and Daed still resting in the front room—Tilly decided now was the ideal time to return Anna's cap upstairs. She reached for her purse on the pantry doorknob and promptly snuck up the back stairs, glad to have written the apology note tucked into the plastic bag next to the *Kapp.*

At the top of the stairs, she noticed what had been little Anna's room, the one nearest their parents'. She was very curious to see her sister's room again. *Such a long time,* she thought, wondering if Mamm had kept any of the dolls Tilly had sewn for Anna. Then again, it was hard to imagine that her mother had kept anything related to Tilly.

Trying the doorknob, she discovered the door was locked and crouched low to look through the large keyhole. To Tilly's amazement, the little rocking chair Daed had made was still draped with the Double Bar–pattern dolly quilt brightening the room—Tilly had made it for Anna's fourth birthday. "Mamm *did* keep it," she whispered, wondering why the room was locked. It hadn't been that way before Tilly left . . . though now that Tilly considered it, she'd never tried to enter. *Maybe it's been locked all this time.*

Doubtless, Mamm had her reasons, and Tilly let herself think how she'd feel if she still lived here and had to see Anna's door closed all the time. Truly, it was impossible to forget that everything had changed after Anna's death. Life had ceased in many ways, just as the clocks in the house were stopped at the estimated time of Anna's fall into the mighty Conestoga.

Feeling forlorn in spite of the mostly happy time downstairs, Tilly made her way to her brothers' former bedroom, the largest of the four rooms upstairs, except for their parents' bedroom, positioned over the warm kitchen. She looked inside and saw Mamm's cutting table for laying out fabric in the middle of the room, her old treadle sewing machine on the window wall. On the west-facing wall were two spool cabinets, similar to Mammi Lantz's own, and a hutch filled with quilting material. Seeing the room as it was now, Tilly had a hard time recalling the double bed, and bunk beds, too, stacked up along the wall, years ago.

Heading back toward her parents' room, she paused in the doorway before slowly stepping inside. The room looked much the same as when Tilly lived there—Mamm was not one to alter the décor. The small oak table was still centered between two tall windows with a sturdy rocker on either side. It was there her parents liked to sit for their morning devotions, especially in the summertime. There was only one difference: a bed quilt she'd not seen before, a Country Songbird pattern in a lovely green, white, and mauve theme. "When did Mamm make this?" she murmured, setting Anna's head covering on the bed and leaning closer to look at the quilt.

She studied the pattern and realized how many quilting bees and work frolics she'd missed out on during the past years. While she did not regret her modern life with Kris and their young daughters, Tilly had completely cut herself off from her family here.

Reaching for the plastic bag, she went to the foot of the bed and opened the blanket chest, thinking she'd simply leave it inside. *For Mamm to find later*, she thought, hoping to bypass any painful discussion.

Tilly could hear laughter floating up the steps—*Mamm, Ruthie, and Josie*, she thought. In that moment, she questioned her decision. Why was she doing this so secretively? Her mother had always been a person she could approach, in contrast to Daed's detachment and seeming disinterest. Didn't she deserve a personal explanation?

Looking down at the little cap, Tilly changed her mind. She closed the lid to the blanket chest, took Anna's head covering and the note, and returned them to her purse before quietly leaving the room.

CHAPTER 15

*B*ack downstairs, by way of the main staircase in the heart of the house, Tilly noticed her mother sleeping in an easy chair over in the far corner of the hallway-like sitting area. Mamm kept her prettiest dishes in the narrow space, like a dining room but without any table. There were two upholstered chairs perched on either side of an old cherry-wood desk Daed had made long ago. Mamm had always said this furniture would go to little Anna when she was married. *"That's what Daed wants,"* she'd told both Tilly and Ruth.

What does Mamm want? Tilly mused.

In the kitchen, Tilly found Ruth cleaning up the dishes. "You're working alone?"

"It's okay, really," Ruth said, mentioning that Sam and Josie had gone out to check on the new calves for Daed. "And Mamm must've needed a snooze, too."

"Here, I'll help you dry." Tilly picked up the embroidered rose tea towel. "When we're finished, let's you and I walk back to Uncle Abner and Aunt Naomi's together."

"Only if Daed's feeling better." Ruth paused. "I overheard Sam say he was ready to call 9-1-1."

"Well, Daed would not take well to it."

"Sam knows that." Ruth stopped washing, her hands deep in the soapy water. Beads of perspiration lined her brow. "Honestly, I think it's probably a good thing we made the trip back here when we did."

Tilly understood. "And I'm beginning to wish I'd stayed in touch better, too. Through all the years away, *you've* been the good daughter, writing letters to Mamm and others in our family."

"Well, but even so, I sometimes think I have a lot to make up for." Ruth paused, suddenly looking at Tilly. "Not pointing fingers, mind you."

Tilly reached for another plate to dry. Mamm had written occasional letters and cards to her, but there had never been direct word from Daed. She had excused it, though, knowing most Amishmen were too busy plowing and planting and tending to the livestock to bother with letter writing.

Ruth shrugged. "Of course, I'm not sayin' I could ever return to the Plain life, if that's what you're thinking."

Tilly wondered why Ruth would say such a thing. Wasn't that a given? There was no turning back for either of them. Not now.

∞

Ruth managed to match Tilly's long stride during the walk to their uncle and aunt's place. They talked about the anniversary party, especially the two new babies present. "Little ones who will grow up not knowing us," Ruth said, feeling a little blue.

"We've obviously made some big changes in the direction of our lives," Tilly offered. "People make choices. Difficult as it was to go, I just couldn't stay."

"That's why we look to the Lord each and every day." Ruth thought back to her younger days when she had been so carefree. Back then, she'd had not a single worry, at least not in her secluded little world in Eden Valley.

A large market wagon piled with pumpkins rattled past, pulled by two road horses. Ruth's mouth watered at the thought of pumpkin pies and sweet pumpkin bread, and she realized how much she missed baking with her mother.

"Goodness, how can everything look so much like home, yet seem unfamiliar all the same?" Tilly said quietly, looking her way. "Do you feel it, too?"

Ruth said she did just as she spotted a gray carriage coming this way with a tall lone driver. "We must look terribly out of place to everyone here," she said, glancing down at her shiny loafers. "Which is downright peculiar, considering this was once our home."

"It's not like we're dressed very worldly, though."

"But in contrast to the Amish here, we surely are." Ruth looked down at her navy blue corduroy jumper. The hem came just to her knee, which must have seemed nearly scandalous to Mamm, who'd made no comment about it. *She bit her tongue,* Ruth thought, remembering a few furtive glances her mother had given her attire and hair.

"Who's this coming now?" Tilly asked, slowing her pace.

Eyeing the buggy, which seemed awfully familiar, Ruth continued to keep up with Tilly's stride. "Well, I sure hope it's not who I think." She could be entirely wrong, not having seen Wilmer Kauffman since she left at twenty.

"You'd know better than I would," Tilly said, picking up the pace again. "If it's Will, what'll you do?"

Ruth wasn't sure and didn't have time to answer, because the carriage was slowing and an arm was waving out of the buggy. Then a sun-tanned, enthusiastic face appeared from the side, and as Ruth had feared, it *was* Will Kauffman, her former beau.

"Hullo!" he called a hearty greeting.

Where's his beard? Ruth was shocked that he wasn't married by now.

She moved closer to the side of the road, her heart beating considerably faster, not knowing what to say to this young man she'd so loved. In that instant, she realized she hardly knew a thing about Will anymore. What sort of person had he become? Had he been ruined by the Jamborees, marked for life . . . spoiled for the Old Order church? She could not even estimate her own previous significance to him, except to remember that he'd wanted to make her his bride, before Lloyd Blank stepped in and steered him toward the wild side of things.

"Tilly . . . Ruth," he said, halting the horse and jumping out of the carriage. He wasted no time in coming around to offer a gentlemanly handshake to each of them. He looked like he'd just had a shower; his blond bangs were clean and fluffy beneath his black felt hat. He wore a long-sleeved light blue shirt and black work trousers with black suspenders.

Not surprisingly, Tilly seemed a bit hesitant to shake Will's hand. Her big sister had clammed right up, leaving it to Ruth to carry the conversation, if there was going to be any.

"We're just out enjoying the day," Ruth said, avoiding saying his name. She didn't feel like looking him in the eye, either, but he was persistent and drew her gaze toward him. *Such confidence*, she thought. *Or is it arrogance?*

"I'd be glad to give you both a lift, wherever you're headin' to," Will offered.

"*Denki*, but we'd like to walk," Ruth was quick to say.

Tilly continued her silence.

"Well, once you're back at your parents', I'd like to talk to you, Ruthie. If you don't mind."

"She *does* mind," Tilly finally snapped, then reached for Ruth's hand and started walking away.

"I mean no harm," Will called after them—after her. "Ruthie, is that how ya feel, too?"

What's to feel? she asked herself. *After all this time, he's of no interest to me.*

"I have something important to tell ya, Ruthie Lantz . . . if you'll give me a few minutes."

Tilly still held Ruth's hand fast. "Don't turn around, whatever you do," she whispered. "Just keep walking."

Ruth had never expected to find herself in such a predicament. She could no more describe what she was feeling than she could describe the smell of the air after a soaking summer rain. And while she purposely kept her head facing forward, allowing her sister to lead her up the road, Ruth felt drawn in two directions, by Tilly at her side, and Will pleading behind her.

"Are ya goin' to be at Preachin' tomorrow, maybe?" Will asked, sounding farther away.

"Just leave her alone!" Tilly hollered.

"Tilly—" Ruth said.

"What?" Tilly exclaimed.

Ruth jerked to a halt. "I'd honestly like to hear what he has to say."

Groaning, Tilly released her. "Oh, Ruthie . . . what am I going to do with you?"

With that, Ruth turned and disregarded Tilly. She raised her chin and walked back toward Will Kauffman, who evidently didn't see her and was getting into his carriage. Oh, but she was still too far away to be heard even if she had the nerve to call out, and she certainly didn't want to make herself look foolish.

"Be careful who you love." The old warning swathed her thoughts.

Watching him go, Ruth stopped walking and stood still as a stone. She would not run after him. No, she'd just let Will go and be done with it. *For good.*

CHAPTER 16

Melvin went back to oiling harnesses once he returned home. It was a rather good thing that Susannah was busying herself, too, inside the house, across the backyard from his shop. The temptation for them to sit and further rehash what had happened over at Daed and Mamm's was all too strong. Overall, things could have gone better between Daed and Tilly, what with the obvious apprehension from everyone. But Daed's weakened state had prevented much interaction. Melvin was thankful Sam and Josie had offered to stay around and keep an eye on Daed. Their children, Sammy and Johanna, had been outside playing on the tree swing when Melvin left for home.

Susannah had mentioned during the ride that she thought there had been a slight improvement in Daed's color and responsiveness after the cup of hawthorn berry tea. Knowing his wife as he did, Melvin trusted her opinion.

Even so, what tomorrow held was a mere guess. Only the heavenly Father knew the end from the beginning. Melvin had learned that he could readily trust that, regardless of the circumstances. Once again, he committed Daed's health to the Lord God, then continued to process the week's orders, wanting to finish prior to the Lord's Day . . . and the Preaching service over at his brother Allen's place tomorrow. Ruth had said she would be attending. *Seeing Ruthie in the house again surely must've bolstered Daed's spirits,* Melvin thought.

Alas, having Tilly there might have had the opposite effect. Melvin was glad Susannah hadn't commented on that, one way or the other. It was hard enough contemplating the past— Ruth's departing the area had definitely increased Daed's anger toward Tilly.

Will he ever forgive her?

Melvin set aside the harnesses to look in on his sick mule. Thankfully, the vet had made time to check on the animal before Melvin and Susannah had to leave for the anniversary cake and coffee. "Thank the Good Lord for doctors," he muttered, wishing Daed might come to the same conclusion.

On Melvin's walk toward the house, he thought he smelled cigar smoke but dismissed it as his imagination.

The day has enough worries of its own.

"Honestly, do you really want to spend time with the likes of *him?*" Tilly said as she and Ruth rounded the bend toward Uncle Abner's property. The three-story house loomed over the expanse of fields bursting with field corn ready for harvest, tassels dried to a golden brown.

Ruth hadn't wanted to, not at first, but curiosity was getting the best of her. What did Will want to say? Apparently, there was something. "I should at least hear him out," Ruth protested.

"Oh, sister . . ." Tilly exhaled, clearly disappointed. "You pleaded with me in your letters, remember? You needed a way out of here, an escape from Will."

"But back *then* I had a say about my life. You didn't *make* me leave Eden Valley." She shook her head. "Today . . . well, you really should have let me speak to Will."

Their eyes met. Tilly took a deep breath and let it out slowly. Her eyes registered regret. "You know what—you're right, Ruthie. It really wasn't my place to speak up back there. I'm sorry."

Ruth touched Tilly's arm. "Actually, I think I would've done the same if the tables were turned."

"I'd just like to spare you more heartache."

She nodded, understanding. "And I love ya for it."

They had reached Uncle Abner's. Ruth opened the rasping side gate for Tilly and waited for her to go up the sidewalk first.

"We could find a church to attend together in Strasburg, if you'd like," Tilly offered. "If that would make things easier."

She's still trying to keep me away from Will.

"You decide," Tilly surprised her by saying. "Meanwhile, let's drive over to visit Mammi Lantz. Would you like that?"

Ruth said, "Sure," and began to ponder the idea of hearing Will out tomorrow, possibly after the Preaching service.

Together, they headed straight for Tilly's car and left for the short ride.

"I wonder how our grandmother will react to seeing us," Ruth said as they rode.

"We'll soon find out."

Ruth gazed out the window, half hoping they might run into Will again, when they came back this way. Of course, he wouldn't realize it was his former sweetheart-girl inside the vibrant red vehicle. Would he?

⚭

Mammi's own parents had once lived in the little *Dawdi Haus* where Mammi Lantz now resided. As was true of all additions built for aging relatives, the new home was much smaller and laid out differently than the main farmhouse next door.

Despite feeling a little disoriented in the space, Tilly was delighted to find her grandmother as warm and affectionate as she'd always been. Soft blue eyes alight, Mammi greeted them with kisses on the cheek and insisted they go and sit in her "cozy room," as she called her sitting area.

"Would you like some hot apple cider?" Mammi asked in *Deitsch.*

Tilly glanced at Ruth, and they followed their grandmother's lead and responded in their mother tongue, knowing it would be easier for Mammi.

As Tilly and Ruth sat, Mammi flitted about, opening several drawers near her large treadle sewing machine. It was heartening for Tilly to see the old spool drawers, as well as a tall bureau Dawdi had built. In the corner, there was a small heater stove, too. It was a welcoming room, indeed.

When Mammi seemed to find what she was searching for, she turned and placed two colorfully embroidered hankies each in first Tilly's hands, and then Ruth's. On top were wrapped peppermint candies. "Here's chust a little something to remember me by," she said, this time in English.

"Aw . . . Mammi, this is so nice of you," Ruth replied first. "*Denki.*"

Tilly thanked her, too, recalling how generous Mammi

Lantz had always been. She wished she'd thought of bringing something for her, too, and just that quick, she remembered the extra wallet-sized pictures of Jenya and Tavani that Kris had stuck in her purse. "Would you like a peek at your twin great-granddaughters?" She reached for her purse.

Mammi poised her tiny spectacles on the bridge of her nose and held the pictures up toward the light. "*Ach*, they look alike to me."

"They're identical twins," Tilly explained. "Not fraternal like our brothers."

Still scrutinizing the photos, Mammi's expression grew solemn, and she frowned as she looked at Tilly. "Goodness' sake, they remind me of your little sister, lost to the river. Ain't so?"

Tilly's heart dropped. She'd forgotten Mammi might think so. None of Tilly's siblings or their spouses had come close to mentioning this at the anniversary celebration. Were they just being kind, not wanting to broach the painful topic?

Tilly felt the wrench in her heart . . . that old sinking feeling that came whenever she thought of Anna's premature death. *The years away haven't healed that wound.*

Belatedly, she realized Ruth was talking, pointing out the slightly different shape to Jenya's mouth. "That's how I've been able to tell them apart," she said, evidently trying to move the conversation away from Anna.

"Yes, and Tavani's hair is just a touch more wheat colored than Jenya's," Tilly said, thankful for Ruth's new direction. "Almost like we put highlights in it."

"Such interesting names," Mammi said, pushing her glasses up on her nose. "Where'd ya ever hear of them?"

Tilly remembered the day she'd first seen the names—and

a few other beautiful, yet unusual names. "In a baby name book, actually."

"What an interesting way to choose a name."

Tilly nodded.

"Now, let's have that hot apple cider," Mammi said, getting up and wandering into the nearby kitchen. Her steps were slow yet determined. "And how would ya like a treat to go with it, maybe?"

Tilly didn't have the heart to tell her they were full to the gills with sweets and treats. "Are *you* hungry?" she whispered to Ruth, who rolled her eyes in answer.

Tilly motioned for Ruth to join her in the kitchen with Mammi anyway, not knowing when or if they'd have another chance to visit with their aging grandmother.

"You still have your piggy salt and pepper shakers," Ruth said, smiling.

"Oh, I remember these," Tilly said as she reached for the saltshaker and looked at it more closely. "I've always loved them."

"They're mighty cute, ain't so?" Mammi said. "One of the few things I convinced my family to let me keep when I moved over here . . . after your Dawdi died."

Tilly could see that it was still hard for Mammi to talk about him; undoubtedly she missed him terribly.

Mammi shook her head. "But that's all part of life's seasons, *jah*? And from what I hear, your parents will soon be vacating their big house, too."

"What do you mean?" Tilly asked, thinking she must have misheard.

"Well, your father's appointed Sam to run the dairy farm."

Tilly realized she should have considered that Daed might

want to transition the farm to Sam, who was renting and no doubt waiting for this moment. It certainly made sense that Daed would want to do this while he was still living, but no one had breathed a word about it today.

"How soon?" Ruth asked.

Mammi didn't seem to know the answer. "But I do know it's all been settled, and what with your Daed's heart condition, I'd be surprised if he puts it off. Sam is itchin' to start."

Tilly could scarcely comprehend her parents' moving away from their first home . . . that wonderful old house passed down through the family for generations.

Ruth blinked repeatedly, and Tilly knew if she looked at her sister any longer, she, too, might be fighting back tears.

Mammi gingerly poured the hot cider into three blue-and-yellow teacups with gold edging. "I fear I've upset you both."

Ruth was quiet, and Tilly was too stumped to say anything sensible. The more she contemplated this news, the warmer her neck felt.

"I spoke out of turn, maybe," Mammi added. "I would guess your Daed will surely say something while you're both home visitin'."

Tilly looked out the window, lost in thought. She saw the old windmill rotating slowly, facing the southeast presently. The view was similar to that from the large farmhouse next door, where she'd so often sat and soaked up all of her grandmother's enduring love. Tilly had never fully appreciated until now what a blessed gift that was.

Mammi broke the stillness. "That's sure one bright automobile you've got there."

Ruth laughed softly. "Tilly figured if she was going to drive at all, she might as well go with something colorful."

"Oh, now, aren't you something!" Mammi was laughing, too. "Are ya sayin' that if you're goin' to step away from the church ordinance, you might as well go whole hog?" Her voice trailed off, and she looked mighty sheepish. "*Ach*, I never should've said that."

Ruth reminded her that they hadn't joined church and weren't under the rules of the *Ordnung*.

"Is that right?" Mammi looked befuddled. "I guess I'd forgotten."

But Tilly wasn't so certain.

"Well, if you don't have plans to go to another church tomorrow, you're welcome to come to ours in the mornin'." She peered over the top of her wee glasses at Ruth.

Ruth stirred her hot cider, which was cooling now. At last she said, "I've actually considered going to Preaching service."

"It'll gladden your father's heart, I'm sure." Mammi poured more hot cider in their cups.

Tilly presumed her sister would definitely end up going now. And soon after, when they had bid Mammi good-bye and she drove Ruth back to Daed's house, Tilly wasn't up to saying more about it. She just wasn't.

While there at the house, she wondered if now was a good time to talk to her mother about how she'd taken Anna's head covering, eager to return it to its rightful place. But she wanted to do this privately, without Ruth around.

How will I ever manage that?

CHAPTER 17

From the hints Tilly had dropped about Ruth's helping Daed in the barn, Ruth was determined to oblige Tilly and make herself scarce when they arrived. *Something's up. . . .*

"Why don't you just come out and say it, Tilly? You want to talk with Mamm alone."

Tilly nodded as she pulled into the driveway. "I don't mean to push you away . . . it's not that. It's about Anna."

Ruth bowed her head. "Sorry, I'm not trying to make things hard for you."

Tilly tried to assure her that it was all right. But Ruth knew it wasn't. Why had it always been that, whenever the topic of Anna's accident came up, it was Tilly who had the final say? It didn't upset her, really, but Ruth had wondered about it. Then again, Tilly had been like a second mother to Anna, the oldest sister naturally looking out for the youngest.

Seems like Tilly still is, thought Ruth.

As they sat there in the car, Ruth asked, "What do you think of Sam and Josie taking over Daed's farm?"

"Sam's always had a good business head. He learned that from Daed."

"But you've been gone since Sam was twenty."

"True, but don't you remember how Sam was in charge of the roadside stand every summer? And the homemade root beer sales, too."

"You're right." She smiled. "He never failed to count the customers' change twice." Ruth felt a twinge of sadness, thinking of those lost summers. "And he's certainly been even more responsible since marrying and becoming a father."

"He'll be good managing all the turkeys and chickens, and with the livestock, too, keeping meticulous breeding charts like Daed does. And having plenty of help lined up to carry fresh milk to the cooler in the milk house." Tilly leaned on the steering wheel, looking at her. "Something else bothering you, Ruthie?"

"I don't know . . . maybe it's just being back here. Our childhood home, you know?" Ruth swallowed. "It's hard to think of Daed and Mamm moving like Mammi Lantz said."

"Not easy, no. But when you think about Daed's health issues, it's probably for the better." Tilly reached over and clasped Ruth's hand. "Retirement's a good thing for a hardworking farmer."

"I guess I just have a difficult time with change." She paused, remembering how tough it was for her after Tilly left home for Rockport, back when. "It's one of the reasons I wanted to come and live near you in Massachusetts." She faced her sister. "I never told you, but I missed you so much, Tilly. I thought leaving Eden Valley and being close to you might help me make sense of my life again."

"Aw, sister . . . that's the sweetest thing."

"I mean it."

"And here I always thought it was because of Will Kauffman's shenanigans."

"That too."

"Which is exactly why I'm thinking you'll want to steer clear of him while we're here." Tilly gave her a sly glance.

"I can't help being curious about what he has to say."

"That I can see . . . but again, I really caution you, sister." Tilly opened her side of the car. "Keep in mind the harm he did to you."

Ruth knew better than to say more and opened the door to step out of the car.

Tilly was relieved when Ruth headed to the stable. Taking this opportunity while the house was quiet, she hurried through the kitchen and into the small sitting space, where she found her mother relaxing with a devotional book. "Is Daed still resting?" she asked.

"*Jah*, but he headed upstairs a little bit ago," Mamm replied. "What have ya been doin'?"

"Well, we dropped in on Mammi Lantz," Tilly said, going to sit near her mother. "She seemed happy to see us."

Mamm pushed one of her *Kapp* strings behind her shoulder. "I'm sure she was. How's she doin' today?"

Tilly said she thought she was well.

"You can't always tell at her age."

"True." Tilly thought then of Dawdi Lantz's last years and how she'd missed out on them . . . including his funeral. *I never even made the effort to come.*

She noticed how calm her mother seemed, sitting so primly in her favorite chair. There had been satisfying moments like this with Mamm through the years, and she was grateful for them even as she settled in to reveal her offense. "Mamm," she began, removing the plastic bag from her purse. "I wrote you a little note, and I'd like you to read it." She removed the white head covering and gave it to her mother. "And this is Anna's *Kapp* . . . I took it when I left home."

Mamm's eyes glistened as she held it to her breast. "I always wondered what became of this."

"I should've asked you first . . . and I'm sorry."

"*Ach*, 'tis all right," Mamm whispered, her lower lip quivering. Tilly was taken aback by her gentle response.

Mamm smiled through tears. "Why not just keep it?" She looked fondly at the small cap and returned it to Tilly. "Maybe your twins would like to take turns wearing it," she said suddenly. "They can see what they'd look like as Amish girls."

"Oh, Mamma." Tilly rose and went to kneel beside her. She felt so tenderhearted just now. "*Denki* . . . thank you. This is so kind of you."

Her mother reached for her hand, and Tilly squeezed it. "Will Daed ever forgive me for leaving the Amish life, do you think?"

Mamm sighed. "Goodness, he'll have to if he wants to be forgiven himself by *Gott*. To tell the truth, ain't something he talks about."

Tilly should've known; she hadn't spoken this openly with her mother in a long time. She reached for her purse and placed Anna's *Kapp* back inside.

"But he is *ferhoodled*, I know that. Maybe upset at the Lord God . . . or himself. Maybe both."

Tilly wondered why her mother was telling her this, and why so freely.

CHAPTER 18

After Tilly left the house and drove away, Ruth wandered inside. She poured fresh milk into a tumbler and looked around for Mamm, who must have gone upstairs with Daed, since the first floor was quite vacant.

While outdoors, Ruth had enjoyed the lovely day, meandering around the back of the barnyard, looking over at the turkey pens—reliving the old days. She'd also noticed the Amish neighbors up the road carrying pots from the back porch to their blue potting shed, all covered in vines on the south side. *They must think winter's coming any minute now,* Ruth had thought.

Presently, she made her way to the front room and got settled on the soft settee, picking up her father's favorite periodical for Plain families, *The Budget.* It felt like such a long time since she'd read the interesting and sometimes humorous homespun stories the Amish scribes shared with Plain readers each week—many downright clever. The story that captured Ruth's immediate attention was a true account of a three-year-old Ohio Amish boy named Jakey, who'd somehow gotten himself trapped inside the family barn while his father and mother and many siblings hunted for him all over their vast property. When at last they found him inside and realized he was quite safe, they saw that he was not the least bit ruffled. To the contrary, little Jakey had occupied himself by putting feed in the horses' trough and grooming the German shepherd watchdog.

Sounds like something Will might've done at that age. But Ruth chided herself, thinking again that Wilmer was not a wise topic to consider. *No more!* she told herself, recalling Tilly's concern and admonition.

The afternoon dream she was having was certainly a pleasant beginning to her nap. In it, she was peeling apples for the cider press along with Tilly, helping their mother. Ruth was just ten years old and humming as she worked in the warm kitchen while dark clouds blew in from the north. The family effort of making cider had always been fun, although lots of work.

In the dream, Ruth felt annoyed by one-year-old Anna's whining. The little one, who'd just learned to walk, kept clinging to Tilly's hem until finally Tilly leaned down and picked her up.

"She ain't really a baby anymore," Mamm scolded. *"Let her sit in the playpen while yous work."*

"Aw, Mamm. Can't ya see she wants to be with us?" Tilly talked back.

"That'll come soon enough," Mamm replied, eyeing Tilly, who nonetheless kept Anna sitting on her lap.

In the dream, Ruth felt terribly tense. And when she woke up, she was perspiring, her teeth grinding. *Tilly often stood up to Mamm without being scolded,* she recalled. *Though it was never that way with Daed.*

Stretching, Ruth stared at a sunbeam across the room surrounded by motes of dust, which Mamm had always called *heavenly powder*. Sunlight touched the tall grandfather clock on the far wall, and she found herself growing misty-eyed.

This time tomorrow, Ruth would be gathering up her things, packing for the trip home Monday morning. And while she was eager to return to her real life . . . and her job, she also felt confused. Drowsy and snug, she was reluctant to leave the shelter of her surroundings.

Just then she heard her mother in the outer room, talking to Josie, who must've come back while Ruth was resting.

"So it's settled," Ruth heard her mother say in the kitchen. "We'll begin sorting through things Monday for the move this next week."

"All right, then," Josie said matter-of-factly. "I'll let Sam know."

Ruth sat straight up, nearly falling off the settee. *Next week? Moving to the* Dawdi Haus *that quick?*

She got up and made her way toward the kitchen, still sluggish from the effects of her nap and the strange flashback of a dream.

A few minutes later, when Sam came to pick up Josie, Ruth asked her mother if she'd overheard correctly. "I thought I might still be dreaming."

"Oh *jah*, I can see why. But it's all comin' together nicely," Mamm said, confirming their plans. "Though I *could* use some extra help with sorting, 'specially in the upstairs bedrooms and the attic. Well, and in the kitchen, too."

Ruth looked about her at all the many high cupboards, wondering how much her mother wanted to take next door. "Do you plan to have an estate auction?"

"We might have to if your brothers and their wives aren't interested in takin' our excess furnishings, ya know. We'll just have to see."

Maybe Tilly would want some of the dishes and linens. But Mamm hadn't mentioned either Tilly or Ruth. Ruth presumed their mother had too many things on her mind. After all, she and her sister were mostly out of sight, out of mind these days. "Well, will Josie and the other women in the family help you?"

"They want to, but I can't expect them to drop everything. They have their own lives and chores . . . and their little ones."

It was hard to imagine the womenfolk not converging over there en masse, like usual. In fact, Ruth was sure they would, but she had the sense Mamm wanted her to stay and help. *For old times' sake?*

"I wouldn't mind staying longer, if that would be a comfort to you, Mamm. Assuming I can get off work, that is. My boss has been encouraging me to take a vacation for some time now—Friday was my first day off since I started there."

"*Ach,* would ya consider it, then?" Her mother smiled briefly, then frowned. "But you rode here with Tilly, so how will that work?"

For a split second, she'd actually forgotten. "I see what you mean." Ruth was surprised at her feeling of disappointment.

"You might ask Tilly if she'd mind extending her time here, too," Mamm suggested hesitantly. "But, even so, it's all in *Gott's* hands." Mamm got up and went to the woodbin near the stove to put several pieces in the grate. "Would ya care for some coffee or tea?"

Ruth smiled. She hadn't sipped so many hot drinks in years. But the offer was her mother's way of continuing their discussion.

And, feeling grateful for their time together, Ruth agreed and went to get some tea leaves from the jar in the cupboard.

"The move's not as sudden as you might think," Mamm told her. "Your father's been talking 'bout it for at least three years."

Since I left? Ruth was shocked. "Really?"

Mamm nodded her head while she filled the teakettle with water. Then, not saying more, she went to get the sugar bowl from the center of the table, poured more sugar inside, and returned it to the table.

"Dairy farmers tend to burn out sooner than others, I daresay. The work is just plain exhausting. And now with your Daed's heart ailing . . ."

Ruth heard concern in her voice. "You must be worried."

"*Jah.* Awful hard seeing him this weak. I worry, too, 'bout how difficult it is for your Mammi Lantz to see her son this way, 'specially being a widow herself. At least she's never alone for long. The family makes sure she's included in all the work frolics and other gatherings, ya know."

Ruth had witnessed this blending of generations even as a child, while playing beneath quilting frames with other youngsters her age. Overhead, the older generations made small talk, sometimes having friendly competitions to see who could get more than five stitches on a single needle by taking the smallest stitches one could imagine. Often, as she recalled, Mammi Lantz won with five or even six.

Mamm resumed talking about the many duties of dairymen, even mentioning that many Amishmen were gathering advice from professionals at Penn State in addition to neighbors and family. The hours, Mamm said, were long and grueling. "Even regular farmwork has its challenges. Just taking soil samples and learning to fertilize and spray properly, or knowing when and how to plant and harvest correctly—all this takes time and knowledge," Mamm told her. "And energy, too."

"Can Sam keep up with everything, do you think?" Ruth asked.

"Well, it helps that he grew up here . . . and he's become accustomed to working at your uncle's dairy farm." Mamm dropped two sugar cubes into her coffee as she took a seat across from Ruth. "And he'll have some hired help, too, from two brothers."

"What about the money? Does he have what he needs to invest in herds or equipment for the field . . . maybe more land for the future?" Ruth asked, curious. "Or will Daed permit him to use all the existing equipment for now?"

"It'll take some time for the changeover, is all I know." Mamm reached for her hankie and dabbed at her eyes. She went on to say that she thought the move to the *Dawdi Haus* would be relatively painless, considering everything.

"The Lord will be with us," Ruth said, surprising herself. It sounded even to her ears as if she were already committed to staying.

"*Jah*, for sure and for certain."

Her mother was winding down, ready to simply sit quietly with the late-afternoon sun drenching her back with warmth and light. Regardless of Mamm's downplaying it, all the talk of the upcoming adjustment had taken its toll. And Ruth was more than sorry she had no way to stay here longer for Mamm's sake.

On a whim, Tilly stopped in at the Bird-in-Hand Farmers Market and perused the aisles, reliving her childhood and later years at this and other farmers markets in the area. Without her Amish garb today, she wasn't recognized as Plain at all, even though there were times when she still felt quite Plain inside.

Glancing down the long aisle, she was drawn to the handmade quilted table linens, and later, she moseyed over to look at the neatly lined up jams and jellies—especially the strawberry and peach, as delicious as they were beautiful.

A number of vendors were interacting with customers, a lively atmosphere permeating the marketplace. She wondered if any of her kinfolk had a booth set up there but doubted it. After all, Bird-in-Hand was a long way by horse and buggy from Eden Valley. It would take some doing to transport merchandise and helpers to tend to the long market tables, something that usually involved calling for a paid driver. Daed was never too keen on car rides, she recalled as she strolled the aisles.

In the far north corner, Tilly noticed Josie's plump brown-eyed mother, Edith Riehl, generally known as Edie. The woman smiled when she spotted her but then seemed to regard Tilly suspiciously, as if she wasn't sure she knew her at all.

"It's Tilly Lantz," she said, leaving off her married name. *Too confusing.*

"Well, for goodness' sake, it sure is." Edith Riehl reached for Tilly's hands and gripped them both, pulling her around toward the side of the table. "I've been wondering 'bout you." She looked her over right quick. "Don't ya miss bein' Amish, Tilly girl?"

A leading question for certain. "Don't worry, you can't take the Plain life out of me . . . not completely," Tilly said politely—and truthfully—although her answer was vague enough not to get her in too deep with her sister-in-law's dear mother.

"And you have little ones, I hear," Edie said, wiping perspiration from her face. "Josie told me about your twins. It wonders me . . . what's it like raisin' a matchin' pair?" She smiled, eyes growing wider as she seemed to lose the battle not to gawk at Tilly.

Tilly explained that what one twin didn't think of, the other certainly did. "It's been like that since they began to crawl—and always in opposite directions, if you can imagine." She had to laugh, partly to relieve some tension. She'd spent so many delightful times at the Riehls' farm during the years she and Josie were like sisters—the best of friends.

"When will ya bring the twins to see us?"

"We'll have to figure out a time." She realized after she'd said it that she might seem as though she was putting Edie off. But what else could she do?

"Time's a-wastin'," Edie said. "I'm sure your Daed and Mamm would enjoy meeting two more of their grandchildren." The older woman fell silent before adding, "I just *know* they would."

Tilly nodded. She had definitely felt bad that her girls were growing up without the benefit of their Anabaptist grandparents. In fact, she'd stewed over it frequently.

"Your Daed might not have much time left, I'm sure you've heard," Edie said, pulling out a chair and waving toward it. "Care to sit awhile?"

Feeling pressured, Tilly respectfully declined. "I need to get back to Eden Valley," she said.

"It's nice you got to see your parents in their place once more. They're movin' right quick," Edie said as if it were common knowledge.

Tilly was shocked at the immediacy but tried not to overreact.

After all, she'd already heard most of this from Mammi Lantz. "How soon?"

"From what I've heard, in just a few days."

"Well, Daed's been hard at work these many years," Tilly said. "There comes a time to slow down, you know."

"For everything, a time and season," Edie agreed. "Such a shame when old age creeps up, ya know. Next thing, health begins to slide, too."

Tilly pursed her lips. Despite Daed's heart, it was hard to think of her parents growing old.

"Don't be a stranger, all right?" Edie said and gave a wave when Tilly mentioned she ought to get going.

Tilly thanked her, but there was no changing her stranger status this late in the game. "Tell Josie I saw you, all right?" Tilly added.

"That I will." Edie walked with her partway down the busy aisle. "Awful nice seein' you again."

On the way back toward Strasburg, it wasn't running into Josie's mother that occupied Tilly's thoughts. Her parents' upcoming move took precedence, and Tilly couldn't help thinking this was partly why Melvin had urged her and Ruth home.

CHAPTER 19

*W*ill Kauffman's open buggy was parked halfway into Daed's driveway, black and sparkling with polish in the early evening light. Just a few short minutes before, Ruth had seen Will dart across the back lawn, then open the barn door and disappear inside. Curious, she walked downstairs to peer out the back door window, wondering what on earth Will was doing there. Since he hadn't come to the door and knocked, she guessed he wasn't there to see her. *A relief.* "Must be returning something to Daed," she murmured, not wanting to snoop.

She'd heard her father's heavy footsteps on the stairs not long ago, so she assumed he was more rested now and out in the barn. *Where Will is . . .*

Ruth refused to stand there and wait for very long. She had other things to occupy her time, didn't she? Things like preparing supper and setting the table. Mamm would be back down to join her in the kitchen any moment—things were running behind this busy day.

She wouldn't let herself think of stepping outside and

calling to Will, if she happened to see him coming this way. No, that was the farthest thing from her mind.

∽

Melvin came across the cold remains of a cigar out near the outhouse. He headed back to the barn and went to the stable, wondering where Caleb and Benny were getting their cigars. Somewhere in Strasburg or Lancaster, no doubt. Of course, there was always the possibility they were rolling their own. One of his uncles had done the selfsame thing when he was a teenager. It wasn't so much Caleb and Benny's smoking behind the trees that irked Melvin, but rather where their sneaking around might lead them. He prayed that, in the long run, it wouldn't lead them out of the church.

Like Tilly and Ruth.

On a happier note, just knowing his sisters were home, even for this short visit, was something of a comfort. And now with word out that Daed and Mamm planned to scale back immediately, and that Sam was definitely taking over the dairy, Melvin couldn't help but think it was nothing short of providential that he'd contacted Tilly and Ruth. The fact that they had actually returned after initially digging in their heels, well, it just seemed mighty surprising, as he thought about it. "Even miraculous," he whispered to himself as he worked to refresh the bedding straw. *Thank the Good Lord.*

∽

Potatoes were boiling in Mamm's big black pot as Ruth carried four plates over to the table and glanced outside. Her breath caught in her throat. There, just outside the window, a young woman was sitting in Will's courting carriage. For the life of her, Ruth didn't know how she'd missed this.

So he is seeing someone! she decided. No wonder he'd asked to talk to her earlier. "He must want to tell me he's engaged," Ruth said right out.

In her mind, she played back the conversation—if she could even call it that—out on the road earlier today. *Will said it was important. . . .*

But did she really want to hear about the pretty girl with strawberry-blond hair just out the window? Ruth turned away with half a notion to pull the blind down so she wasn't tempted to gawk.

Puh! Why should he have to tell her of his engagement? There was simply no need!

∞

Tilly returned just in time for supper. Daed nodded at her as he came indoors for the meal, and Tilly did her best to greet him cordially, though the words sounded stilted even to her. She was uncertain what to do and was relieved when it was time for all of them to take a place at the table, followed by the silent prayer.

When the blessing was finished, Tilly passed the mashed potatoes to Mamm, who in turn handed them to Daed. The thick chicken gravy followed.

The first part of the meal passed mostly in silence until they'd eaten their fill, and Tilly was encouraged by her father's appetite after his earlier sick spell. The color in his face had returned somewhat, and he seemed to be feeling better. *An answer to prayer.*

Ruth, however, appeared almost nervous. Tilly wondered

if her sister was already feeling homesick, realizing their visit was drawing to a close. Or was she simply tense due to this being their first meal together, the four of them? The latter seemed more likely.

As Tilly had expected, Daed was aloof and only glanced at her now and then, not saying much. She recalled what Mamm had said about Daed's being upset at God and shuddered a bit.

Then, without warning, Ruth sat up straight in her chair and announced, "I'd like to stay the week and help Mamm sort things, Tilly." Ruth looked at her, then at Daed. "If that's all right."

"Why, sure 'tis," Mamm was quick to say. "But how will you get home?"

Shyly, Ruth replied, "I've thought it over. I'll take a bus. No need to worry about me."

Tilly was baffled beyond words at this sudden news.

"I'd planned to miss work on Monday anyway, and my boss told me before I left to take extra time if I wanted. I just need to let him know."

"Well, wasn't that nice," Mamm remarked.

"You're welcome to stay, too, Tilly." Ruth's eyes were pleading.

Daed brusquely cleared his throat and looked toward the window.

He'd rather I was on my way, Tilly thought.

"Sure, you're welcome, too, dear," Mamm chimed in. "Why not sleep on it . . . decide tomorrow, on the Lord's Day. *Wunnerbaar-gut* things can happen on His day, ya know."

Tilly had heard this plenty of times growing up, but she wasn't so sure it would prove true in this case.

"Please think about it." Ruth reinforced her campaign.

"Mamm's right," Tilly said at last. "I'll sleep on it."

144

A smile blossomed on Ruth's face.

She thinks I've decided, Tilly thought, not so amused. Quickly, she changed the subject. "Guess who I ran into at Bird-in-Hand market this afternoon?"

Mamm looked startled. "You went all the way there today?"

"Must've been Edith Riehl," Daed said, finally joining in the conversation.

Tilly nodded. "Yes, and Edie happened to say you were moving soon. I expect that's the reason for the sorting Ruthie wants to help with."

Mamm sighed loudly. "Well, for pity's sake. The word's out." She began to unfold the plan to sort and pack up on Monday through Wednesday, then move to the attached *Dawdi Haus* on Thursday. "Lord willing, of course."

"*Jah,* if *Gott's* hand's in it, we'll move just thataway," Daed said, wiping his mouth on his sleeve cuff. His eyes squinted nearly shut as he looked Tilly's direction.

"Melvin's offered some boxes he has sitting around in the cellar," Mamm mentioned. "And muscle power, too."

"Just don't walk to Melvin's through the woodlot after dark," Daed said, eyes serious as he glanced first at Ruth, then Tilly. "Or anytime, really." He emphasized this with a deep frown.

Usually, it was Mamm saying it wasn't smart to cut through the woodlot. "*Better to go out on the road, or around through the pasture,*" she'd often advised.

Tilly had ignored the admonition more times than she cared to disclose, knowing that both alternate routes took longer. She'd never seen anything to worry about in there. But what did she know? Maybe someone had gotten bitten by a wood-chuck or a snake.

"How much work can you really afford to miss, Ruth?"

145

Tilly asked, wondering if her younger sister had money socked away somewhere.

When Ruth didn't reply, Tilly decided not to take it up at the table, not with their parents observing. She did intend to get to the bottom of Ruth's sudden change of plans. It was hard to fathom that Ruth merely wanted to help Mamm and Daed move. There had to be more behind it.

"Will Kauffman stopped by to return some tools," Daed said then. "Forgot to mention that earlier."

Will was here?

Tilly wondered if Ruth's conniving former beau had cornered the poor, vulnerable girl and talked her into taking him back. And looking now at her sister's blushing red face, Tilly guessed she might be on to something.

I leave here for a couple of hours, and Ruth's lured right back to the Plain life.

CHAPTER 20

*F*eeling out of sorts, Tilly retired early that night. She was so rattled, she didn't even accept Aunt Naomi's invitation to sit and have some decaffeinated tea before bedtime. Later, she fretted, unable to sleep, and finally wandered out into the front room and sat there in the dark.

This can't be happening. After everything, is Ruth willing to give up her wonderful modern life? Has she forgotten what Will did to her? Does she relish the thought of being totally submissive to someone like him?

Tilly's mind ran wild with all sorts of worrisome thoughts. Nighttime hours had a tendency to stir up such thinking.

Yet truthfully, she was beginning to think her sister had never gotten over Will Kauffman, which was downright confusing. All those letters flying back and forth between her and Ruth, and all the many months of counseling her away from such a young man and his questionable leanings. Was it all for naught?

Tired, she trudged back to her room and lifted the quilts to get into bed. She fought sleep, even though she was worn out, though more from the energy that went into the stress and frustration of such a day.

Eventually an idea hit her like lightning, and she sat up in bed. *I have to stay, too! To protect Ruthie.* Yes, tomorrow she would call Kris and ask his opinion. *Surely he won't mind . . . and neither will his mother.*

"My mother-in-law will be happily running the ship by the time I get back," Tilly whispered, smiling into the darkness. "But I'll be *here* with Ruth, talking sense to her. Like always."

Ruth shed her covers and rose to light the small lantern, anxious to write a prayer in her small notebook, something she did when she was this keyed up. Although she had been quick to spout off her wishes, despite what she'd said, she had fears that her job might not still be waiting when she returned to Rockport. Yet staying to help her parents with this transition seemed important, especially now, and she prayed that Tilly might see the light and stay around, too. The extra days might give Tilly and Daed an opportunity to reconnect . . . before his health worsened. At supper, she'd witnessed anew the unspoken tension between her father and sister. *Why has it always been that way?*

She began to pray about that, as well as the other things that slipped unbidden into her mind. *O Lord, bless Will and his sweetheart . . . give them a good life together. And many little ones*, she wrote.

Then, wanting to do the right thing by her former beau, she decided to hear him out tomorrow after Preaching service and the shared meal. Yes, she would take the high road. It was the gracious thing to do, after all.

The next morning, Tilly got up, washed, and dressed quickly so she could help Aunt Naomi prepare breakfast for Uncle Abner before the couple headed off to church. Tilly knew for certain she would not be attending the Preaching service up the road. She was far too sleepy to last through such a lengthy meeting.

"Didn't ya sleep so *gut?*" Aunt Naomi asked when she saw Tilly come into the kitchen.

"Hardly at all."

"Guess you'll be noddin' off in church, then."

"Actually, I'm staying home to rest," she told her aunt. "If you don't mind."

Aunt Naomi smoothed her gray work dress and apron and gave her a nod. "Well, then you can keep your uncle company, maybe, since he didn't sleep much either last night."

"Is he under the weather?"

Her aunt explained that he sometimes had bad headaches, but she thought they were caused more by stress than anything. "Growin' older ain't so easy," she told Tilly. "You'll find out, in another few decades."

Tilly wasn't looking forward to it. "Sure, I'll be happy to keep him company, if we don't both fall asleep in our coffee."

This brought a big smile to Aunt Naomi's face. "You should just go back to bed after breakfast. A full stomach should put you right out," she said. "I know it does me." She went on to say she'd been known to fall sound asleep during the sermons, but as far as she knew, folk thought she was just being pious, keeping her head down in prayer.

"Mammi Lantz used to do the same thing," Tilly mentioned.

"Back when you were still Amish?" Naomi said out of the blue. And just as quickly, her dear face turned cherry red. "I didn't mean . . ." she sputtered.

"Don't fret about it, Aendi." Tilly cracked farm-fresh eggs into a bowl and stirred in some raw milk to make scrambled eggs, Uncle Abner's favorite.

"He likes a piece of cheese on top," Aunt Naomi mentioned. "Guess I've spoiled him."

"It's wonderful to be spoiled now and then," Tilly thought out loud. "That's something I never really experienced until I married Kris."

A peculiar look altered Aunt Naomi's expression. "You weren't made over much when you were little?"

"By Mamm, sure."

"Not your Daed, too?"

"If he did, I don't remember." The painful words spilled out.

"Oh now, Tilly, how could that be?"

It just was, she thought, recalling all the love Daed showered upon both Ruth and Anna and their brothers. Again, it was simply a fact . . . not something to fuss over. "No need to feel sorry for me," she told Aunt Naomi.

"Well, but I do." Her aunt glanced back over her shoulder at her as she carried coffee to the table. "I truly do."

It was enough that someone believed her and didn't assume that Tilly was sorely mistaken. *Always wrong,* she thought sadly.

⚭

The church gathering was well attended, but Ruth felt strange sitting in the back row, dressed as she was, though quite modestly by English standards. On the opposite side, to her right, a row of young men in their late teens and early twenties sat together. Will Kauffman and Lloyd Blank were at the far end of the row.

They must still be friends . . . and on the edge of the church, Ruth thought, aware of someone's cologne. If Will planned to marry soon—and the girl in his courting buggy was certainly Old Order Amish—then he would be joining church somewhere. Whether or not it was Eden Valley, she had no way of knowing.

During *"Das Loblied"*—the praise song and traditional second hymn—she looked about to see if she could spot the pretty young woman she'd seen with Will yesterday in his open carriage—surely a sign they were at least courting, if not engaged. Was she also attending church here today?

Ruth looked for Tilly, as well, but didn't see her sitting in back with the other Englishers. She looked up now toward the front to Mamm and two of Mamm's older sisters. It was fascinating to see the large number of young women with babes in arms—girls she'd grown up with who'd already settled down and married. *Are they happy?* she wondered, then, chagrined, she realized she was not being reverent. She ought to rein in her thoughts at this holy hour. *I'm like an unruly filly!*

<hr />

After a good long rest, Tilly wandered back downstairs and found Uncle Abner sitting at the kitchen table with his German *Biewel* open next to his King James. He was practicing his English, and then his German, by doing so. He looked up when she came in, and she noticed he wore a white long-sleeved shirt and a black vest and trousers—his church clothes—in honor of the Lord's Day even though he'd stayed home. He motioned for her to join him.

She sat without speaking, feeling somewhat refreshed from the extra sleep following breakfast. She'd definitely eaten more than she was accustomed to at home with Kris and the twins.

"You look bright-eyed now, Tilly."

"Did you rest, too?" she asked quickly.

"Quite a bit, *jah*. Not sure what kept me awake last night." He smiled. "Might've been the full moon. I tend to be more wakeful during that phase."

"I didn't sleep that well, either," she admitted. "Lots on my mind, I guess."

"Well, it must be a bit strange comin' back here," Abner suggested. "'Specially when there are some sad tokens from things long past." His solemn look was gentle.

She didn't wish to rehash her past troubles relating to Daed. Just the awareness of his standoffishness toward her was difficult enough. And not much seemed to have changed, although he had been a bit more talkative than she'd expected.

"If ya don't mind, I'd like to tell you a story," Uncle Abner said, folding his hands over his German Bible.

She nodded, interested.

"I was just a boy, oh, maybe nine or ten," he began, a smile on his wrinkled face. "I happened to overhear my father talking to the preacher in the stable, and, lo and behold, if it didn't sound like he was braggin' on me. He said, 'Well now, Preacher, I'd have to say my boy Abner's a mighty hard worker. Dependable, too.' And right then and there, the Preacher decided, based solely on *Dat's* account of me, that he wanted to hire me to groom his road horses."

Uncle Abner sighed, the recollection clearly meaningful to

him even now. "My father's opinion of me gave me the determination to always take my work seriously and be responsible. His words changed my life that day, Tilly. I wanted to live up to his expectations. I honestly did. And I hope I have."

She wondered why he was telling her this when he must surely know about her own sour father-daughter relationship. "I've made it a point to say positive, affirming things to my children," she told him. "My husband's the same way with them."

"That's important. Life-changing, really," Abner said, nodding so his thick beard bumped his chest.

She was at a loss, still not understanding what he'd intended for her to glean from the story.

"Your Daed may not have said the kinds of things that made ya want to strive for certain higher qualities," Abner said. "And for that, you must be willing to forgive him."

She hadn't thought of it quite that way.

"Your return here, 'specially at this feeble season in your Daed's life, well . . . it might just be timely."

Tilly wasn't ready yet to put all that aside and forget. But she found it remarkable that her uncle still had that way about him that could peer deep into her heart. "I hear what you're saying."

"*Jah*, but hearin' and doin'—are they the same?"

She sighed. It would have been easier going to church this morning.

He continued. "I daresay you oughta consider what I've told ya. You've got less than a day till ya leave for home," he urged. "Better to make amends before someone passes on than to kick yourself for waitin' and end up too late."

She folded her arms. "I think you know me nearly as well as I know myself." Even so, she felt pressured.

Uncle Abner cupped his hand to his ear as though he wanted her to repeat it, sporting that mischievous grin. "What's that?"

She couldn't help but smile. "I'll think on it."

He reached over and patted her arm. "That's my girl."

Tilly looked away quickly, concealing the start of tears. In spite of the fact that the Lord of heaven and earth never made errors, there had been days years ago when she'd secretly wished—even prayed—that somehow or other God had gotten her and her parents mixed up. That Uncle Abner was, in all truth, her father instead of Daed. In this moment, Tilly felt the same stirrings. *"Denki,"* she whispered, looking back at him. "I just don't know how to go about it."

"Let me just say that, from what I've learned, offering forgiveness doesn't have to go according to any plan." He ran his fingers through his bushy beard. "I'd say it's a matter of the heart."

Tilly let his words sink in.

Later, when she returned to her room and opened her Bible, she was amazed to stumble onto one of the verses her grandmother Lantz had read to her many times when Tilly was little. "For if ye forgive men their trespasses, your heavenly Father will also forgive you: but if ye forgive not men their trespasses, neither will your Father forgive your trespasses."

How long will I harbor this bitterness against Daed? she thought forlornly.

CHAPTER 21

At the shared meal following Preaching, Ruth sat with Mamm and across from her grandmother, glad to see Mammi Lantz again. "*Denki* for the pretty hankies," she said, pulling one from her purse. She showed it to her mother, pointing out the delicate embroidery.

"*Ach*, it looks exactly like one I made for *you*," Mamm said to her mother-in-law with a soft laugh.

Ruth's grandmother's face turned nearly as red as a boiled beet. "Well now, I never intended to give away—"

"*Puh!* Don't fret," Mamm said.

Ruth was secretly glad for the mix-up. This way, she had something of her grandmother's, and one that Mamm had made, as well. "I'm just ever so grateful."

"To be back in Eden Valley?" Mammi asked, her eyes sparkling.

"Well, *jah*, and that, too," Ruth admitted, holding up the handkerchief again. "I should brush up on my embroidery skills. The stitching on this is nearly perfect."

"It's never too late to pick up where ya left off," Mammi Lantz said.

"Why not tomorrow?" Ruth's mother suggested with a twinkle of a smile.

"Thought we were going to begin sorting." Ruth was puzzled.

"I was teasin' you," Mamm said.

Ruth giggled, happy to be with these two women once more, even for a short while. *To think Tilly and I almost stayed away. . . .*

Much later, after apple pie was served, Ruth noticed Will heading for the back door without Lloyd, who was still talking with other young men his age at the end of one of the tables.

This is my chance, Ruth thought, hoping it wouldn't appear that she was running after him. In spite of that, she excused herself and nonchalantly slipped outside.

Melvin was sipping his black coffee when he noticed Ruth leave by way of the back door. Oddly enough, it wasn't but a few moments after Wilmer Kauffman had left, as well. There had been rumors some years back that Deacon Kauffman's grandson was mighty sweet on Ruthie, but then Will quit going to church for the longest time and Ruth left Eden Valley. Melvin hadn't thought much more about it other than to thank the Good Lord that his sister hadn't gotten herself hitched up with Will, considering what he'd heard later.

"You see that?" Chester leaned over and whispered at him.

Melvin waved his hand. "*Ach*, might not be anything, really. Ain't like Ruthie to chase after—"

"No, and she ain't Plain no more," Chester added. "Will'd have to be awful desperate to let a right fancy girl catch him—our sister or not."

"Young folk." Melvin reached for his pie, glad for it. His

stomach had done its share of rumbling off and on all during the second sermon.

No matter his exchange with Chester, one thing was certain: Young people had few hesitations when it came to love. *Few, indeed.*

Ruth didn't have to walk fast to catch up with Will, who was the picture of piety in his black vest, white long-sleeved shirt, and black broadfall trousers. He turned and saw her coming, then, removing his black hat, he began to walk back toward her. A breeze swept his blond hair over his eyebrows. When he came closer, he suggested they go around the barn and walk where they wouldn't be seen. "Thought maybe I scared ya off yesterday," he said quietly.

They were both still thinking about that brief encounter out on the road.

"I wonder if congratulations are in order," she said when he looked her way. "I'm ever so happy for—"

"For what, Ruthie? For me finally getting your attention, maybe?" He gave his usual tuneful chuckle.

She was confused. "What do you mean?"

He stopped near a shade tree, motioning for her to join him. "Like I told ya yesterday, I have something important on my mind." He paused to glance at the sky, then back at her. "It's been a long time comin', but now that you're home again, I want you to hear this directly."

His expression was so serious, she had no idea what he was about to say.

"I have to tell ya, Ruth, I feel like I've been reborn," Will continued. "And I'm not sure I can explain what actually happened . . . but I'll try."

Even more curious now, she kept her eyes on him.

"I've made peace with God," he told her. "Some months ago, I realized you were right—the Jamborees gang was a bad fit for me. So while it took some doin', I've started over with a new buddy group. We're far more conservative, I can assure ya." He leaned against the trunk of the tree, looking more humble than pleased. "I never should've followed Lloyd back then—should've made up my own mind."

Hearing all this from Will was nearly unbelievable. The peer gang a person chose during *Rumschpringe* was the group that a person followed throughout life. You paired up with your mate in that group and worked side by side with those friends, who became a sort of extended family. Typically, there was no breaking away from the group, no saying, *"I changed my mind."*

"I guess I don't understand," Ruth said. "How'd you get out?"

"It required a lot of time on my knees in prayer. And even then, it wasn't so easy." He explained how he'd gone to his parents and the ministerial brethren for advice, then talked to the few adult sponsors of the rowdy group, explaining his situation—how he felt convicted of having a radio and a camera, for starters, and eventually a car, and water skis. He was thankful he hadn't gotten caught up in drinking alcohol or using drugs. Some of his friends would tell him they couldn't remember what they did the Saturday nights they drank too much. A few of them got caught one way or another, and Will just didn't want that sort of wild life before marriage—or afterward.

Ruth was relieved for Will, but she was baffled by why he was telling her this now.

"There's more." His voice grew soft. "You might not believe it, but I haven't forgotten you, Ruthie. Not at all."

Considering the pretty girl in Will's carriage yesterday, his admission was bewildering. Wracking her brain, Ruth was sure she knew all of his cousins—the young woman was *not* a relative. "Have you forgotten, Will? I'm no longer Amish." It wasn't the only thing she wanted to say, but it was the first thing that came to mind.

"Well, I wonder if, deep down, you've actually turned your back on the Old Ways."

"I'm enjoying a good life," she answered. "Involved in a church I love, learning more about Christ's teachings—and I have lots of new friends . . . a great job. And I really like living near my sister and her family."

"That's not what I asked, though." Will's eyes penetrated hers. "Have you abandoned the Amish ways in your *heart*?"

Such a thing was nearly impossible, she'd discovered. The Amish world would always hold special meaning for her, no matter how worldly she might appear. She did appreciate that he still seemed to care for her, and oh, how she'd missed talking to him. There had been a time when she could hardly wait to do just that. Even so, Ruth wasn't going to let Will think she'd come rushing back for him. That was another thing altogether.

"Remember the old saying—Go *far from home, and you'll have a long road back*," he quoted.

She hadn't forgotten.

"You know what, Ruthie? It's been a long while since we've shared our thoughts like this. So askin' questions is a *gut* thing," he reminded her. "For both of us."

Ruth wondered if she ought to bring up the young woman— she didn't want to seem jealous. "Well . . . aren't you seein' someone, Will?" she asked hesitantly.

He shook his head no, then rubbed his forehead.

So, is this little talk merely for old times' sake? She stepped back, feeling awkward and still puzzled.

Just then they heard rustling behind them, and footsteps, and she turned to see the very girl she was about to inquire of. When Ruth looked back at Will, she caught him smiling suddenly at the appearance of the younger woman.

"Oh, there you are," the slight woman said, eyes alight. "I've been lookin' all over for ya, Will."

"I didn't realize you were in church today." His neck and face looked flushed. "Honestly thought you'd—"

"I wasn't. Just walked down to see if you were still around," the girl with the strawberry-blond hair said, eyeing Ruth. "One of the men inside said they'd seen ya head this way."

Will looked embarrassed, but he must have remembered his manners, because he began to introduce them. "Ruth, I'd like you to meet Arie Schlabach, here from Mount Hope, Ohio. And Arie, this is Ruthie Lantz, who grew up just a few farms over."

"Ah, we meet at last." Arie stepped forward and shot out a stiff hand. "Will's spoken of you from time to time." She took in Ruth's modern attire without even trying to hide her curiosity. Or was it disdain?

The three of them exchanged comments about the enormous size of Allen's farm and the upcoming cold weather. Then Arie asked if Ruth was going to the evening Singing in the barn behind them.

Ruth didn't have the heart to say she wasn't interested. "No, not me," she said instead. "But I know you'll have a fine time. I'll be visiting with my parents later."

By now, Will looked even more uncomfortable, as if he were feeling claustrophobic with two women near.

"I'll catch up with you later," Will told Arie, his voice firm. Was it his way of telling her to leave him alone with Ruth? Such a prickly, peculiar situation this was! Ruth wished she had stayed back at the house.

Arie raised her eyebrows and nodded, then turned and walked back along the dirt path toward the barn.

Ruth asked, "Is that . . ."

"*Jah*, she was with me in the carriage yesterday when I went to bring a bunch of boxes over to your father."

"Arie obviously likes you, Will. Quite a lot, in fact."

He removed his black hat and rubbed his hand over his clean-shaven chin. "S'pose she does, and she's nice enough. But she ain't . . ." He glanced back toward wherever Arie had headed.

The other girl was nowhere in sight, and Ruth felt more awkward than ever, standing there alone with Will. She wanted to ask if he'd rather go after Arie—it sure seemed that way.

Then, just as she opened her mouth, Will excused himself right quick and darted off to head around the barn, leaving Ruth standing there, quite befuddled.

She scratched her head, wondering if Will even knew his own mind. *The silly boy!*

Ruth turned and rounded the opposite side of the barn, in case Will and Arie were on the other side talking privately, or who knew what else. She did not care to see the two of them together again. And as she walked toward the meadow, deciding not to return to the house just yet, she knew without a doubt that Jim Montgomery would never, ever treat her in such a flippant way!

CHAPTER 22

*I*nstead of remaining at the house with Uncle Abner, Tilly got in the car and headed to Central Park in Lancaster. She didn't feel put out by her uncle's earlier remarks, knowing it was simply his bold and frank way. The man loved her beyond measure; she knew as much. But she wasn't sure she could manage a wholesale act of forgiveness toward Daed, and even if she could, she didn't have the slightest inkling of how to attempt it. Worst of all, what if he refused her effort to reconcile?

All too likely, she thought.

Tilly walked the expanse of the picnic area at the familiar park. Ribbons of tall grass swayed near the banks, with craggy driftwood scattered over the leaf-strewn ground. The sound of the water struck her as she approached the river, the swift movement as it flowed, ever moving, tossing, churning. From her vantage point, it was impossible to see into the water beyond the reflection of the twisted black bark of ancient trees, though its crest was far lower than the swell of that terrible day.

For the life of her, she couldn't remember the exact place where she'd last seen Anna walking with Ruthie and Josie, following the picnic that day. So many details were lost to her. She hadn't forgotten, however, the sting of her baby sister's words earlier that Sunday morning. In the privacy of Anna's room, her sister had looked up with her wide blue eyes and shouted, *"Ya act like you're my Mamma!"*

Hurt, Tilly had hardly known how to respond, though she had urged Anna to be more gentle with her words. Still, she had been astonished and realized her young sister must be too doted upon to talk so. After all, Anna was expected to obey her elders, and Tilly was truly that.

Earlier that week, Anna had tried her patience, spilling a full pan of snapped peas on the kitchen floor, the tiny green pods scattering every which way, after multiple warnings to be more careful. It was a good thing Mamm had been out delivering homemade cottage cheese to her cousin up the road at the time so she could not see Tilly's frustration over the incident.

Even now, Tilly disliked that Anna, the little darling of the house, had been able to push her buttons like that. There was no way Anna would have ever let their father see her misbehave so. Tilly recalled how Daed had carried Anna on his shoulders for nearly an hour some weeks before, Anna giggling as she ordered Daed around. Tilly couldn't imagine her father putting up with the same from her at that age. *Anna was obviously Daed's favorite*, she thought now.

"Mamma always wants ya to look after me." Anna's words that final morning came back to her now. At the time, Tilly

had made herself take in a few slow breaths, then went to sit on the cane chair near Anna's little rocker. She'd purposed in her heart not to retaliate and held out her arms to Anna instead, trying to demonstrate unconditional love, like Mamm. *"Kumme, Anna. . . . Hock dich naah!—Sit by my side."*

Anna had stared back mischievously. *"Nee."*

"Ich liebe dich," Tilly said softly, tears welling up. *"I love you. Honest, I do."*

But Anna refused to budge.

It was normal for a five-year-old to exert her will—Tilly had certainly done that, too, and even long after her early years. Yet she was very sure neither Daed nor Mamm had seen their youngest daughter behave so.

Tilly wondered if her clingy little shadow was merely testing her. *"You're just going to have to obey, Anna, and learn to do so more often,"* she'd said.

After a few tense moments, Anna had nodded her sweet head and meekly apologized as Tilly declared again how much she loved her. Creeping forward, Anna had come and wrapped her arms around Tilly's neck, then sat on her lap. Later, she'd begun to jabber about starting school that fall—first grade— saying that she was no longer a *Bobbli*.

Did we spoil her? Tilly wondered now. *Did I?*

Presently, standing on the brink of the windswept spot— eerie with its tattered treetops and broken branches—she finally paid her last respects. Too distraught to attend the funeral, Tilly had remained in bed for the service, which was minus a casket—unheard of in the Amish community. But Bishop Isaac was insistent there be a fitting funeral for Lester and Sylvia's youngest child, no matter the strange circumstances.

Tilly stared now at the red and gold leaves swirling like her thoughts in the rapidly moving river. She felt off balance, as if she were the one moving. The large body of water traveled on for sixty-one miles, yet in places, it was shallow enough to walk across. *Not that summer, though.* She recalled its elevated crest and trembled. What was it like for poor Anna to drown? Had she suffered for long?

All my fault . . . If only I'd kept a closer eye on her!

Crouching in the high grass, Tilly's years of pent-up anguish flowed freely. She sobbed and wished she'd done everything differently. *Everything.*

When she rose at last, brushing away tears, she looked once more at the dreaded river. Since Anna's death, it had been such a barrier . . . a place and a moment she could not seem to move past.

A line I can't move beyond . . . like my relationship with Daed.

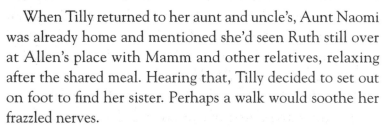

When Tilly returned to her aunt and uncle's, Aunt Naomi was already home and mentioned she'd seen Ruth still over at Allen's place with Mamm and other relatives, relaxing after the shared meal. Hearing that, Tilly decided to set out on foot to find her sister. Perhaps a walk would soothe her frazzled nerves.

Tilly recalled again her uncle's advice, unable to dismiss the things he had said that morning. Numerous times as a child, she'd huddled in the dark corners of her room and whispered her admissions of guilt to the heavenly Father. "I carried the weight of being wrong all the time," she murmured as she walked toward her brother Allen's house, where church had been held. How had things gone for Ruthie this Lord's Day?

Tilly pictured her running into Will Kauffman, him gazing into her sister's eyes. No—she had to shake off that notion.

As she walked the road, Tilly waved at each of the boxlike gray family carriages that passed her, the quaint sound of *clip-clop-clip* wonderful-good in her ears. Absently, she decided if there was anything she missed about Amish life, it was the appealing sound of horses pulling buggies in the early hours on a market-day morning. But not much else . . . not the Plain attire, nor the hard work of running a home without electricity or indoor plumbing, nor the required attitude of *Gelassenheit*—turning one's back on individuality and wholly yielding to the community and to God. She certainly did not miss the fattening foods, either, as delicious as many of them were. *I'd be as big as Uncle Abner's two-story barn if I'd stayed,* she mused.

On the other hand, she was fairly sure her sister did miss various aspects of the life she'd left behind. Their family here, especially Mamm and her siblings, was a given . . . and the little ones she didn't even really know and might not see again until they were half grown or older. Ruth had also enjoyed the work frolics and gatherings of the womenfolk—cornhusking and canning bees, too. Tilly knew that well.

But Ruthie left to escape her disappointment over Will.

Tilly heard the clatter of carriage wheels, and looking up, she saw two black courting buggies coming at a fast clip. The first buggy was occupied by a tall driver with a shy-looking girl next to him. As they approached, the pair bowed their heads in unison, not wishing to be identified, undoubtedly newly courting. Tilly recalled doing the same thing as a teenager with her first beau—hardworking Abram Stoltzfus, with his hearty laugh.

Oh, the bliss and madness of first love. Tilly was relieved now that she hadn't married young Abram, although he had been fun to be with and knew what type of farmer he wanted to be when he was older. Joy and determination were two important traits for a good Amish match. At the time, however, she had been nervous about her father's strict rules and tendency to dominate the house, and she wasn't thrilled at the prospect of handing over the reins of her life to another man, at least not an Amishman.

Now the second buggy, directly behind the first, came near the shoulder, carrying none other than Will Kauffman. Tilly wasn't sure if she should catch his eye or not, guessing he might still be annoyed with her from yesterday, but Will gave a friendly wave. She nodded, not wanting to be rude again.

He slowed and asked if she wanted a lift.

"*Denki*, but I'm headed that way." She pointed toward the northeast, the opposite direction he was going.

"I don't mind turning," he said, his bangs fluttering in the breeze. "I'll come back for ya."

Surprised, Tilly agreed to let him take her to Allen's farm. "I thought I'd go and see if Ruthie wants to walk with me—it's such a nice day."

"*Schee, jah?*"

She agreed the day was beautiful.

"Wait right there," he said, sounding chipper.

While he made his way up the road to turn, Tilly hoped she wasn't erring by accepting his offer for a ride. If Ruth saw her with Will, would she understand that Tilly was simply trying to make up for her earlier detachment?

Standing and waiting, she took in the impressive reds, oranges, and golds of nature's autumn palette; there weren't many more days before the brilliant leaves would vanish from the trees. *I must talk to Kris about staying to help Mamm pack,* she reminded herself as Will returned this way. *Won't Ruthie—and Mamm—be pleased if I do?*

Of course she didn't have to wonder how Daed might react to the news. That was another thing altogether.

CHAPTER 23

*R*uth was in a cloud, still reeling from her peculiar conversation with Will. "*Go far from home, and you'll have a long road back,*" he'd quoted, and its truth rang in her ears.

While her parents enjoyed visiting, she had been meandering through the meadow and was heading back toward the house when she spotted her sister riding with Will. As Tilly got down from his open carriage, Ruth couldn't believe what she was seeing. Was her sister having a change of heart? And had Will already decided against spending time with Arie?

Bemused by this odd turn of events, Ruth waited for Tilly to come this way. "Looks like you got yourself a ride," Ruth greeted her. *A silly thing to say.*

"Will talked me into it," Tilly answered, waving to him as he backed out of the lane. "Thanks again, Will," she called after him. Then, lowering her voice, Tilly said, "Merely courtesy on his part."

Ruth wasn't convinced. "Did he say anything I should know about?"

"He didn't mention you, if that's what you're wondering."

Tilly reached for her, slipping her arm around Ruth's slight shoulders. "Would you like to go for a walk with me? It's been a very unusual Lord's Day."

"Weren't you feeling well this morning? Aunt Naomi mentioned something."

Tilly said she hadn't slept much.

"I had trouble, too. Probably not for the same reason, though." Ruth glanced toward their brother's house.

"How's Daed seem today?" Tilly asked.

"He came to Preaching service, so I guess he's feeling some better. Right now he's over talking to Chester and Allen, if you want to see for yourself."

"No, I want to talk to *you*."

Ruth nodded. "Wait just a moment, and I'll tell Mamm I won't be riding back with them."

In a few minutes, Ruth returned and mentioned that Mamm seemed tired and was looking forward to a nap.

"Sounds like a good time for our walk," Tilly said, as if urging her away.

"Fine with me." *She's got something in mind. . . .*

Together, they headed out to the two-lane road. Ruth remembered how, before Anna had died, the three of them often walked home from house church, Tilly and Ruth taking turns carrying Anna when her little legs grew tired. It had been a time of harmony and quiet rejoicing.

Not so now. There was something bothering Tilly. Ruth saw the way her sister was working her jaw. "You all right?"

"I thought I was . . . but . . ." Tilly paused, then began again. "I just have a lot on my mind—it's nothing at all about Will, though." Tilly gave her a sideways glance. "Did you end up talking to him, after all?"

172

"Oh, we talked, all right." Ruth had memorized everything he'd said . . . especially that he'd never forgotten her.

They walked without saying more for a time. Then Tilly said, "If Kris doesn't mind, I'm going to stay and help you and Mamm with the move."

Ruth was thrilled. "I'm happy to hear it. But also surprised."

Tilly shrugged. "Honestly, I'm worried you'll fall right into your former beau's arms if I leave you here alone, Ruthie. There, I said it. Are you mad as a hornet?"

She shook her head. "There's so much you've missed today." Ruth began to share what had transpired between her and Will behind the barn . . . his talk of a spiritual rebirth, for one, and even his introduction of his Ohio friend, Arie Schlabach.

"Goodness, you're right. I missed a lot."

"Well, I hope you won't decide to head home tomorrow now that I'm safely out of Will's grasp."

"No, I want to stay put."

Ruth felt ever so good about this. "We'll have Mamm and Daed moved and settled in no time."

Squinting into the sunshine, Tilly seemed to agree. "I may sound conflicted, considering what I said when we first arrived here, but I think it was a good thing, our coming."

"In many ways."

Tilly didn't reply to that, and Ruth was deeply touched when her sister reached for her hand. It was very much like old times. *Almost.*

They walked a long ways without speaking. Was Tilly re-living their growing-up years, too?

The old woodlot was coming up on the left. Ruth had always obeyed their father and resisted the urge to take a shortcut through there. Daed had certainly been smothering in his approach to raising daughters, never seeming to let them out of his sight, but she'd tried very hard to mind him. "There's that spooky wood," she said, wondering what Tilly might say about it.

"It's not spooky, for pity's sake . . . whatever Daed says." Tilly rolled her eyes like a pair of marbles. "I've gone that way plenty of times, even explored it some for critter holes."

Ruth sucked in air. "You have?"

"Always the rebel, I guess."

Ruth wrinkled her nose. "I've never thought of you that way. Why do you?"

"Maybe because that's how Daed thought of me . . . and still does." Tilly shook her head. "My sins didn't have to find me out; Daed always did. He was always on the alert for any misstep."

Ruth wished now she hadn't brought any of this up. The last thing she wanted to do was remind Tilly of her difficult childhood.

When they arrived at the house, Ruth was glad to just sit in her room with Tilly and talk further about their parents' move next door. More relaxed now, Tilly sat cross-legged on the bed while Ruth perched on a chair near the dresser.

"It'll be interesting to see how much Mamm wants to cut back on furnishings and whatnot," Tilly said. "This house has nearly a lifetime of accumulation . . . and that's not including the attic."

"Good thing they have a larger *Dawdi Haus* than some families do."

"Wonder if Mamm will keep Anna's things in her room

here—or at all. It's like she has a shrine up here behind locked doors."

Ruth ran her hand through her hair, feeling glum. "I really don't know what Mamm will do about that. There's not enough space to set up a room full of just Anna's things next door." She wondered if that would be the most difficult part of the move for Mamm.

"Are you okay?" Tilly touched her sister's arm.

"Honestly, being home again and talking to Will today has set me back some. I never thought . . ."

"What, that you might still have feelings for him?"

Ruth looked away, toward the window. "Feelings of frustration, mostly. He acts like he did before we broke up. Confident one moment, and mixed up the next." She shook her head. "I doubt he knows what he wants in life, even now. Well, I should say, *who* he wants."

Tilly nodded and patted the bed beside her. "Come sit with me, sister."

Ruth saw the concern in her sister's eyes and went to sit at the head of the bed, smooshing the pretty pillows.

"You know, there are only so many people who will love us during our lives," Tilly said softly. "But even so, there are some we'd do well to simply forget."

Ruth sighed. "I realize that . . . believe me, I do."

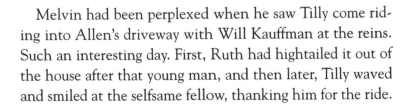

Melvin had been perplexed when he saw Tilly come riding into Allen's driveway with Will Kauffman at the reins. Such an interesting day. First, Ruth had hightailed it out of the house after that young man, and then later, Tilly waved and smiled at the selfsame fellow, thanking him for the ride.

Why is it that Tilly wants to make nice with the Kauffman boy? Surely not for Ruthie's sake . . .

Melvin's thoughts were in a tangle as he drove Susannah home, leaving Caleb and Benny to fend for themselves, wherever they'd headed off to. Melvin presumed Caleb had likely hitched a ride with one of the older courting-age fellows. As for Benny, Melvin hoped he wasn't crouched somewhere behind the stable, lighting up a cigar on the Lord's Day. *Wouldn't put it past either of them.*

"Awful nice seein' Ruthie at church again," Susannah said as they passed Bishop Isaac's house. "Ain't so?"

"It was."

"A little odd, I'll admit, seein' her in *Englischer*'s clothes at church, no less, and all dolled up, her hair cut off to her shoulders."

He had to agree, even though he wouldn't have expected otherwise. "At least my sisters are still mindful of modesty, unlike some outsiders."

"Well, your mother raised her girls right on that account."

"And there's no blame on her for their choices, either. If a person's blessed enough to grow up Plain, it's up to them to earnestly choose that life." He sighed loudly. "Or another one."

Susannah turned to face him, eyes wide. "You sound rather casual 'bout Tilly and Ruth leavin'."

"Ain't that a'tall. The heart's the key, ya know. We all have to choose—one way or t'other."

"Still, it ain't right to just dismiss someone makin' the wrong decision, *jah?*"

His lovely wife sometimes spoke her mind. Melvin knew other husbands amongst the People who would have flat-out rebuked her for such spunk, but he was glad for Susannah's opinion.

"Every one of us will stand before the Lord God on the Judgment Day," he said. "The intent of our hearts will be determined by the Almighty—and no one else."

Susannah sat up straighter on the carriage seat beside him. "Those who tend to judge here on earth are just wastin' their time and breath," she remarked sagely.

How he loved his *schmaert* wife! He reached over and clasped her dear hand. "Couldn't have said it better myself."

Susannah gave him a sweet smile, but as they drove home, he could not shake the feeling that something was hovering in the air, about to stir things up—something involving Wilmer Kauffman.

CHAPTER 24

*R*uth stood near her old bedroom window, looking out at the farmland as she brushed her hair. Tilly was still relaxing on the bed, droopy eyed.

"See the little nick right here?" She stopped brushing and pointed to the small notch. "Will Kauffman tossed a pebble one night, six months after I started going to Singings."

"You were just sixteen?"

Ruth nodded her head. "Way too young for a proposal."

"He should've known better," Tilly said disdainfully.

Ruth didn't blame her; she was still feeling torn about her own encounter with Will today. "He said that night I was the girl for him. Even hinted that the Lord was in it."

"But now, of course, things have changed so much for you both. Everything, really." Tilly scooted near the edge of the bed.

Ruth agreed, though she struggled with the possibility that Will must be living in a fantasy world. "He actually started talking like he wanted me back today—but only for a moment. It was the strangest thing. Like old times."

"Maybe he wishes it but can't follow through."

179

Ruth didn't know. Certainly the noticeable way he'd come alive when Arie appeared seemed to point to a young man who was quite befuddled. *How long did Arie observe us?* Ruth wondered even now.

She heard soft humming—one of the hymns sung at Preaching—and Mamm's familiar gait on the wide plank floor. Ruth had left her door ajar, and she could see Mamm putting a key in the lock across the hall.

"Mamm?" she called.

"Just thought since both you girls are here, I should open up Anna's room." Their mother didn't turn to look at them, just unlocked the door, then gently pushed it open.

Filled with curiosity, Ruth moved toward the doorway of her own room. Then, thinking better of it, she turned and motioned for Tilly to come, too, moving aside to let Tilly go first, since she was older.

Entering the room was like stepping back in time. Anna's faceless cloth dolls, in various sizes and colors, sat on the bed, one still perched on the wooden rocking chair where it had always been.

Mamm ran a finger across the dresser and murmured, "Even though no one uses it, I like to keep this room nicely dusted . . . 'specially clean, ya know."

Tilly was silent, and Ruth glanced at her.

"But I left everything as it was—even her clothing," Mamm said, as if making a confession of sorts. She inched her way across the room like it was hallowed ground. "Other than me, no one's been in here for a long time. 'Course that's all going to have to change with the move." She sighed loud enough to be heard and reached up with a trembling hand to touch the little dresses on hangers distributed across the four wood pegs. Everyday dresses with matching aprons and for-good dresses with one white organdy apron for Sundays.

Tilly sniffled, and Ruth did her a favor and didn't look her way. Knowing her sister, if they made eye contact, it would make things harder for them both.

Ruth looked at the bed quilt, one Mamm had made years ago. "Wasn't this Anna's favorite?" she asked, treading lightly.

"*Jah*, she thought it was the prettiest pattern," Mamm replied, her composure intact. "Double Nine Patch."

Ruth hadn't heard that quilt pattern mentioned since she'd gone to Rockport, and hearing it now made her feel cheerless. It was the pattern they'd worked on at her first-ever quilting bee, over on Mammi Lantz's big quilting frame.

"Anna liked the reds and blues in this one," Tilly said softly.

"The brighter, the better," Mamm agreed, standing over near the window.

Just then Daed's voice broke the ponderous moment as he called to Ruth and Mamm from the bottom of the stairs. Mamm gestured for Ruth to join her, and they hurried into the hall. Ruth wondered why Daed hadn't included Tilly. Didn't he know she'd walked home with Ruth?

By the tone of Daed's voice, Tilly assumed that someone had dropped by to visit. She stepped to the window in Anna's room and saw her brother Joseph below, and his wife, Rachel, holding their baby. They were outside sitting in their gray family carriage and talking with her parents and Ruthie.

Daed must think I'm spending the afternoon at Uncle Abner and Aunt Naomi's, she realized, watching as Joseph conversed with Daed. She'd never forgotten how outraged Joseph was when she'd announced she was leaving Eden Valley. Tilly wondered now if her brother's indignation would find its way to her ears yet again.

"Maybe that's why he's stopped by," she muttered, suddenly overwhelmed, especially here, alone in Anna's room. Turning away from the window, she went to the top drawer of the dresser and quietly opened it. She held her breath at the sight of the remainder of her little sister's clothing folded neatly inside. *Mamm can't part with them*, Tilly thought.

She'd never forgotten how endearing Anna looked after she was snug in her little pink cotton nightgowns, ready to be tucked in. How many times had they sat nestled on this very bed, leaning into the soft, plump pillows and reading Anna's favorite Bible stories?

Finding two nightgowns she had sewn herself, Tilly held first one, then the next up to the light, letting the sunshine hit them. *Remnants of a short life*, she thought. *Too short, because of my negligence.*

The room was as familiar as Tilly's own reflection in a mirror, and she carefully refolded the gowns and returned them to the drawer. Pausing, she thought better of opening the next drawer . . . and the next. Not with Mamm so protective of the room and its contents. What would her mother think of her, prowling about?

But stepping to the window again and seeing her family still outdoors together, she returned to the dresser and dared to open the second drawer. There, on the right side, she saw a wooden box. She reached slowly to open the lid and peered down at a single envelope with her mother's handwriting on the front, lying against the dark blue velvet lining.

Daed helped Anna make this little box, she recalled.

Looking more closely at the letter, she saw that her mother had written Tilly's name on the front.

To be opened after I die was written at the bottom.

What on earth? "A death letter?" Tilly whispered, holding it reverently. "Why?"

Her heart pounding, she stepped to the window once more, feeling breathless. The horse and carriage were backing out of the driveway, and Daed, Mamm, and Ruth were no longer in sight.

Frozen with disbelief, she stood there, aware of her racing pulse. Then, just when she thought she might need to sit down, Tilly heard voices coming into the kitchen. Soon Mamm, at least, would return to lock up Anna's room.

Not wanting to risk being found snooping, Tilly placed the letter back inside the little wooden box and closed it.

CHAPTER 25

*T*he last peachy glaze had faded from the sky. Tilly began
to think about getting back to Uncle Abner and Aunt
Naomi's and mentioned this to Mamm and Ruth as the three
of them sat at the supper table.

"You aren't goin' back on foot . . . not unless your Daed
goes with ya," Mamm said decisively.

Daed was nowhere around, but that didn't seem to matter
to Mamm. The women had been making Tilly a list of the
names and birthdays of all the nieces and nephews, something
Ruth planned to copy for herself, too.

The gentle mirth and overall happiness that seemed to
pervade the kitchen was a marked contrast to the emotions
Tilly had experienced upstairs.

Mamm wrote a letter for me to open after her death?

Ruth seemed especially lighthearted and had once or twice
attempted to drop some hints that Tilly also planned to stay
into next week.

Finally, when Ruth looked like she might burst, Tilly told
their mother what she'd decided. "We're both staying as long

185

as it takes to get things sorted and moved," she said. "Till Friday morning, if need be."

Mamm's face shone, her pleasure at this news evident.

"I do need to contact Kris, though." She'd nearly forgotten, there with Mamm and Ruth. The shock over the letter she'd found in Anna's room had momentarily pushed everything else from her mind.

"Well, why don't ya bring your things over here tomorrow, then?" Mamm suggested, her eyes smiling. "You can sleep in Anna's room, if ya like."

Tilly found this very sweet. "*Denki*, Mamm . . . are you sure?"

"Never more."

"All right, then, I'll let Aunt Naomi know when I return tonight." Tilly said it with faith that all would be well while she was under Daed's roof—and thumb—once again.

"So, you'll join us here after breakfast?" Mamm asked.

Tilly could've wept, she was that moved by the unforeseen invitation. "If that's what you want."

Later, Ruth grabbed Tilly before she went out to help Daed hitch up his horse and carriage. "This is all working out nicely, isn't it?" she whispered.

"I can hardly believe it." She shooed Ruth out the door. "Remember Daed's bad heart. Don't let him do much of the hitching, ya hear?"

Ruth tittered. "You're starting to sound Amish to me."

"Oh, get going, will you."

Still grinning, Ruth headed out the back door.

The sound of her sister's laughter lifted into the twilight. And Tilly suddenly realized what she had agreed to do in order to get back safely to her uncle and aunt's. *Ride alone with Daed.* More important, he'd consented.

She remembered Uncle Abner's advice. *Will I regret my choice to stay?*

"I think this is the first time in ages that Daed and Tilly have been in the same place at the same time without bickering or worse," Ruth mentioned to Mamm as they prepared for a light supper of soup and sandwiches.

Mamm gave Ruth a worried look. "I sure hope it goes well on the ride up to the phone shanty and then Abner and Naomi's."

"Me too." Ruth thought about that, hoping there might somehow be a breakthrough in their relationship. "Why do you think they've never gotten along?"

"Ain't something we oughta discuss," Mamm said quickly.

Is Tilly too much like Daed, maybe? Ruth looked at her mother, beginning to understand what she never had before. "You must feel constrained to stand by whatever Daed says or does, isn't that so?"

"'Tis the right thing to do," Mamm said, which gave Ruth pause.

Oh, Daed . . . still as overprotective as ever, Tilly thought as her father got out of the carriage and took her to the phone shed in the dark, his flashlight shining on the dirt path. Though she hadn't always appreciated his watchful presence, she was a little touched that he was going out of his way for her, as he had when she was a girl living at home. She thanked him, but he said nothing in return.

Kris picked up the phone on the second ring, and when she talked about her plans, her husband was all for it. "Mom won't mind at all, and I think you need this time to really catch up with your family." Eventually he put Jenya and Tavani on to talk, and while Tilly could tell they missed her, they were also caught up in chatter about Sunday school. More important, they seemed to be enjoying having Grandma Barrows around. Tavani let it slip that Grandma was letting them bake cookies and other treats. "We just ate a couple," she said, giggling.

Tilly said nothing to discourage their pleasure. *This is good for them*, she thought, relieved.

After she and Kris said good-bye, Daed walked back with her to the carriage. Tilly filled him in on the lively conversation with her twins, hoping to lighten things up between them.

"Your twins don't sound much at all like Jacob and Joseph at their age," Daed stated.

"My girls *are* pretty easygoing compared to my twin brothers. They don't mind a change in plans." Tilly wondered if Daed might say why Joseph had stopped by earlier. She recalled that Joseph and Chester had given her the hardest time about her inching her way out of the church. *Well, flying out, really.*

"By the way, what sort of names are those ya gave your daughters?" Daed asked. "Never heard the likes of 'em, even amongst fancy folk."

She bristled but tried not to let it show. "Lots of people think Kris and I made them up, but we didn't."

"Sure sounds like it." Daed's voice had the familiar edge to it. Was he actually going to scrap with her now that they were alone? "Whatever happened to *gut*, solid Amish names?"

Oh boy . . . here we go.

She wouldn't say what she was thinking—that people could name their children whatever they wished. Besides, she and Kris weren't Amish.

For the sake of harmony, she let it go, and a miserable,

tedious silence filled the carriage just like it always had when her father was disgruntled with her.

When they were nearing the halfway point between the phone shed and Uncle Abner's, Daed brought up Anna's *Kapp*. "I'm disappointed in your mother's decision for you to keep it, considerin'." His expression was one of distrust, like the glare he'd directed at her when she was a naughty child. "Why'd ya have it anyway?" His words pierced her.

You, of all people, he meant. *You, who have been wrong your whole life long.*

"It was all I had of my sister, Daed. *All*." She felt like she might cry, but she wouldn't let herself. Not now. Not with her father peering down his nose at her. Hadn't she come to expect this?

"Sorry, Daed," she muttered. They were the words she'd repeated so often during her growing-up years. Sorry, yes, but never able to improve or measure up.

Her moment in the sitting room when Mamm returned the *Kapp* to her had been so dear. *Why must Daed go and ruin that?*

She leaned forward, suddenly determined to speak her mind. "Why isn't Mamm's opinion on the matter good enough for you?" she asked. Frustration continued to build until Tilly could no longer contain it. "Why has it always been this way, Daed?" she lashed out. "My entire life, you've made a point of making me feel like I've never been good enough."

He was silent for a moment, his expression stricken, and Tilly feared she had been insensitive and unwise to upset him further, given his heart condition. "It was my job to raise ya in the ways of the church, Tilly . . . accountable under *Gott* for how you've turned out." Daed's jaw was tight, and his eyes remained firmly fixed on the road ahead. "And here you

are, living far from the People. What does that say about me?
About you?"

She cringed, her toes curled in her shoes.

"Must I name off your transgressions?" He turned his stern
face toward her.

Tilly shuddered as a whirl of possibilities filled her head.
Anna's death; my leaving the Amish, then Ruth . . . It was no
wonder her father was bitterly disappointed. "No need to,"
she muttered, chagrined at her own nerve and feeling as small
in his presence as if she were a young girl again.

One more offense on the endless list . . .

As soon as Ruth heard her father's horse and carriage pull
into the driveway, she hurried out to offer to help with the
unhitching process. Daed promptly refused, a thorny tone to
his voice. *Something must've happened with Tilly,* she thought,
concerned.

Puzzled, Ruth returned inside, where she alerted Mamm.
Sighing, Mamm confided that Daed was still terribly miffed
at Tilly. "It's eating away at him that Tilly took you away from
Eden Valley. Perhaps that's why he's tetchy tonight."

"She didn't *take* me, Mamm. I wanted to leave."

"Well, it still gnaws at your father . . . and Chester and
Joseph, too—all of them. It's just that no one else is as out-
spoken about such things."

Ruth took it all in, finding it odd that Joseph had skirted
the issues that surely burned in him when he dropped by that
afternoon. She guessed he had been more easygoing with his
wife and baby there in the carriage. *Just maybe.* She had noticed, however, when Mamm mentioned that Tilly was in the

house, Joseph flinched and frowned so deeply it was nearly a scowl. *"Don't entertain those who say they are of like faith, but live a life of deceit."* The words from a long-ago sermon came to mind now.

Later, during family worship, Ruth felt perturbed as she listened to Daed read from the Bible in English. Gone was his formerly relaxed demeanor. If anything, he was visibly on edge.

"'Children, obey your parents in the Lord: for this is right,'" he read. "'Honour thy father and mother; which is the first commandment with promise; that it may be well with thee, and thou mayest live long on the earth.'"

Ruth wondered if Daed would continue on to read verse four, about fathers not provoking their children to anger. She glanced at Daed, wondering what things he and Tilly had said to each other on the way to Uncle Abner's. Observing the grumpy sternness in their father, Ruth was quite sure they were back to their old standoff.

Later, after she'd said good-night to her parents, giving Mamm a warm hug, Ruth went to her room and opened her Bible to read alone for a while. Through the half-open door, she saw her mother go over and lock up Anna's room. She was definitely a creature of habit.

Then, pondering again how very aloof her father had seemed after his return this evening, Ruth wondered if it wasn't a mistake to have Tilly stay here the rest of the week. Oh, she wished there was something she could do to pave the way for a compromise between her father and sister.

Dear Lord in heaven, what can be done?

CHAPTER 26

*J*osie was over here earlier today," Aunt Naomi was saying as Tilly set the table for a late-night dessert. "She's arranged for her older sister to watch Sammy and Johanna tomorrow and Tuesday, so she can help you and Ruth and your Mamma with sorting and whatnot."

Tilly liked the idea of having Josie there, too. She was a busy bee if there ever was one.

"Won't it be nice for the three of you girls to work together again? It's been a long time." Naomi's eyes twinkled. "Ya know, Josie never really found another best friend to replace you, dear."

"Oh, I'm sorry to hear it." Tilly truly was.

"A close friend ain't something you can substitute at will, of course," her aunt added.

Tilly knew as much. She had experienced the remarkable joy of marrying her best friend, yet there was also something special about a close girl friend. For her, that was Ruthie. In fact, Ruthie had managed to squeeze right into Tilly's heart over the span of years the sisters had shared their thoughts in letters.

Regarding letters, Tilly almost said something to her aunt

about the one she'd found in Anna's drawer, curious as to when her mother had written it, and why.

Because of Anna? Tilly thought unexpectedly. After all, for a parent to experience the death of a child was a life-changing occurrence—totally the opposite of the way things should be. *A mother should never outlive her child*, Tilly thought solemnly.

"I wish you could've seen Josie when she dropped by," Aunt Naomi said, nudging Tilly back to their conversation. "She looked mighty happy. More so than I've seen her in a while."

"Well, if Josie's happy, then I am, too." Tilly went to the counter and scooped some homemade ice cream to go with their apple cobbler.

Has Josie forgiven me for my long silence?

Waking earlier than usual, Tilly rolled out of bed the next morning and tiptoed across the room to raise the blinds. She stretched her arms high over her head as she spotted the first predawn streaks of white in the sky. Stepping closer to the window, she squinted into the mist. Uncle Abner was driving the cows out to pasture after milking, while nearer to the house, a couple of men chopped wood. She marveled at this very natural and beautiful world the Lord had entrusted to her family and to other Plain folk in the area.

Tilly turned and lit the lantern, delighting in its dusky glow. Then she bowed her head and thanked God for this new day—a practice her mother had ingrained in her as a child.

Later, once she'd read her devotional book, she padded downstairs in her bathrobe and slippers to make some coffee, even before Aunt Naomi was up and stirring. Was she making the right choice by accepting her mother's invitation?

I'll do my best to make it work, she decided, all too conscious that no matter how hard she'd tried in the past, it was seemingly never in her power to do so.

Tilly stayed awhile after breakfast to help her aunt redd up the kitchen before she returned to the guest room to pack her suitcase. She stripped the bed first, then gathered up her things. She thanked Aunt Naomi for having her and invited her and Uncle Abner to visit in Rockport. "And I promise to write to you when I return home."

"But this ain't good-bye, remember—we'll be seein' you yet again this week. I'll pro'bly bring supper over Wednesday night, once your Mamm's kitchen is packed up."

"I'm sure Mamm will appreciate that." Tilly reached to hug her.

"Well, if she does things the way I would, she'll want things set up in the new kitchen first."

Tilly said she'd do it that way, too. "Please tell Uncle Abner thanks for his good advice, like always," she said before giving her aunt a kiss on the cheek. "I've never forgotten a single story he's ever told me."

"He's always had a soft heart for ya, honey-girl." Aunt Naomi squeezed Tilly's arm. "I hope you know he teases ya because he loves ya, ain't?"

Tilly smiled. "This world needs more people like you two."

Aunt Naomi slipped an arm around her and walked out to the driveway. As Tilly got in the car, her aunt stood and waved as Tilly backed out, then waved in return. *She's exactly what I needed here,* she thought as she turned onto the main road, fighting a lump in her throat—the dear woman looked so forlorn to see her go.

Kris and the girls would love to meet Aunt Naomi and Uncle Abner, she thought. *Maybe someday.* But of course, if they made the trip to visit them, she and Kris would naturally be expected to stop in and see Tilly's parents, too. She wasn't ready for that.

Not far up the road, a horse and carriage were coming toward her in the opposite lane. Driving carefully, she wanted to be cautious not to spook any road horses. She'd had her share of struggles with horses when she lived here, many times thanks to reckless English drivers.

Still pondering her father, she wondered why he couldn't be more accepting of the life she'd chosen. At first he had been nice enough last evening while escorting her to the phone shanty, shining his flashlight as he had. Yet, when it came to actually relating to her the way a father and daughter should, he seemed to have no clue.

Reliving their carriage ride, she again felt guilty for having lost her cool with him like a teenager. Hadn't she matured at all since living here? After all, she was a married woman now . . . though she'd never thought to ask Daed's blessing upon Kris and her union . . . never cared enough to bring their twins to meet her parents, either. *No,* she thought, *I wanted to shield my precious little family from my father.* Still, that didn't take away the sense of loss she felt for what might have been.

As a girl, she remembered looking forward to the Lord's Day, particularly the off-Sundays from Preaching service, when Daed took them to visit relatives, mostly her grandparents and Daed's and Mamm's siblings. During those times, Tilly saw a very different side of her father's personality emerge, and she liked the cordial, talkative man that he became seemingly at will, friendly and kind to everyone in their large extended family.

So was it something in her that caused him to react so differently at home? Tilly had wondered this since she was about nine years old, when she first began to sense the strain. Whenever they'd gone together in the market wagon, Daed seemed intent on finding fault, advising her to stick right by his side, or not leave his sight, as if she were completely irresponsible and unable to make wise decisions. It never made sense—just wasn't fair when her brothers had the freedom to roam at will when not tending the market table.

This didn't just confound Tilly; she found it annoying. She had often wondered why he'd scowled when her girl cousins and others at the little schoolhouse said how much she looked like Mamm . . . right down to the shape of her face and eyes. She'd even dared to ask Daed why he didn't seem to think so.

She remembered even now his suspicious look, as if she were bent on no good. *"Never thought much about it,"* he'd declared.

Tilly then made an attempt to tell him what others in the family had said, but he interrupted and asked if she'd brought along the big basket of yellow onions to be sold at market. *"Time now for work,"* he'd said brusquely.

After that, Tilly decided not to revisit the topic. No matter what anyone else said about her looks, it clearly didn't matter one iota to Daed.

As she neared her parents' house, Tilly felt increasingly glum. Without a doubt, she had done herself a disservice by contemplating the past just now.

The clouds spread out like a flowering tree in springtime, with gleaming splashes of sunlight toward the east. She lowered her car window as she crept along, taking her time. The wind stirred the grove of trees along the roadside, and she recalled her many walks there.

Just ahead, she noticed her nephews Caleb and Benny headed this way on foot. They were dressed like twins in black work trousers and brown jackets—she was certain the jackets, like the pants, were homemade. Black felt hats were centered on their heads, allowing just a small line of bangs to show. Caleb, being older by a year, was slightly taller.

Spotting her, they waved her down, and she pulled over.

"Mind if we have a look under the hood?" Caleb asked with a mischievous grin.

She played along. "Is something wrong with my car, do you think?"

"Might just need a look-see," Benny said.

She switched off the ignition. "What are you two doing out here on the road?" she said as she obliged them and pulled the lever inside to pop the hood.

Like wasps to sweets, they rushed underneath, talking in *Deitsch* all the while.

Tilly opened her door, breathing in the crisp and tantalizingly fresh air. She got out and wandered around the back, amused at everything the young men were saying to each other under the covering of the hood. Had they forgotten that she spoke their first language fluently? She had to smile at what was being said.

"Ever think she'd let us do this?" Caleb asked his brother.

"Never in my best dreams" came Benny's exuberant reply.

"Listen, fellows, I need to get going," she said, coming around the other side on the shoulder. She stood near Benny, whose hands were black from his happy exploration. "Mamm's expecting me."

Before she realized what was happening, Caleb had skirted to the opposite side and opened the door, slipping in behind the wheel. He told Benny to close the hood, which Benny did. Next thing she knew, Benny had stepped out of the way, and Caleb started the car, peeling out.

"Sure has a lot of get-up-an'-go, ain't?" Benny said, staring in sheer adoration at the soon to be speck of red flying up Eden Road.

"Looks like he knows how to drive," Tilly said feebly, not wanting to imagine what Kris might say if he saw their new car roaring up the road like that.

"*Jah*, you saw him take to it, didn't ya? Real natural like."

That, she had. "Does he have a driver's license?"

"Not yet, but he will."

She didn't know whether to shudder or to laugh.

"I guess he won't be back anytime soon," she said, starting to walk. *Should I be worried?*

"Oh, he'll be back, Aendi." Benny still looked dazed with glee.

"I suppose you want your turn next?" Considering the situation, she wasn't sure she'd let Benny drive.

"*Ach*, could I?"

"Won't the bishop frown on this?"

"Only if he knows."

Benny's response was just what she would expect from a teenage boy who hadn't yet joined church. She wasn't much different in her thinking at his age.

"Let's keep walking . . . see how long he's gone." Tilly allowed herself to be lackadaisical about the car. Still, it was high time to get over to help Ruth, Mamm, and Josie. They would have an extra-full day, since Mamma would also tend to her usual Monday chores.

"Don't think he'll take it out on the main highway." Benny offered a bashful smile.

"I should hope not." She slowed her pace, thinking it wasn't wise to have her nephews tearing around in her car anywhere near Daed's house. "We'd better wait right here, then."

Benny complied and stopped with her. "If ya don't mind me asking, how long did it take ya to feel comfortable in the outside world?"

"Quite a while."

"So did ya have it all planned out?"

She shook her head. "Not much planning, no. More than anything, I did a lot of praying."

Benny looked befuddled. "You *prayed* 'bout leaving here?"

She gave Benny a sad smile. "I realize how strange that must sound to you. But yes, I wanted God's help and guidance . . . and most of all, I desired His blessing on what I was doing."

"Never heard such a thing." Benny sighed and ran his fingers along the rim of his black hat. "Seems to me we hear 'bout guidance and blessing leading folks to stay *put* with the People."

She nodded. "You know I was raised like you, Benny. The church expects you to believe there's only one way to live out your life before God. Only one." She wasn't sure how much more she should say.

"Right, which means bein' Plain." He looked down at the road, pushing a pebble around with his foot. "Uncle Joseph seems to have a bone to pick with you. Uncle Chester, too."

"Not surprising."

"Then you must know they think you weren't searchin'

for spiritual truth . . . that you were just itchin' for a chance to go fancy."

"Actually, I had other reasons to leave."

Benny blinked his eyes. "Dat says it was partly because of your little sister's death." He frowned. "That so?"

She felt limp. "Anna's death was the worst thing that ever happened to our family." She didn't feel the need to say that she was responsible, that Anna's loss had been just one blow too many in Tilly's young life. Melvin had undoubtedly filled his son in on his own theory about what went wrong that day.

"Was there another reason you left, Aendi?"

Tilly refused to delve into that. She couldn't bring herself to say that her father despised her, or close to it. There was no need to risk introducing *that* to the Amish grapevine today.

CHAPTER 27

*F*ollowing her nephews' car-driving adventure, Tilly finally arrived at Daed's house. Ruth must have seen her arrive because she came running from the clothesline, wearing jeans. It was *Weschdaag*—washday—after all, and Ruthie had evidently just finished hanging out the washing for Mamm. *Bless her!*

"Josie's already here," Ruth said, greeting her. "We hung out the washing together."

"It was a busy morning for me, too, in more ways than one." Tilly felt bad about not showing up earlier, but she was still smiling inwardly at the unanticipated encounter with Caleb and Benny.

Cows were lowing in the meadow near the fence as Tilly and Ruth headed inside. She was greeted cheerfully by Josie, who had kitchen utensils scattered over the counters, her hair bun covered by a plain blue kerchief instead of her white *Kapp*.

"Ruthie and I had fun telling humorous stories from childhood while we hung up the clothes," Josie said, eyes dancing.

Ruth looked like she might burst. "We sure did."

"Sorry I missed that," Tilly said.

Josie recounted the time she and Tilly had climbed into the haymow in her father's barn and discovered a nest of barn swallows. "Remember that?"

"Those birds were awfully cozy up there, as I recall. It was the middle of July, right?"

Josie nodded, grinning. "We named 'em all . . . then decided on names for all ten of our future children, too. Five boys and five girls for each of us."

Ruth glanced at Tilly but didn't say a word.

The names Jenya and Tavani were never on that *list,* thought Tilly. "Where's Mamm?" she asked, changing the subject.

"Upstairs counting quilts," Josie said, her eyes searching Tilly's. "She's deciding how many she'll need to take with her."

Ruth added, "She says one of us can start boxing up the hundreds of canned goods in the cold cellar, too."

"We'll get to all of that, for sure," Tilly said, removing her jacket and putting her purse under it on the wood peg around the corner. "It's nice of you to help out, Josie."

"I wanted to spend more time with you both." There was a glimmer in Josie's pretty eyes.

"Where's your suitcase?" Ruthie asked.

"In the car," Tilly said softly, glancing at Josie and groaning inwardly.

"Are you . . . ?"

"Same old issue." It was Tilly's code—her sister would know what she meant.

Ruth frowned and shook her head slightly, stealing a glimpse at Josie, who was back to sorting utensils. "Tiptoe lightly, is what I'd suggest. You can leave your things out in the car till you're more certain."

Tilly agreed, then moved to the opposite side of the kitchen, taking an empty box and sitting on the floor in front of the corner cupboard. She marveled at running into Caleb and Benny, thankful the car had been returned in one piece. Hopefully that was the end of their keen fascination with it. But she doubted it.

Josie asked Ruthie about her job as a medical records assistant, and Ruthie explained that she'd already called her boss this morning about staying longer.

Tuning them out, Tilly wished there was a way to sneak upstairs. Not necessarily to work alongside Mamm, but to get back in Anna's room . . . especially if she decided not to stay tonight, after all. Truth be told, she could not put the letter in Anna's drawer out of her mind. It was such an unlikely thing for her mother to do. Then it occurred to her: Was the letter the reason for the locked door?

⸺ ∞ ⸺

"*Nee*, ain't a *gut* idea to confront Tilly with any of that," Melvin told Joseph when he stopped by on his way to the smithy's. "Just ain't."

Joseph shot back, "But there's no tellin' if she'll ever come back to the valley again."

Melvin looked at his younger brother by four years; Joseph was all disheveled, like he hadn't slept too well last night. His oily bangs clung to his high forehead. "I'd like to suggest that if you haven't said whatever's on your mind to her in the last eight years, there's no need to start now."

Joseph frowned, his blue eyes intense. "It's almost like you think Tilly's in the right."

Melvin regarded him solemnly. "Now, Joseph, you know

that's not what I'm saying. I just wonder what the point is in mentionin' anything now."

Joseph opened his mouth as if to speak, but Melvin hurried on. "It's time we open our hearts more, I daresay. Judge folk less. Treat others like you wanna be treated."

Joseph pulled on his tan suspenders. "*Puh!* You're soundin' too much like Tilly used to, back before she left here. There's nothin' wrong with clearing the air."

"When it stirs up more trouble?" Melvin stopped to cough. "Friction rips families apart, Joseph. It causes more strife, and the whole thing just goes on in ugly circles. We sure don't need more of that."

"In any case, I have a few things to say to Tilly, and that's that." His brother turned heel and nearly ran to his wagon.

"Won't ya pray 'bout it?" Melvin called to him.

"Fer was?"

"Whatever happened to 'a soft answer turneth away wrath'?" Melvin replied as kindly as he could, sorry Joseph had decided to stop by, turning the whole morning to the color gray.

❧

Ruth was starting to fret. Tilly seemed distracted as she kept to the corner of the kitchen.

Josie kept glancing over her shoulder at Tilly, making Ruthie feel even more ill at ease. She felt sorry for Josie, with her once-strong ties to Tilly. But Ruth also felt tenderhearted toward her sister.

Ruth believed that if she could just talk to her sister in private, she might be able to find out what was gnawing at her. *Surely it has something to do with Daed.* Hadn't Tilly hinted as much earlier? *Maybe if Mamm occupies Josie somehow, I can talk to Tilly after the noon meal,* she thought. No doubt dinner would be uncomfortable with Daed and Tilly again at the same table. Yet with Josie present, things might be less tense.

"My husband heard from Will Kauffman this morning," Josie said just then, her voice soft. "Before breakfast."

Tilly made a little gasp and left the room.

"Why are you telling me?" Ruth blushed as she realized she'd snapped.

"I wasn't sure if I should mention this," Josie said, hesitating before saying that Will had somehow heard that Josie was coming here to help today. "He wanted me to pass along word to you."

This was reminiscent of the Amish life Ruth had known, at least amongst the womenfolk—passing word from one person to the next in order to reach the intended ear.

"Will wants you to know that his friend Arie's gone back to Ohio. And she won't be returning here, neither. That's just what he said, according to Sam."

Clear out of the blue? Ruth thought, but she couldn't let this news faze her. *Besides, why should I care what Will wants?* She shrugged the whole thing away. Her life had taken a fork in the road—and a major one, at that. And it did not include him. "Not sure how this pertains to me," she said.

"That's what I thought," Josie replied.

Ruth glanced out the kitchen window, standing now to take a short break. She noticed Melvin's sons, Caleb and Benny, peering into Tilly's car, of all things. Then each boy placed his hands almost reverently on the top of the hood and grinned at the other as if they somehow shared a secret.

When Caleb caught Ruth watching, the boys darted away like they'd been caught stealing or worse, their faces the color of new beets. They walked briskly up the path toward the turkey and chicken pens, and when her father came out to meet them, she figured he was expecting them.

The last time she'd seen these nephews before leaving the valley had been at a watermelon feast over at Melvin and Susannah's place. After they'd eaten their fill, a number of the family had decided to sing some faster hymns, like youth at a Singing. As Ruth recalled, they were well into the third song when her brother Chester had decided to zero in on Ruth, coming over to sit with her, asking probing questions about Tilly. He'd heard she was getting quite a lot of mail from Massachusetts, and also made it clear that he wasn't any too keen on her keeping in touch with their wayward sister. *"She's a bad influence on you,"* he'd said quite adamantly. *"And you know it."*

His words had soured an occasion otherwise marked by sweet watermelon and jovial talk. She'd been thankful at the time for cheerful Caleb and Benny, who had been two of the stronger voices during the hymn singing. It had been later that day that she'd heard through the grapevine that Melvin was starting to have his hands full with his eldest son, Caleb, at just fourteen.

So now, after seeing Caleb and Benny gawking at Tilly's car, Ruthie wondered if perhaps they were unsettled about their future. She believed they would find their way eventually, with God's help and their father's loving direction. As long as they were sincere in seeking the Lord as their Redeemer and true Guide. *"Gott works in ways we can't always see,"* Dawdi Lantz had often said. *"Never forget, nor doubt it."*

Mamm came into the kitchen from upstairs, and Ruth went to pour some cold meadow tea for her, as well as for Josie and Tilly.

Mamm accepted the drink. "*Denki*, dear." She took a sip. "Would ya mind taking some hot tea out to your father?" She directed Ruth to put it in a thermos. "He'll be expecting it."

Ruth wondered if this was the herbal tea Mamm was convinced was helping Daed. "I'll take it whenever you're ready."

At that moment, Mamm glanced toward the front room, where Tilly evidently was, and a small frown came and went.

Ruth wouldn't reveal that her sister seemed to have gotten up on the wrong side of the bed, nor would she blow the whistle on Caleb and Benny for their curiosity over the car. "*Life is too short to tattle*," Uncle Abner had told her long ago. And thinking suddenly of her father, who was waiting for his specialty tea, Ruth sighed. *Much too short.*

Tilly had left the kitchen, upset at Josie's reference to Will Kauffman. She yearned for some sunshine and the feel of the wind on her face. She'd once ridden an English neighbor's bicycle down a nearby hill, her arms outstretched. *Glorious*, she recalled the summer afternoon. Daed had never found out. Even now, it was one of her private triumphs.

We all have secrets we keep to ourselves, she thought and again wondered why Mamm had written her a letter that she'd then hidden. It was nearly impossible to fathom, and she was eager to see the envelope once more—enough so to consider staying just so she could sleep in Anna's room. Maybe once she got herself settled, she'd look again. No matter what, she'd have to wait.

Walking across the backyard with Daed's thermos, Ruth remembered being little and accidentally dropping the mail near the spot where she was presently walking. She'd so wanted to surprise her father, who'd witnessed the mishap and came running out the barn door, repeatedly saying it was all right. He'd scooped her into his arms and carried her, crying, back to Mamm in the warm kitchen. Later, he'd gone back to pick up all the letters that had fallen from her little hands.

At the time, she hadn't yet discovered that if this very thing had happened to Tilly, her sister would have been rebuked in front of all of them and sent to her room without supper. *Not a morsel.* The glaring difference in Daed's treatment of the two of them had long troubled Ruth. *Terribly sad.*

When Ruth pushed open the barn door, she found her father there talking with his brother Hank, planning a big turkey slaughter for the Thanksgiving season next month. She hung back and noticed Daed was pushing the earpiece of his glasses into one ear as he sometimes did when preoccupied. In spite of the thermos, she felt funny about standing there, so she changed her mind and pushed the door back open to head out.

But her father called, "Ruthie?"

She turned and held up the thermos. "Mamm sent this along . . . said you'd be expecting it."

He motioned for her to approach and Uncle Hank quickly excused himself, leaving Ruth alone with Daed. He accepted the thermos and smiled at her. "Tell your mother I'm grateful for it. One other thing—let her know I'll be away for dinner this noon."

Not sharing the meal with us. Ruth's heart dropped. Was it because Tilly had come? She deliberated on what to say, wishing she might ask him something to clear up the query so often in her mind since arriving. Why did Daed seem so put out with her sister?

"What is it?" Daed studied her, then poured the hot tea into the plastic cup. He began to sip it, his eyes still on her. "Daughter?"

She noticed how he seemed to enjoy the tea. "Are you goin' to get better, Daed?" she asked at last, ignoring his questions.

"Well, that's up to the Good Lord, ain't?"

"But you aren't opposed to taking medicine, are ya?" she asked, pushing the words out. "I mean—"

"I went once to the doctor . . . I s'pose I could go again." He paused and visibly inhaled. "And if I consider it, maybe you'd consider something, too."

She was unsure what he meant.

"My daughters have both left the faith of our fathers." His voice wavered. "I've lost you and Tilly both to the world. It just ain't right."

Ruth shook her head. "I'm sorry, Daed, but what does that have to do with going to the cardiologist again?"

"Not much, I guess. Just that I might be more inclined to go if ya came back home, Ruthie . . . for *gut*. Won't ya think on it?"

Ruth's shock and frustration grew as his meaning sank in. Was Daed really saying that her return might prompt him to seek treatment? She decided to ignore that possible implication. "Can't you just go again for Mamm's sake?" Ruth asked suddenly. "She's so worried. . . ."

He threw up one hand. "Everyone's worried. What can I say?"

She'd never been one to speak up to her father, and she could see that he wasn't going to budge. He was merely using her fancy life against her, and it seemed cruel . . . and unnecessary. While she'd expected her parents might ask her to reconsider returning to Eden Valley, she hadn't anticipated this.

Exasperated, Ruth decided to press in a direction she'd never have dared otherwise. "Frankly, Daed, this may sound disrespectful, but I think I know why you and Tilly never got along."

His head jerked up. "What're ya sayin'?" He looked terribly worried.

"You're both awful stubborn."

Daed frowned yet looked strangely relieved. "Well, now, I 'spect you're right." He lifted his cup to his mouth again.

She didn't know what to think. Now was as good a time as any to make her exit, or she might regret opening her mouth again. As Ruth left, she glanced back and saw her father reach for his wooden stool and sit down with a moan. Then, ever so slowly, he raised the thermos cup and took another drink.

CHAPTER 28

Tilly volunteered to check the clothes on the line after the noon meal, well aware that Daed had disappeared just minutes before Mamm put dinner on the table. *I'm invading his territory. . . .*

Josie's presence at the meal was a pleasant memory of former days when she sometimes came to visit. Once Josie graduated from the eighth grade, Tilly's younger friend was always most happy to help, glad for any excuse to be around.

The white and gray towels still needed a bit more time to thoroughly dry, Tilly decided. She noticed Uncle Hank waving from the barn's entrance and wondered what he wanted. Then, of all things, he came rushing over, right up to the clothesline.

"Don't mean to stick my nose in, but your grandmother can't seem to stop talking 'bout your visit the other day," Hank said, hazel eyes shining. Small pieces of hay were stuck in his brown beard, and his black work coat was frayed at the sleeves.

"I enjoyed seeing her, too."

Uncle Hank stepped back a bit, as if appraising her. "I don't s'pose you might drop by again, before you leave for home."

Tilly liked the sound of it. "Tell her I'll plan to do that."

"All right, then." He paused, a frown flickering on his brow. "I have to say it's mighty odd seein' you and Ruthie so fancy."

"It must be quite a shock to everyone."

"I know your Mamm misses ya," he said.

"It's good to be back, even for a visit." Tilly was hesitant to say more.

"Well, I'd best be returning to work, then." Hank nodded slightly, face flushing a bit, and turned to go.

For some odd reason, Tilly thought of Ruth's old dresses hanging in her room, where she'd seen them yesterday. It was remarkable that Mamm had kept them. In hopes of Ruth's returning, perhaps? Tilly's own dresses, of course, were nowhere to be seen. Even if they had still been around, she wouldn't think of trying to dress Plain to lessen the shock for her Amish relatives. In an attempt to honor her parents, the clothes she'd brought for this visit were skirts and dresses—floral and solid colors. She'd purposely left her blue jeans and polyester slacks at home. Ruthie, on the other hand, had worn jeans this morning, showing off her small waist and straight hips. *Is she trying to make a statement that she's truly English?*

It was hard to know what Ruth was up to, but Mamm certainly hadn't shown them the door yet. So that was as encouraging a sign as any.

∞

After Ruth and Josie removed the washing from the line and brought it into the house to be folded, they resumed their work of boxing up the canned goods in the cold cellar—everything from fruit preserves and vegetables to homemade soups.

Later, Sam came by to take Josie home, and Ruth helped Mamm and Tilly make supper. It was their mother's idea to cook one of Daed's favorite meals—sausage loaf and mashed potatoes. They also heated up some canned lima beans and sliced carrots, which Mamm buttered only lightly.

She must be trying to make up for Daed not being around at dinner, Ruth thought, glancing at Tilly. *Poor sister . . . always getting the brunt of Daed's moods.*

When her father eventually came indoors, he was standoffish and silent, going to sit at the head of the table with his arms folded across his chest. Ruth had always pictured him in that very spot, after she moved to Rockport and sat mostly alone in her little kitchen. *At my minuscule table.*

Tilly seemed to wait until the last moment to be seated, first carrying the remaining hot dish over and placing it on the table. When she finally sat down, it was on the right side of Mamm, farthest from Daed. Ruth sat to her father's left, across from them.

"Let's give thanks," Daed said, bowing his head.

They joined in the silent grace. Ruth prayed that something good might come of the mealtime encounter.

After the amen, the stillness was so palpable Ruth felt the need to cough or make a small sound. Anything. The odd situation played out for many minutes, until Mamm asked if anyone wanted something that wasn't on the table.

She feels the awkwardness, too, Ruth thought, looking at Tilly, who kept her head down, eating quietly, almost hiding over there beside Mamm. *Like always.*

No, on second thought, Tilly looked more defiant than sad. Her sister was put out in a big way.

Ruth wondered how long the charged atmosphere would

continue. Mamm had taught them to be peacemakers, although she couldn't remember her mother ever making an effort to bring a peaceful resolution between Tilly and Daed. Why not?

About the time Mamm got up to bring over the warm apple crisp, Daed spoke for the first time. *At last.* Tilly had actually wondered if this was a contest to see who'd talk first.

"Your brother Joseph is droppin' by to see you later on." Daed glanced at Tilly, but he didn't frown or look agitated. "Thought you'd want to know."

"Well, he's taking a chance on coming, because I doubt I'll be around," Tilly replied right quick.

Ruth cast a fleeting look at her.

"But aren't you and Ruthie both stayin' here?" Daed asked. "I thought yous—"

"If we're welcome." Tilly didn't look at him as she reached for the server to dish up some of Mamm's delicious dessert.

"Joseph's visit has nothin' to do with where you're sleeping tonight." Naturally, Daed had to have the last word, and Tilly let him. *Gladly,* she thought, anticipating that Joseph's visit was about his need to vent his opinions with her. She was fully prepared to be lambasted yet again. It was as if she had never left.

After supper dishes were washed and put away, Ruth excused herself and slipped on her jacket and left the house. The tension with Tilly there under the same roof as Daed was already becoming a trial, and her sister had just begun her stay. Ruth needed to get out for a while, and this was the ideal time to do something she'd had in mind since arriving.

There was still some light in the pale sky as she walked up

the road to the Amish cemetery. She remembered the peculiar sort of service they'd had for Anna. In lieu of a burial, Daed had given the bishop a newly chiseled headstone that the men had sunk into place while a hymn was spoken. Bishop Isaac had said a prayer of committal, but without speaking the familiar words *ashes to ashes, dust to dust.*

What had left the greatest impression on Ruth was the enormous group of Plain folk from as far away as Strasburg, Nickel Mines, and Gap—Amish, mostly, and their many Mennonite relatives and neighbors. The blurry assortment of different-colored dresses and cape aprons amongst the womenfolk, representing all different church districts, was still vivid in Ruth's memory. There were even black head coverings mixed in with a sea of white heart-shaped ones. All the dear people had come together for a single cause: to say farewell to the petite girl who was Lester Lantz's last child . . . and Tilly's little shadow. *Till we meet again.*

Ruth had observed how the young folk from other families seemed less somber on the walk back to Daed's house for the funeral supper that day. Some of them had managed to laugh, even to tell a few quiet jokes, talking as if life had somehow returned to normal.

She'd felt nearly sick with heartache that day as she stared at the little white stone marker, Mamm's gentle hands on her shoulders as if Mamm needed steadying.

Ruth's haze of grief had been so deep, it was all she could do to hold herself together. And oh, she'd missed Tilly, who had been home and ill that day, heartsick from the loss of Anna.

We still miss Anna. Ruth was a little surprised that Tilly had declined coming with her now but had taken Daed's comment to heart and was waiting for Joseph to arrive at the house. *Brave soul that she is.*

Truth be told, Ruth didn't know why anyone would still hold any animosity about Tilly's leaving—or Ruth's following her in the end. Truly, Joseph just needed to drop it and mind his own business. Sure, the Amish carried a deep sense of duty to their community, but Tilly and Ruth had long since left the People.

She shrugged off the tension in her shoulders, relishing the mild evening accompanied by intermittent breezes, wishing they might blow away the dust of concern from her head. Ruth hoped never to have to endure another challenge like they'd just sat through at supper. What was the matter with Daed anyhow? It was downright ridiculous.

In the near distance, dark trees clutched the fading sky as she made her way to the small mound—"cemetery hill," the older folk called it. *It's a hard walk when anyone is feeble or sorrowing,* Ruth thought.

Stepping through a heap of newly fallen leaves, she could see the turnoff to the narrow dirt path where the hearse carriage always led the way. Now that she was there, she wished she hadn't come alone. But she knew she might not find another opportunity, so, determined, she made her way up the murky knoll.

It was easy to find Anna's headstone—the third one in on the left, in the third row. Having memorized the spot, Ruth could have found it in the black of night, but it was only twilight . . . plenty of time to get home before dark. She remembered Daed telling her not to be gone long, or he'd come looking for her. But her father had always been like that, nearly scared to death of the dark, or so it seemed . . . at least where his daughters were concerned.

At that moment, she heard the crackling of leaves and turned. A rush of adrenaline shot through her. "Who's there?" Ruth said it loudly to sound confident but startled only herself.

"Didn't mean to frighten you," Will Kauffman called. "I saw you out walkin'."

That quickly, her heart jolted, like a motor just set off. "What're you doing here?"

"I could ask you that, too, Ruthie."

Her heart's powerful pounding made it so she could not think straight, not for anything. *"Arie's gone back to Ohio. And she won't be returning here,"* Josie had said some hours ago.

"Mind if I come up there with you?" His voice was urgent.

"That's fine," she said, then stiffened. *What am I doing?*

"Odd, ain't it, running into each other in a cemetery?"

She couldn't have agreed more, but she felt so overwhelmed with emotion, she couldn't come up with a sensible answer. How had he known she was there?

For what seemed like a lengthy time, they stood side by side, their coat sleeves brushing. She stepped away, not wanting to encourage him.

"You must be here for little Anna," he said. "Ain't so?"

"I needed to visit this place, *jah*." She couldn't stop thinking about all the time she'd missed with him. *Has Will been someone else's beau while I was gone?* The question plagued her even as he stood there.

"Ruthie, I don't want to upset ya, but I have to say this—I made a mistake. I threw our love away," he confessed dolefully. "Trampled it and tossed it to the wind." Will paused. "And I can't begin to say how sorry I am. I really am."

"You don't blame me for leaving?" She had to voice this, had to get it out into the air.

"I might've done the same thing."

"Honestly?" She turned to him.

He paused, grew silent. Then he said, "I was the one to blame, Ruthie."

Her thoughts were all jumbled up like never before. How she'd once dreamed of a day like this. He must still care. Yes, he *did* care. And, quite unexpectedly, Ruth was leaning her head against his shoulder. Then, just that quick, she realized what she'd done and straightened. "Sorry," she murmured. "Truly . . ."

"It's all right," Will said, reaching now for her, gently pulling her into his familiar embrace. "I'm here . . . Ruthie. It's me, the boy you loved."

He held her like she might fall if he didn't. And while she'd never have expected to be so close to him like this in the daylight, the covering of night seemed to embolden her . . . them.

Will whispered her name. "Oh, Ruthie, there's so much I want to make right with you. Will ya let me?"

She tried with all of her heart to push Arie Schlabach far out of her mind. For this moment, all that seemed to matter was Will's nearness . . . and what his strong arms were telling her. *Forget the past. . . .*

CHAPTER 29

"Why'd I come here tonight, you ask?" Joseph mocked Tilly as they stood out near the stable. "After all I've just told ya, ain't it obvious?"

She'd had enough of his accusations. "You've made your point," she said, giving him that much. "I'm going inside now." She moved in the direction of the house, recalling Mamm's mournful look as she'd followed Joseph out there earlier.

"You've forgotten that you're not in the English world here, Tilly," he called after her. "On the outside, womenfolk do as they please, disregarding their men . . . their sacred covering under *Gott*."

His voice was becoming fierce, like Daed's could be. And his words were inflexible . . . demanding.

She kept walking. "I've chosen a different way, brother," she said over her shoulder.

"But you *will* have to answer for your actions . . . at the Judgment," her brother declared. "Remember this day—this very moment, Tilly. Remember it and you will weep later."

She turned just then, stopping to wait for him to start reciting something from a recent sermon; he sounded that fired up. But nothing came. Tilly looked at him, his mouth pressed into a firm line, his sharp eyes narrowed to near slits. "Christ Jesus has set me free," she told Joseph. "And while I didn't leave here in search of a strong faith, I certainly have found it. I've found love and acceptance in my Lord and Savior. And I have a husband and children who share that faith."

Joseph stared at her, openmouthed. "Given all of that, don't you feel the need to repent? Return to the Old Ways—not be so prideful?"

"Actually, I don't. I was never a member of the church here. I haven't broken any vows."

"But ya stole Ruthie away."

"It was her idea from the start. There was no coercion from me," she insisted. "None."

Slowly he shook his head, eyes holding hers. "I don't believe you."

"Joseph, do you really think you know Ruthie? Do you?" Tilly tried to keep her voice calm, to not let her emotion get the better of her. "You never were one to spend much time with her. When our sister's heart was breaking, did you ever try to understand her? That's what loving siblings do."

"So you think you're the perfect sister because she wrote to you, is that it?"

"Ruthie sought my counsel."

Joseph spat on the ground. "And just what constitutes a good counselor?"

He was egging her on, enjoying the battle too much. *Daed's son.*

"The fact remains, Ruth needed someone and she chose me. She asked for a one-way ticket out of here, and I cared enough to help. End of story." Tilly turned boldly and kept walking this time, not interested in hearing more.

He'd left one thing unsaid and untouched: Joseph hadn't brought up the topic of their little sister's drowning. But it was there all the same—she'd seen it in his pained eyes. Surely he blamed her for that, as well.

Not saying good-bye, she hurried to the house. There, she restrained herself and closed the back door quietly, even though everything within her wanted to slam it.

The evening star looked like a tiny white spotlight in the darkening sky, and Ruth pointed it out to Will as they wandered down the grassy slope, making their way toward the road.

"I'd like to walk ya home," Will said suddenly. "If that's all right."

Ruth didn't want to say no, not as connected to him as she felt just now. Strangely, it was as if they'd never parted. "My family won't understand if we're seen together," she said, hoping he'd respect her desire for caution.

"You're prob'ly right. I'll walk ya just to the end of the drive-way." He was quiet awhile, then reached for her hand. "It's time I did better by you, Ruthie . . . did things the right way."

"I'm settled in my new life, a long ways from here," she reminded him.

He squeezed her hand gently. "What would ya think if we talked about that?"

Her heart started to leap again, nearly out of control. "What do you mean?" *Do I even want to know?*

"Just simply this—I love ya and would like to have the

chance to court you properly, Ruthie Lantz, now that I'm back on a straight path here."

After all the heartache, this was so much to take in, so fast. "I'm an Englisher now, Will. I go to a community church, have a job, and live in a house with every modern convenience." Ruth held her breath, their fingers intertwined. "And something else."

"*Jah?*"

"Can you tell me what's become of Arie?" It was impossible to forget Will's happy reaction to seeing the gregarious young woman on Sunday after Preaching.

"I'm glad you asked that," he said quickly. "I want everything to be out in the open between us, from now on. My friendship with Arie is strictly that. She's not my girlfriend."

Will went on to say that Arie had come to visit her uncle and aunt for a few weeks, during which time Will had befriended her. "I heard she was struggling in her Old Order church back in Ohio, longing for more freedoms. She had some leanings toward a faster group, one kind of like the Jamborees." Will looked mildly embarrassed at the reference to his former buddy group. "But because I experienced a conversion—or so the bishop calls it—someone thought I might be able to help Arie. That's all there is to it," he insisted. "No romance at all."

"Maybe the interest is more on her side?" Ruth suggested, unsure why she was pushing so.

Will acknowledged that it might be possible. "I haven't led her on, if you're wondering."

Should Ruth believe him, in light of his supposed change of heart? Will had never been deceitful about other girls before, though he'd let Lloyd Blank lead him off track. But that was over and done with, wasn't it? And, by the looks of it, Will had brought Lloyd back to the Eden Valley church, too. Ruth recalled seeing them together yesterday at Preaching, their expressions solemn—no smirks like from some of the younger unbaptized fellows.

"Have you joined church, then?"

"I've been in touch with my Dawdi Kauffman, the deacon, ya know, and Bishop Isaac, too, lookin' ahead to my baptism next fall, after the instruction classes." Then, stopping on the road, he asked, "What 'bout you, Ruthie? Has there been anyone for you up there in Massachusetts?"

She didn't know why, but she was pleased he'd asked. She told him about the singles group she attended once a month. "I've gone out with a couple of nice young men, yes. And more recently, one in particular." She thought of Jim Montgomery. How would he feel if he'd seen Ruth so snug in Will's arms this evening? She felt sad . . . maybe even a little guilty.

"I worried 'bout that," Will said quietly while the moon peeked its white face over the eastern horizon. "You're so pretty, Ruthie, and kind, too. I thought for sure I'd lost ya forever."

Speechless, she felt the same wonderful-good emotions again, knowing his gentle look and words were for her. Oh, her poor mind was so mixed up!

"Would ya ever consider joining church back here, Ruthie? In due time, maybe?"

Her heart pounded in her ears. He must really care for her, to want an Amish-turned-English girl for his sweetheart. "It would mean giving up a lot," she replied, feeling tentative. "That's not something I can decide overnight. It would take some serious thought."

"I'd do my best to make sure you were never sorry. I can promise ya that."

Ruth's head was filled with the things Tilly, especially, would be saying. Oh, she needed to slow things down, didn't she? She must, somehow. Without a doubt, there would surely be a big discussion about this with her close sister. *No one knows me better.* "I'm not ready to make a decision, Will. Please understand."

"Take your time, then, dear."

It surprised her greatly, knowing Will as she had, that he did not press for an answer. *So unlike him.*

"I know the idea of us as a couple could take some gettin' used to," he said boldly.

People would think I don't know my own mind if I come back here to live, she thought. But Ruth knew the bigger question was where God wanted her to be. She pondered all of this as she glanced toward her father's house. "It's so complicated," she said before they parted.

"Will ya think 'bout it—pray, too?" he asked.

She agreed, albeit reluctantly, and turned to hurry up the driveway.

⧜

Tilly was getting settled in Anna's room and decided to utilize some of the space in the second drawer for her few items, knowing it was more an excuse than a need. She opened the drawer and caught her breath.

The wooden box was gone. Was she mistaken about which drawer?

Breathing faster, Tilly pulled open the third drawer and found nothing.

Did Mamm move it?

She was stumped. At the sound of Ruth's footsteps in the hallway, she quickly rose to stand in the doorway, wanting to greet her. "You were gone so long. Are you okay?" She noticed Ruth's very rosy cheeks . . . too red to be from just the evening's relatively mild air.

"I ran into Will Kauffman near the cemetery." Ruth shrugged, looking sheepish. "I know, an unlikely place to meet." Then she reached for Tilly's hand. "I need to talk to you, sister."

Tilly had a peculiar feeling, dreading what might be coming. "Sure, Ruthie, come in." She stepped away from the door to let Ruth pass.

For as long as Tilly could remember, Ruth had been plainspoken about most everything in her life. Tonight was no exception as she began to lay out the matter regarding Will Kauffman. "He says he's never stopped loving me."

Tilly pulled the only chair in the room over next to the bed where Ruth sat, her long legs dangling off the edge. "Well, I guess one of the questions you must ask yourself is, Do you still care for *him?*"

Ruth listened, apparently receptive.

"And furthermore, do you care enough to return to Amish life?"

"How can I possibly know that?"

"About loving him or about returning?"

"It's always been a bit hard for me to think of marrying anyone other than Will. Maybe because he was my first love, you know."

"But?" Tilly prodded.

Ruth sighed and pushed herself up toward the head of the bed. "He's not interested in going fancy—he made that pretty clear—so I'd have to give up everything back in Rockport."

"Including your church friends . . . and living near me," Tilly pointed out to see what she'd say.

"And many other things I've come to appreciate and enjoy." Ruth's face was solemn. *And wonderful Jim* . . .

"You'll have to count the cost, I guess."

Ruth was quiet for a moment. She leaned her cheek against her hand. "This has come up so fast, Tilly. I just don't know what to tell Will. It's not that he's putting pressure on me, though. Not really."

"That's a good thing. I'd hate to see him push you into something you're not sure of." She didn't want to add to Ruthie's strain, either.

"I said I'd pray about it."

Tilly smiled, touching her sister's knee. "Do you really need to, Ruthie?"

"You must think I already know my heart."

"Well, from what you've told me these past few years, I think you probably do know. You've moved in a different direction from the Plain life."

Ruth slid off the bed and gave her a hug. "Thanks, Tilly. You're the best sister ever."

Tilly watched Ruthie shuffle across to her room, still concerned. *If she's not careful and spends more time with Will, she'll likely become even more confused.*

Feeling all wound up, Ruth sat in her room long after she'd put out the lantern. She pinched herself twice to make sure she hadn't dreamed the meeting with Will. "He says he loves me," she whispered.

Her mind was turning. What should she do first? Or should she do anything? After all, this was the very man who had broken her heart before. Could she really trust that he had changed his ways . . . and that his interest in her now was for the good of both of them?

Should I confide further in Tilly? Or Mamm? Oh, to think Will wants to court me!

Ruth's pulse raced. She did not know her own heart. One minute she was elated; the next she was eager to return to Rockport . . . and to Jim.

Oh goodness, it had not been easy, all this time apart from Will. She'd thought for sure she was long over him . . . that he'd forgotten her. What did it mean that he hadn't?

Dear Lord, what would You have me do?

CHAPTER 30

Alone once more in Anna's room and trying to regain her bearings, Tilly realized things with her sister might possibly be on the brink of monumental change. She set the chair back between the windows with a great sigh, then returned to the dresser drawer where she'd seen the wooden box nestled just yesterday afternoon.

She waited until the rest of the house was dark and still before she began to search in earnest. Just to be sure, she looked in all the other drawers again first before moving over near the maple washstand that had belonged to her maternal grandmother. She searched the cedar chest, too, then opened the only drawer in the table next to the bed.

Not seeing any other options in the room for concealing the box, she found the flashlight in the top dresser drawer and turned it on. Then, getting down on all fours, she peered beneath the bed as the flashlight bumped against the floor. There, on the far side, back under the headboard, she spotted the wooden box. Feeling strangely relieved yet also bemused, she went around to the other side and fished it out.

She rose and sat on the bed to open it and saw that the same letter was still very much there. Not knowing what to think, Tilly closed the lid and replaced the box where she'd found it and got ready for bed. Just knowing she hadn't been wrong about seeing it before was enough to rest her mind—at least for now. Dutifully, Tilly put away the flashlight and snuffed out the lantern.

Ruth's ears strained. She thought she'd heard a sound in Anna's room. Was Tilly still up? Was she perhaps fretting over the things they'd discussed?

Holding her breath, Ruth waited, listening. Surely Tilly wasn't staying up late and kneeling at the bedside, praying about all of that? Ruth climbed out of bed to check on her sister. Tilly had always looked out for her in this big old house. Shouldn't Ruth do the same now? Thinking it was the sisterly thing to do, she made her way to the door of Anna's former bedroom and quietly opened it.

To her shock, Tilly was down on her hands and knees with a flashlight, looking under the bed. Thinking it odd, Ruth stepped back, not wanting to spy on her dear sister. Yet she'd never felt so curious. *Did she hear a mouse?*

Ruth tiptoed back to her own room, shuddering at the thought of a rodent on the loose. She flew into bed and pushed her bare feet under the covers. Oh goodness, she hoped Tilly managed to stun the nasty critter with her flashlight.

Rodents were just one of the troublesome things Ruth would have to look forward to, living in a breezy old farm-house—if she returned to live amongst the People, that is. *An enormous* if.

A permanent return to Eden Valley would mean she'd

have to toughen herself up. *I've gotten too soft living in the English world.*

∞

The next morning, Tilly was surprised to hear Ruthie talking about the possibility of a field mouse skittering about the upstairs, going on and on about it during breakfast, no less. Finally, Mamm asked her to just sit and think for a while, which Tilly thought was out of character for their mother, and a little comical, too.

Tilly kept wondering when Ruth might reveal that she'd spoken last evening with Will Kauffman. Or would she abide by the Old Ways and remain secretive, even though Ruth was clearly a modern Englisher now? No, Tilly doubted she'd keep it mum from at least their mother.

Not long afterward, Daed dashed in and said he was too busy to sit and eat with them, snatching up a banana and a sticky bun, along with a cup of coffee. From Mamm's expression, Tilly guessed it was a rarity for him to do such a thing, and had he stayed, there would've been no more talk about Ruthie's fear of mice. On the other hand, a dreaded undertow was always present when she and Daed were in the same room, so perhaps it was better this way.

Mamm got down to business after Daed left for the barn. "I think we should be able to finish sorting everything this afternoon," she said.

"Next comes the packing," Ruth said, her blue eyes wistful, though surely not over the challenge of the work ahead. No, she looked like a girl who was mighty flustered over her long-lost beloved.

"You seem befuddled today, dear." Mamm prolonged her gaze on Ruthie.

She notices, too. Tilly kept her head lowered for fear her frown would give away what she knew.

The meal of dippy eggs, crispy bacon, and toast with Mamm's smooth apple butter was memorable. Despite that, Tilly found herself contemplating her mother's mysterious letter again, wondering over the possibilities. Had Mamm heard of someone else writing a loving farewell to a child? Yet if so, why weren't there letters for all of her children?

Tilly could not imagine any of Mamm's many sisters or cousins writing a letter meant to be opened only upon their death. Had it been Anna's sudden passing that had prompted Mamm to do this? If so, Tilly felt guiltier than ever.

Ruth went to feed the poultry, and Mamma and Tilly were doing up the breakfast dishes when Mamm asked her, "Was Joseph harsh with you last evening, dear?"

"Oh, you know how brothers can be." Tilly had no need to bash him, but didn't feel it was necessary to repeat the conversation, either.

Mamm stopped washing the dishes and turned to shake her head. "I should think the passage of years might have soothed Joseph's anger some . . . and your visit here with Ruthie, too." Mamm filled the sink with more hot water. "I, for one, have forgiven ya, daughter. I truly have."

Tilly drew in a deep breath—she'd already sensed the mercy in her mother's sweet demeanor. "That means a lot to me, Mamm."

Her mother smiled a little. "It wasn't so easy after you left . . . not at first, I'll admit."

"And I compounded all of that by not keeping in touch with you. It was terribly wrong of me."

"Well, and knowing Ruthie was getting mail from you when I wasn't, nearly made me *ab im Kopp*—crazy in the head."

Tilly had never considered this and felt awful. "Oh, Mamm . . ."

"I'm not sayin' this to make ya feel bad, Tilly. Shouldn't have said it at all. Let bygones be."

Thinking it was the first talk of this kind they'd had in years, Tilly embraced the opportunity to say more. "It's past time we aired all this, isn't it?"

"Just so we don't put up more walls by doin' so." Tears threatened to spill over as Mamm kept her hands deep in the hot, soapy water.

Tilly put her dish towel down and leaned her head against her mother's shoulder. "If only it were possible to talk openly like this with Daed. . . ."

"*Jah*, without getting his ire up." Mamm shared a knowing glance. "He's easily irritated, that's for sure."

Around me, she means.

Mamm bobbed her head and kept glancing up sheepishly, and Tilly suspected she knew what had set Daed off in the carriage.

"You should know that he told on himself 'bout the other night," Mamm said. "Couldn't keep it in, I guess."

Tilly felt less animosity toward Daed, just hearing this.

"I took your side—informed him that you most certainly could keep Anna's little *Kapp*, since the two of you were nearly joined at the hip."

Tilly was astonished. "You spoke up?"

"And lest ya think otherwise, his sharp response to you

has been eatin' away at him." Mamm finished washing the last of the dishes.

Daed must *care*. But if so, why did he seem to be taking great pains to avoid her at the table? *Now's not the time to ask. One hurdle at a time.*

She contemplated the little wooden box again, not wanting to reopen a rift with Mamm by bringing it up. Tilly also recognized that the subject of Anna's drowning had gone almost untouched between the two of them.

"You all right?" Mamm leaned forward to pull the plug to drain the water. "You look awful sad, dear one."

Tilly shook her head. "There's a lot on my mind, coming home and all."

"Well, I certainly hope it's not a hardship, bein' here."

Tilly put her arms around her mother. "You've endured so much because of me. Especially Anna's drowning." She paused to swallow, her chest tight with so much emotion. "I really hope you know how much I love you."

Mamm kissed her cheek. "And it's a joy to have you and Ruthie here, believe me. But I certainly hope you don't blame yourself for Anna's drowning, dear. There's no reason for that."

"I do struggle with it," Tilly admitted. "It's one of the reasons I left. It was so hard to be here, with her dear memory all around."

"Tilly . . . *nee*, you must not fault yourself. Has someone else blamed you?" Mamm's concerned eyes searched her own.

Only me, Tilly thought sadly. "No one else," she answered, still secretly wondering if Daed didn't hold it against her. But she wouldn't ask. With all the faults her father had found with her over the years, why would that be any different?

CHAPTER 31

*J*osie tucked her arm through Tilly's after arriving that Tuesday morning. The endearing gesture reminded Tilly of their days as dear friends.

"Mind if we work together?" Josie asked, her eyes hopeful.

"I'd like that." Tilly smiled.

Mamm had assigned them to the attic, to bring boxes down to the hallway on the second floor, where they were to make designated piles—giveaways, discards, things to save, and items to be set aside for a future auction.

To Tilly, there had always been something intriguing about their attic, although it wasn't a typical one, like that in Mammi Lantz's old farmhouse. The whole expanse of one side of her parents' attic was partially finished, complete with a darling dormer window. As a youngster, Tilly had imagined what it might be like to have her room up there, perhaps with white lace curtains over the dormer, although Mamm would never have heard of it. Of course Tilly knew enough not to ask.

"Do you remember slipping away up here to tell secrets?" Josie asked, her voice hushed, as if entering hallowed ground.

Tilly smiled. "How can I ever forget?"

They talked quietly of all the fun they'd had growing up, nearly like close-in-age sisters. And amidst the busyness of emptying trunks and boxes, Tilly realized what a mistake she'd made not keeping in touch with Josie, the most helpful person she'd ever known, and sweet as shoofly pie.

As they worked, they finally began catching up with each other's lives. Eager to tell her former best friend about Kris and their twins, Tilly took the lead in removing the barrier her silence had long created.

"You might be surprised that I've taught Jenya and Tavani how to sew a little." Tilly glanced at her, checking to see if Josie looked surprised, but she didn't. It was perfectly normal for an Amish mother to put a needle in her tiny daughter's hand at the twins' age.

"Will ya show them how to quilt, too, as they grow older?"

"It's still one my favorite pastimes, so I want to, yes." Tilly laid out some ecru-colored linens on the floor, unsure whether they were family heirlooms. If they were, Mamm would surely have had them downstairs in her sitting room, on display. She decided to set them aside and ask her mother later.

"My girls like to sing together, too," Tilly added. "Mostly little worship songs from Sunday school."

Josie didn't comment directly on that. "I wish I could meet your daughters," she said, her soft blue eyes bright.

"Wouldn't that be fun?" Tilly paused. "And your *Kinner* . . . it'd be nice to get to know them better, too." With the lingering uncertainty between her and Daed, she had no idea what the future held as to visiting there again . . . but she could hope.

❦

"Lots of folk meet their one and only well after their teen years," Mammi Lantz was saying as Tilly settled in for the second visit at her grandmother's later that afternoon.

"You must mean Ruthie?" Tilly smiled.

"Who else?" Mammi tittered and pushed her small reading glasses up the bridge of her nose. "She's how old now . . . and no prospects for marriage?"

Tilly pointed out that Ruthie was still fairly young at twenty-three, according to the English world. Tilly herself had been twenty-five when she married Kris, and she knew two young women who were going back to get their master's degree, after working for several years. *They're still single*. While Ruth wasn't interested in pursuing much more higher education, Tilly didn't think her sister was at risk of remaining a *Maidel*. And from what Ruthie had told her privately that afternoon, once Josie left for the day, she wanted to talk things out further with Will before supper. *Right about now*. Tilly checked her wristwatch.

"Well, you must've finished up early over at your folks'," Mammi said, glancing at the wall clock. "I would've expected ya to still be pokin' through all the disarray in the attic."

"With four of us, counting Mamm, we made fairly short work of it." Tilly explained how they'd organized everything from old sets of dishes to Anna's baby clothes. "You should see the sorted piles of things everywhere."

"Oh, I remember my own move . . . and hope to never have to go through that again," Mammi said. "Such a *Marasch* it was, truly a mess for days on end."

They talked about the tendency to accumulate things,

sometimes unwittingly. Tilly thought of her mother, who had thus far been unwilling to relinquish Anna's things.

"Well, chust remember, havin' doesn't bring happiness. Never, ever does," Mammi said, as if Tilly hadn't heard it repeated during her childhood. "Investing time in family and friends and fellowship with *Gott* is what adds up to happiness on this earth, ya know."

Tilly agreed. She also knew full well the value of such blessings as compassion and joy, goodness and faith, and peace and patience. *And gentleness and cheerfulness*, which Tilly observed in Josie. There was just no one as happy as Josie Riehl Lantz. And Tilly could hardly wait to in some way make up for lost time with her sister-in-law and friend.

"You're awful quiet, Tilly. Your mind must be somewhere else." Mammi angled her head questioningly.

"Oh, sorry."

"Are ya worried 'bout something, my dear?" Tilly's mother had always said that Mammi had a way of seeing a person's heart through their eyes.

"Ruthie's meeting someone today." She let it come rushing right out. "Just don't say anything, all right?"

"Must be a young fella, then."

"I probably shouldn't have said."

"Well, that answer told on ya." Mammi gave a shrewd grin.

Tilly sighed. "I'm a bit concerned, actually," she said, deciding she could trust her grandmother with more. "Ruth's seeing her former beau today."

Mammi's eyes lit up.

"I just hope Ruthie's not impulsive about such an important decision."

"Does she want to return to bein' Amish, maybe?" Mammi asked. "That's the first thing for her to consider, ain't so?"

Tilly couldn't have said it better herself.

Will Kauffman insisted he and Ruth talk sensibly and not let their emotions guide their time together as he and Ruth walked toward the big pond between his father's grazing land and the English neighbor's cornfield.

"Are you sure we aren't being too public about our meeting?" Ruth asked, glancing around them.

Will shook his head. "No one but the heavenly Father can see us walking out here together." His tone was gentle.

But if I can glimpse the road from here, surely we can be seen, she thought, though she kept her opinion to herself.

"If you're worried, then we can head up to the woods over yonder." He pointed in the direction of the dark forest.

"Well, the pond's so pretty," Ruth said, feeling more comfortable in the sunlight.

"You seem anxious."

"Do I?" She smiled at him.

"Maybe it'll help if I tell ya that I know of a rental house with electric," he said, a grin on his handsome face. "What do ya think of that?"

"That's thoughtful of you, Will, but electricity alone isn't enough to make me decide to return."

"What do ya mean?" He gave her a confused look. "Help me out here."

She felt sorry that she couldn't be as confident as he was that they had a future together. To come back to Eden Valley was her decision alone, after all. "I really don't know if I can embrace the Old Ways again."

But he wasn't listening. "We're young, Ruthie . . . we don't have to figure everything out this second . . . or this week. We have our whole life together, Lord willing."

It was clear he didn't understand her need to ponder things . . . or that she might feel rushed.

"If I'm to return, I need to come back for the sake of the Amish way of life, for the church," she said. *Not because Will wants to court me.*

"Ach, let's stop right now and pray about that, all right?"

"I have been praying, Will. I even prayed about us the last time, when we went our separate ways." She paused a moment. "Besides that, we're starting over as friends, getting reacquainted. We really don't know each other anymore."

But he seemed bent on his agenda. "I'm not talking 'bout praying whether or not we should be together."

Well, I am! she thought, glad she hadn't voiced it. "Go ahead and say a prayer," she said, trying to show a smidgen of meekness. Goodness, she needed to be more submissive. If she was entertaining the idea of being courted by a young Amishman, she must start putting on the adornment of a gentle and quiet spirit—a priority she'd lost touch with in the English world. Her female friends, even the ones from church, rarely talked about deference to the men in their lives. *Only to God.* In fact, most of them would have been shocked if they knew she was thinking about giving up her modern life to go back to Plain farmland. But then, they didn't know of her past affection for Will . . . or his for her.

So long ago, she thought.

Will stopped walking and bowed his head. "O Lord God, I

come before You, askin' for our paths to be made straight, and ever so clear—'specially for Ruthie. We need divine help in finding our way through the obstacles ahead. We know that where Your presence is, we can find peace. And we look to You for all that we need for our body, mind, and spirit. In the name of Your Son, Jesus Christ. Amen."

Ruthie wiped away a tear—she'd never imagined hearing Will pray aloud, especially not in such a reverent, heartfelt manner. It was heartening and a real blessing, too, seeing how much he'd changed. "*Denki*, that was beautiful."

He reached for her hand. "We'll get through this together, with the Lord's direction."

"If God's in it," she reminded him. *An echo from the past.*

"When we put Him first, everything will follow. Ain't so?"

Ruth studied him at that moment . . . his sincere eyes, the confidence he exhibited in his faith now. But could she trust Will as her beau? His present behavior was certainly light-years better than the way he'd carried on before. God forgave; but could she?

Thinking about Will's prayer for her—for them—a covering of peace settled over her. "*Jah*," she said. "I do believe the Lord will guide us, whether we're together . . . or apart."

CHAPTER 32

After a supper of scalloped ham and boiled potatoes; and a side dish of cabbage, pepper, and carrot salad; Daed read aloud from Second Corinthians, chapter six for family worship. Tilly noticed how quiet, if not contemplative, Ruthie looked over in the corner of the front room near the heater stove.

Mamm, on the other hand, looked bleary-eyed and ready to call it a day while Daed read verse seventeen, "'Wherefore come out from among them, and be ye separate, saith the Lord.'" There was not a speck of expression in his voice.

I could fall asleep to his monotone, thought Tilly as he read the Bible. It took her back to the days when her older brothers were still living at home, and this room seemed much smaller with all of them present. Joseph and Jacob were always the most relaxed during evening Bible reading and silent prayer, as she remembered. *Was it that they were less interested?* She also remembered later, when Anna was old enough to calmly sit on Mamm's lap and fold her little hands while Daed read to them.

Thinking of her baby sister still took her breath away, as if Tilly were realizing yet again that Anna was gone.

Later, when they knelt for silent prayer, Tilly asked God what to do about Mamm's envelope with her name on it. She knew better than to open it without permission, but asking Mamm about it would mean admitting she'd been poking around Anna's room. *Especially embarrassing now that I'm a grown woman. . . .* Perhaps she should just go about her business, get the house packed up tomorrow and moved over to the *Dawdi Haus*, so that she could get herself back to Kris and the girls, where she belonged.

Then again, maybe this was an opportunity for Tilly not to run from confrontation . . . to open her heart to Mamm again. After all, she might not have another chance.

Ruthie shuffled across the hall to talk with Tilly after their parents headed for bed later that evening. Both young women had slipped into their robes, but neither felt very sleepy. "Do ya mind if I sit and talk with you for a while?" asked Ruth, seeming almost reticent about asking.

"Make yourself comfortable."

"Where'd you go this afternoon?" Ruthie asked as she got settled on the bed.

"Over to visit Mammi Lantz again." Tilly shared how Uncle Hank had urged her to stop in there before leaving the area.

"It's probably a good thing—she must get very lonely." Ruth pushed her hair behind her ears. "I'd make a point of seeing her often . . . that is, *if* I should decide to move back."

Tilly swallowed her relief. "So you're taking it slow and easy."

"As much as Will wishes otherwise." Ruthie smiled demurely. "I need to take one day at a time for now."

"It's always a good idea to let tomorrow worry about itself."

Ruthie nodded. "To be honest, when I think about not seeing you and Kris and the twins, I feel sad."

"Oh, but you'd still see us," Tilly was quick to say. "Just not as often."

Ruthie sighed. "It wouldn't be the same, though. And I'd face a lot of challenges."

"At first, sure. Like when you left here and got settled in Rockport." Tilly gave her a small smile as she remembered. "But you haven't decided to move back. And you know what I think about it, for what it's worth."

"Well, it's worth ever so much to me. You've always helped me make sense of things." Ruth looked away. "There's just so much at stake."

A silent, unruffled moment passed.

Then Ruth said, smiling at Tilly, "Can you actually picture my colorful sofa and chair in a farmhouse?"

Tilly laughed. "No, but even more than that, I can't picture you living out your life as an Amish wife and mother . . . let alone as a church member."

"Sincerely?"

"You're entirely settled as an Englisher, my sweet sister. And it's a good fit, in my opinion." Tilly appreciated her sister's humor—Ruthie was on a more even keel than three years ago, for sure. And from the sound of it, she was leaning toward dismissing the idea of returning for Will alone. If, however, Ruthie decided to make the leap back, she would have to embrace the Old Order Amish tradition, leaving the English world behind completely. There really was no middle ground.

"I'm glad you know what you're up against, Ruthie." *For sure and for certain!*

∽

The room was pitch-black when Tilly awakened before midnight. She felt terribly restless. It was impossible to sleep, knowing that the wooden box was just a foot or so beneath her head and pillow. It was as if the box demanded her attention.

After several more attempts to get comfortable, Tilly sat up in bed for a few moments, staring into the darkened room. Then, exasperated, she went to the window and opened the blind, but the moon was shrouded by thick clouds. She had little choice but to get the flashlight, not wanting to light the lantern.

Is anyone else sleepless?

She stepped lightly on the back staircase, heading down to get a drink in the kitchen. The house seemed to moan at night, something she remembered from growing up here. Back then, the nighttime sounds had seemingly come from deep within the house and always made her scurry to get back into bed.

At the creak of a floorboard, she turned and was surprised to see Mamm standing in the opposite doorway. "Heard someone up," she said in a sleepy voice. "You feelin' all right, Tilly?"

"Not really." She sighed, wondering if now was the best time to talk about the strange letter. She crept to the long wooden bench near the table and sat down, letting the flashlight shine onto the corner cupboard. "I found something in Anna's room," she began, then mentioned the lone letter. "I haven't opened it . . . though I really wanted to. Would you mind telling me about it, maybe?"

During the silence that ensued, Mamm looked so troubled,

even agitated. A hint of suppertime scents still hung in the atmosphere, and Tilly felt almost sorry for putting her mother on the spot.

"*Ach*, maybe 'tis best, after all, if ya know this awful hard news now," Mamm replied quietly, shaking her head. "It might help you understand your Daed better, for one thing." She sighed. "You were my very first daughter, and I'm ever so grateful for your life. In fact, every day I give thanks to God for you."

Tilly listened, as moved by the faltering of her mother's phrases as the words themselves.

Her mother continued. "I've thought for many years whether to tell you this . . . wanting to spare you the trauma of your earliest beginnings—the memories I carry silently, deep in my heart." Mamm sighed and came to sit beside her on the bench. "I wanted to take them to my grave, honestly. But then I decided perhaps it was better for you to know . . . at least once I was gone."

Tilly shuddered, suddenly fearful of what her request had set in motion . . . what Mamm was about to reveal.

"One moonless night, I was violated, daughter. My pain and horror was such that I did not expect a child to come of it . . . certainly not my darling Tilly." Her mother reached for her hand, holding it tightly. "I scarcely know how either of us survived, dear. It was an alarming time for us—for you and for me. The stress I bore surely affected you, my tiny babe, as you grew protected beneath my heart."

Tilly scarcely believed what she was hearing. If her mother hadn't been right beside her, real and solid, she would have rejected it as an appalling nightmare.

"Maybe now you'll understand why Daed has always kept you at arm's length, an added heartache for you and for me.

249

Jah, I noticed that, believe me, I did . . . I always have. And no one but Daed was ever told of what happened in the woodlot that night. For your own sake, we made a pact to keep it just between us . . . a pact I've broken now." Her mother let go of Tilly's hand and wiped her eyes.

"The woodlot?" Tilly managed to ask.

Mamm nodded her head slowly, sadly. "The man was an outsider passing through the area. Not Amish, for certain."

Tilly's lip quivered. Oh, the pain her poor mother had suffered! And no wonder Daed had warned her and Ruthie against that woodland area, making it seem as though he never trusted them to go anywhere without him. *No wonder* . . .

"I can surely see how the torment of that night colored your life, my dear. Daed's overprotectiveness . . . our concern that ya turn out right. Daed was harder on you than my other children—never could forget what happened. I witnessed it all through your growing-up years." Mamm was weeping now. "It was wrong of your Daed and me to let that happen. I am sorry, Tilly. So very sorry."

Shaken to the core, Tilly sat like a pillar on the bench. Her fingers trembled as she struggled to turn off the flashlight. It was so difficult to breathe, to pull air into her lungs as she and her mother sat there in the now dim kitchen.

Poor, dear Mamm! Tilly thought, her mother's words tearing at her heart. *To think I never suspected* . . .

Tilly felt a cool hand on hers at that fragile moment, and slowly, she let herself lean into her precious mother.

CHAPTER 33

I think my sister's still sleeping," Ruth told Mamm while stirring pancake batter early the next morning.

Mamm nodded. "Well, *you* certainly look fresh as a flower." She regarded Ruth, seemingly measuring her expression. "Makes me wonder if there might not just be something interesting comin' . . . well, in your near future."

Ruth was startled. Had Mamm somehow seen her with Will?

"I can certainly hope, can't I, that maybe you and your former beau might be thinking of getting back together, *jah?*"

So, Mamm *had* seen them. "I don't want you to get your hopes up, but I'll tell you something to keep private for now." At Mamm's quick nod, Ruth went on. "Wilmer Kauffman has asked me to return home here. He wants to court me."

"My dear girl . . ." Mamm's eyes were ever so hopeful that it pained Ruth a little.

"I haven't made up my mind, though."

Mamm wiped her hands on her apron and reached to give her a hug. "Oh, Ruthie, when will ya decide?"

"I'm taking my time . . . praying, too."

"Well, it sounds like you just might be persuaded."

251

Ruth felt a flutter again at the thought. "I don't want to jump into anything too quickly."

"Very wise. And if you ask me, dating someone for all four seasons is a *schmaert* idea, too—my own mother counseled me to do that."

Ruth's mother must not realize she had already been Will's sweetheart-girl for far more than twelve months. But that felt like a world ago. "It would definitely be a huge adjustment to leave my English life behind, but with God's help, I'm willing—if that is what He wants for me."

A big tear rolled down Mamm's cheek, and she shook her head like she could hardly believe it. "It would be such a *wunnerbaar-gut* answer to my every prayer."

Ruth wondered aloud how the rest of the family would receive the news, if it came to that.

"I can tell ya that your Daed would greet the prospect of gaining you back to the People with such joy." Mamm smiled. "He'd pro'bly even shed a few tears."

Ruth couldn't imagine her father moved to tears over this, but perhaps he was more tenderhearted than she knew. "I still remember a thing or two about living Amish. Bet I could even hitch a horse by myself if I had to," she joked.

Her mother laughed. "Well, and you'd be wantin' a place to stay, too, I would guess."

"*If* I decide to return . . . and if that suits you."

"What do ya mean, child? Of course it does. Oh, Ruthie, do you know how delighted I would be?" With that, Mamm threw her arms around Ruthie and held her near.

Tilly yawned and sat up in bed, getting her bearings. She sighed and dragged herself out from under the covers, still shaken by the stunning thought that Daed was not her father. *And poor, sweet Mamm . . . what she went through that horrid night so long ago!*

Earlier, Tilly had awakened out of a deep sleep to the sound of laughter from somewhere in the house. The sounds were muffled and coming from the kitchen.

Long before dawn, she'd returned the letter to Mamm, still unopened. The terrible secret was in Mamm's safekeeping now, hidden from other eyes. Why her mother hadn't concealed the letter in a more secure place, she did not know. To think Daed was not her flesh-and-blood father . . . that her violent beginnings had colored his view of her, his treatment.

The miracle was that Daed hadn't insisted that Mamm get rid of her before the birth. Thankfully, he was a God-fearing man who valued all life. Still, the truth remained: Tilly was a constant reminder of what had happened to his beloved wife.

"I'm grateful to be alive," Tilly whispered, reaching for her morning devotional book. Wearily, she went through the motions of reading it, and of praying, too, but her heart was in neither.

Peals of laughter echoed up the stairs yet again. Tilly braced herself, wondering how she could sit at the same table with her family this morning, knowing what she did.

Ruth rang the dinner bell several times, just as Mamm requested. Yet for whatever reason, Daed hadn't come in for breakfast as usual.

"The waffles and eggs will get cold," Mamm fretted, "and your father is not one for eating cold anything, ya know."

"I'll run to the barn and let him know we're ready." Ruth

took time to slip on her jacket, wondering if Tilly was ever coming downstairs. Now that everything was sorted, they had so much packing left to do; they really needed to get started.

The morning felt nippy, a far cry from the warm temperatures yesterday when she and Will had basked in the sunshine of late autumn. The hour they'd spent together walking and talking had been something she'd never anticipated, but she still had so many things to consider . . . including her relationship with Jim Montgomery.

Ah, Jim. Their friendship had been growing in such a promising way—somehow Ruth knew she wouldn't need to wonder about whether she could count on his word and intentions. She had observed his caring concern for others in their congregation, including the elderly couple whom he drove to church as needed. Jim was certainly a man she could depend on, whereas Will . . .

But he's changed, hasn't he? Ruth thought. The serious tone of their conversation was certainly an indication of that. Even so, it would take time to know for sure. And time would be in short supply unless Ruth moved back home.

Could I really give up so much just for the hope of a happy life with Will?

Ruth contemplated what Mamm had said earlier. The thought of pleasing her parents with her return—possibly causing Daed to weep. The idea touched Ruth profoundly, and she couldn't imagine her father wiping salty tears from his ruddy face. As for her mother, even the slimmest possibility of a permanent reunion between Ruth and her family had lifted her spirits nearly to the sky.

Still, tempting as all that was, Ruth knew she needed to

proceed carefully, with wisdom. She was thankful Tilly was there to keep her mindful of that.

I don't want to raise everyone's hopes only to dash them.

Tilly felt unsteady as she made her way down the steep back staircase and into the kitchen. She found Mamm alone there, standing over the cookstove, her face pink with the heat, small beads of perspiration on her brow. "Mamm?"

"Well, *Guder Mariye* to you, my dear." Her mother looked her way, her expression amiable, though she, too, looked sleep deprived. "Were you able to rest . . . after we talked?"

Tilly yawned. "It wasn't the best night I've ever had. How about you?"

"Oh . . . at my age, I get my sleep when I can." Mamm sighed. "But no. Rest was hard to come by."

Tilly took four paper cups out of the cupboard, needing to keep busy and wanting to be useful. "We certainly have a big day ahead of us." She felt it wise to change the subject. Enough gloomy talk.

Mamm nodded and smoothed her apron. "Melvin and Susannah will be over to help, squeezing in work over here before picking field corn. And Caleb and Benny are comin' to help with barn duties—doin' double duty, bless their hearts. And I hear Naomi's bringin' supper. She and Abner will join us—ain't that nice?"

Tilly nodded. "Is Daed around?" she asked. "And Ruthie?"

"Your sister's out alerting your father 'bout breakfast." Mamm eyed the stove. "Which is not going to be very good if the waffles get soggy."

Your father . . .

Tilly trembled at the word. Mamm was right—the pain had

found its way into her own life. The heartbreaking knowledge she now possessed only deepened her hurt.

She was just making her way toward the icebox to get some orange juice when Ruthie dashed into the house, breathless.

"Come quick, Mamm. Something's wrong with Daed!"

Mamm gasped and dropped everything to follow. "I'm comin'!"

Tilly hurried to the back door, offering to phone for help.

"*Jah*, or if he's in need of a hospital, can *you* drive him, maybe?" Mamm called back as she rushed out to the barn with Ruthie.

Tilly stood there, paralyzed, not knowing what to do first. Wouldn't Mamm prefer an ambulance? Then, suppressing her emotions, she darted out to the barn to assess the situation. She was shocked to see Daed lying on the cement floor, not far from the calves' birthing pen. Melvin was already performing CPR.

"Someone better call 9-1-1," Melvin said louder than Tilly had ever heard him speak. "*Graades wegs!*—Right away!"

Tilly moved quickly, running to the car, her heart pounding so hard she could scarcely hear herself think. *Oh, dear Lord, will Daed live?*

CHAPTER 34

*M*elvin had only performed CPR on a dummy in the class he'd taken on the sly. It wasn't something he'd ever thought he would have to do on his father. Even so, he was relieved to see Daed beginning to respond now as Melvin pumped in the steady rhythm he'd been trained to do.

Hurry, Tilly, he thought, aware that if this was an arrhythmia problem like he thought, there was no time to waste. He was thankful, too, that the Almighty had directed him this very day to drop in early to help, after accomplishing some of his own chores at his farm.

He looked at his once brawny father lying on the floor. Daed had stumbled forward while they were forking hay together, saying he was awful dizzy. Melvin had eased him carefully to the ground, speaking firmly yet calmly to Daed . . . telling him everything he was going to do to help him. *Everything I learned at the class.*

"Medical help's on the way," Melvin said, more to reassure himself than Daed, who had lost consciousness. He took his father's pulse and then resumed pumping his chest again. *We'll get you out of the woods yet. . . .*

257

Meanwhile, Mamm and Ruth had stepped back, and he heard a whispered prayer falling from his mother's lips. *Jah, pray, someone please pray!*

"Ruthie, why don't you go on out to the road and wave down the paramedics? Direct them in here, won't ya?"

Immediately, his sister left the barn.

"Will he be all right?" Mamm asked, her voice sounding terribly weak. Weaker than when she'd had the flu two winters ago and lain in bed for days.

"He's a Lantz, ain't he?" Melvin answered, not wanting to add to her anxiety.

"He certainly is," Mamm replied, catching Melvin's spirit.

"Keep prayin'," he added, waiting for the sound of the siren. *Hurry, hurry!*

~~~~~

Tilly pushed the speed limit all the way back down Eden Road. She tried not to assume the worst, even though the image of Daed sprawled out like that, unconscious, was impossible to push from her mind.

She had quickly called 9-1-1 at the phone shanty, so now it was just a waiting game. If the ambulance arrived soon enough, Daed had a better chance of surviving. Arrhythmia wasn't the same as a heart attack, she knew, but it could be fatal if his heart didn't get back into rhythm with CPR or an electrical shock. If the paramedics dallied, Daed might not make it.

She pulled into the drive and sat in her car, not knowing how to feel or what to think. She wasn't Daed's biological daughter, but it didn't change the fact that he'd raised her as his own. Well, nearly. And even that made no difference now, not at such a critical time.

258

On top of Daed's sudden episode, Tilly was still reeling from the repercussions of her mother's shocking revelation. The fact remained: Her very existence was a thorn in Daed's flesh. *The ugly duckling* . . .

She pleaded for divine help, for God's will to be accomplished. Daed certainly needed heaven's intervention, living in the country, so far from town. *How far away is the ambulance service?* she wondered, anxious.

Then, incredibly, moments later, she could hear the sound of a siren and breathed a thank-you to the Lord. "They're almost here," she said, ever so relieved.

Tilly and Ruth encouraged Mamm to ride along in the ambulance, grateful Daed was now conscious, although very disoriented.

When the ambulance left with their parents inside, Tilly and Ruth hurried inside the house and choked down a few bites of the cold breakfast, then put away the leftovers. They would finish cleanup later.

Melvin, for his part, had declined eating, saying he and Caleb would take care of things outdoors, covering for Daed till other men—neighbors, mostly—came to take their place once Benny returned from getting word out next door.

Tilly had thanked Melvin profusely, suggesting that he had saved Daed's life with his quick thinking and CPR.

My half brother, Tilly thought now. She couldn't help looking at her siblings far differently, even dear Ruthie.

"Why are you staring at me?" Ruth asked, frowning as they went to grab coats and purses.

"Just thinking." Blood kin or the strong bonds of the heart—

what did it matter, really? She loved Ruth as if she were her full-blooded sister. Same with her brothers.

"You all right?" Ruth still seemed concerned. "You've asked *me* that more than once since we arrived here. No doubt you're worried about Daed."

"Well, it's not a day I'll forget anytime soon." *Nor last night . . .*

Ruthie nodded and walked with her out the door. "I wonder if we shouldn't have taken Mamm in the car and just followed the ambulance. She must be thoroughly confused."

"You're right. Let's get going," Tilly replied, thankful they didn't have to rely on horse and buggy. "Mamm can benefit from our experience in the English world." She didn't like the idea of Mamm not knowing what to do there amongst strangers, although medical professionals. She felt terribly protective of her as she remembered again the startling things she'd learned from her mother's lips in the wee hours just this morning.

Dear, dear Mamm . . .

Tilly swerved out of the way of a white-haired man driving along the narrow streets of Strasburg as she headed north toward the Lincoln Highway. The older gentleman gripped the steering wheel with both hands, spectacles all the way down on the tip of his nose as he squinted through the windshield at the road.

"Isn't he too old to be driving?" Ruth asked, her tone serious.

"We'll all be like that someday." Tilly glanced at her sister.

"To think I might not be driving anymore . . . and soon."

"Are you sad about that, Ruthie?"

Her sister sighed. "It wouldn't be the hardest thing to give up, I'm sure. My friends and my overall freedom would be much harder to leave behind. And I'm not sure I could leave our church, either. It's so different from the Amish meetings, as you know."

"Have you thought of discussing any of this with Will?" asked Tilly. "What about making a compromise? After all, if he really wants to be with you, he could meet you halfway."

"I don't know. He seems very set on joining church here." Ruth folded her arms, and for several miles she was brooding and quiet.

When she spoke again, Tilly changed the subject. "Just think what we might have missed by not coming to our parents' anniversary celebration."

Ruthie agreed. "Amazing, isn't it?"

"We wouldn't have enjoyed visiting with Mammi Lantz again, or seeing our new nieces and nephews, either."

"And Uncle Abner and Aunt Naomi, too, don't forget," Ruth said. "And Will Kauffman," she added more quietly, confiding that Will wanted to take her out in his courting carriage that evening. "Of course I won't go unless Daed is doing better . . . but if I do, I've thought of wearing one of my Amish dresses to surprise him. What do you think?"

"Well, nothing says you have to." Tilly didn't know whether to smile or frown, though she was certain Will would see it as a step in the right direction. "First, let's find out how Daed's doing."

Ruth agreed.

"And sometime before we leave for Rockport, I might stop at the cemetery to see Anna's headstone," Tilly said.

Ruth nodded, saying she probably wouldn't do that a second

time this visit. "But I'd like to go to the river . . . near the spot where Anna fell in."

Tilly shivered and admitted she'd already gone on Sunday but would have to take Ruthie there before they left town. Hard as it would be.

"Melvin mentioned wanting to go, too," Ruth said suddenly. "Do you mind?"

Tilly found this peculiar. "Why does he want to go?"

Ruthie shrugged and looked at the sky. "He didn't really say. Just needs to sort out some things that have nagged him for years, is all."

I understand. Yet Tilly felt overwhelmed at the thought of returning to the scene of Anna's accident. It was almost too much to take as she drove to the hospital as fast as the speed limit would allow.

Please, Lord, don't let Daed die, she prayed, struggling with tears for the man who was her father in name only.

CHAPTER 35

At Lancaster General Hospital, Tilly and Ruth found their mother sitting in a chair next to Daed's bed when they stepped into the semiprivate room. Mamm looked so pale, Tilly told her not to get up but to preserve her strength. "Daed needs you strong," she whispered as she leaned down to kiss her cheek.

"Such a lot of papers to read and sign in the ER," Mamm whispered, waving her hand before her face. "I hope I didn't make any mistakes."

"I'm sure everything will work out just fine," Ruth told her, assuring her that the People's benevolence fund would help with the medical costs, like always. No one in their Old Order community had health insurance.

"Well, it seems that your father may not be in longer than overnight. The nurse said his cardiologist has ordered more tests. Might even be that medicine alone will help him. We can hope and pray."

Tilly glanced at Daed, who was resting. Now and then, he raised one eyelid and peered over at them. She saw the IV in his arm and the heart monitor charting his pulse. Unable to bear it, she ambled to the window across the room, near the other bed, which was vacant.

"Tilly, you all right?" her sister asked softly.

She waved absently, without turning around, and stared out at the sky . . . still thinking of the Conestoga River and the fact that Melvin wanted to go back there. The whirling, churning river had carried Anna downstream, out of their reach. Life felt like that, too, sometimes. An unpredictable yet powerful flow of circumstances—some appalling, like Mamm's experience in the woodlot, and now Daed's brush with death—some good and even sweet, like her marriage to Kris and the birth of their twins.

She wondered if she shouldn't get word to Daed's siblings about how he was doing, or that he was even here. She walked back to the foot of the bed and suggested this to Mamm, who sat stiffly, pressing her fingers into the edge of the hospital bed. She looked like she might cry.

"*Gut* thinkin'." Mamm wiped her eyes. "And Abner and Naomi planned to bring supper over tonight, too, don't forget."

Daed raised his head slightly. "Naomi's cookin'?"

"Oh now, you . . ." Mamm sputtered a soft laugh. "We'll save you some . . . if they even come at all."

"Sure they will," Ruth said. "They won't want you to do any cooking. And anyway, they know we've packed up most of the kitchen for the move."

A few moments later, the doctor appeared, looking both professional and serious in his long white coat and with a stethoscope dangling from around his thin neck. He politely informed them that only two people should be in the room at a time, so Tilly took this as her chance to exit. She waited in the hallway, wondering what was happening inside while the doctor examined Daed, feeling yet again like she was on the outside looking in. *All my life.* Truly, she'd been an outsider long before she left the valley.

Nurses bustled back and forth. A patient lying on a gurney, returning from surgery, was pushed past her. The hallway suddenly smelled of antiseptic, and it turned her stomach. *I'm too sensitive*, she thought. *I could never be a nurse.*

After what seemed like a long while, the doctor exited the room and caught her eye but didn't stop to fill her in. A bit later, a tall, slender nurse, like a magazine model, approached her with a pleasant expression and suggested that she relax in the family waiting room.

Tilly thanked her and headed in the direction the nurse had pointed.

Another half hour passed, and eventually Mamm poked her head into the small waiting room. "If Naomi and Abner still want to come for supper, you should welcome them," Mamm suggested. "All right with you?"

"If they're fine with that. Or . . . if they'd rather, I can drive them here to be with you and Daed instead."

Mamm smiled. "*Denki*, Tilly. It's such a blessing to have ya here just now. But before ya go, dear, your father wants to see you. Alone."

There it is again—"*your father*," thought Tilly as she accompanied her mother back to the room. Again, she waited while Mamm went inside to ask Ruth to come out to give Daed privacy with Tilly. *What's on his mind?* she wondered.

Ruthie's eyes looked pink and puffy as she moved into the hallway with Mamm.

"We'll wait right here, dear." Mamm motioned for Tilly to go inside.

Tilly crept in and noticed again how vulnerable Daed looked in the hospital bed, elevated more now than it was earlier.

"*Kumme*, Tilly, to the other side." He motioned for her to sit where Mamm had been before.

He must feel better.

"Mamm wants your brothers and sisters to know you're in the hospital," she started the conversation, feeling jittery. "I'll head back as soon as—"

"Tilly," he stopped her. "Listen to me once." He frowned at the needle in the crook of his elbow. Then, with an exasperated-sounding sigh, he turned to look at her. "While I'm able, I want to say this to ya."

She listened, and if she wasn't mistaken, his lower lip quivered.

"I shouldn't have talked like I did the other night—in the carriage, ya know." He drew a labored breath. "I've had some time to think about everything," he said. "For one thing, what ya name your children is your business. And I don't mind if ya want to keep Anna's *Kapp*."

Tilly was too shocked to speak.

He looked pained. "There's something else, too. You might not know it by the way I acted, but I'm awful glad you and Ruthie came for the anniversary get-together." Here, his eyes filled with tears. "I know it maybe wasn't the easiest thing for you to do, daughter. But it means a lot to your Mamm and me."

Daughter . . .

Still unable to say what was in her heart, she reached up and placed her hand on his. "*Denki*," she whispered. "Thank you, Daed, for telling me."

Tilly waited for him to say more. But when she was certain he'd said all he wished to, she found her voice at last. "Da

266

Herr sei mit du, Daed—God be with you." She tiptoed to the door and quietly left the room.

∞

Respectfully, Tilly drove to each of Daed's eight siblings' homes after leaving the hospital. Thanks to the Amish grapevine, five had already heard, and the rest said they were grateful for her dropping by and were eager to call for a van driver to take them to Lancaster General Hospital as soon as possible.

"We'll do everything we can so Lester's not alone in this," Uncle Hank was quick to say. He thanked her repeatedly for coming. "Mighty nice of ya."

The Amish way, she thought. *Rallying around someone in need.*

At last she headed to Uncle Abner's, where she broke down and cried, despite acting so outwardly strong earlier.

"You just go ahead and let it all out real *gut*," Uncle Abner said as he motioned for Aunt Naomi to come and embrace her—together, they formed a small circle of compassion. "Your father will be all right," he said. "We've been prayin' ever since Benny ran by and told us the news."

"Word travels fast round here," Aunt Naomi said.

Tilly dried her tears and headed for the door, indicating that Mamm had said they could still come over to the house with supper as planned.

Aunt Naomi seemed to like the idea. Then, moving to the icebox, she said. "You might need a bite to eat now, too, ain't?"

Tilly thanked her but wanted to get back to the house. She needed to finish packing up the kitchen for Mamm, and the breakfast things needed cleaning up, too. "Not sure what I'd do without you two. *Denki*."

"That's why *Gott* gives us big families, *jah?*" said Uncle Abner. "We can be like the Lord Jesus to each other."

Tilly had never heard it put quite like that.

"We'll see you around six o'clock, then," Aunt Naomi said. "After Abner's all cleaned up from milkin'."

"I'll look forward to it."

While driving down Eden Road, Tilly remembered Daed's remarks to her at the hospital, and the almost gentle expression on his face, usually so stern when she was around. *Nearly always*, she recalled.

"To think he apologized," she whispered, struck by the reality. Her Daed seemed to have given as much thought to their stormy time together as she had.

Was this a new beginning?

CHAPTER 36

*W*hen she arrived at her parents' house, Tilly finished up what was left of the kitchen, leaving out a few essentials, then packed Anna's former room, except for her own things. Mamm had asked her last night if she wouldn't mind doing so—it was too emotional a task for Mamm herself to tackle.

Not long afterward, several relatives arrived to help Tilly finish the packing and begin the work of carrying things over next door and placing boxes in the specific rooms, according to Mamm's instructions. Many hands made light work, and by the time Uncle Abner and Aunt Naomi arrived with a single large hot dish, Tilly's stomach was rumbling. She'd only taken time to eat an apple and two oatmeal raisin cookies when she arrived back from the hospital, wanting to make good use of the time Mamm was with Daed in town.

Tilly had set the table with paper plates, missing Mamm's pretty white dishes with blue edging, already packed. Her aunt lifted the lid from the casserole and the steam rose, filling Tilly's nose with the tantalizing smell. "Ah . . . your baked chicken mushroom dish."

"Abner's mighty fond of it," said Aunt Naomi. "I made enough for seconds and more." She and Tilly sat with Uncle Abner at the far end of the table so as not to usurp either Daed's place at the head or Mamm's spot.

Uncle Abner seemed to want to get Tilly's mind off her father's situation, telling stories during the meal. "Now then, have I told ya this one?" His soft eyes shone as he leaned forward and folded his arms on the table. "My older brother was out visiting the Grand Canyon last winter when a curious tourist came up to him and asked, 'You're from Pennsylvania somewhere, right?' to which my brother nodded and said he was.

"'Lancaster County?' the man persisted.

"'*Jah*, that's right,' my brother said.

"'Does everyone there wear beards?' asked the tourist.

"'Not everyone, no.' Then my brother grinned mischievously. 'The women sure don't!'"

Tilly had to laugh right along with him; he was getting such a kick out of telling the tale.

When they bowed their heads for the second silent prayer, she thanked the Lord not only for Aunt Naomi's delicious food, but for her aunt and uncle's comforting presence at this, her mother's long table.

⤸

Melvin was well into the milking process at Daed's when he stepped outside for some air while the rest of the fellows hauled milk to the milk house cooler. He'd noticed Tilly on the back sidewalk, over there talking with Uncle Abner and Aunt Naomi.

Paying closer attention, Melvin saw that the three of them were actually laughing. *What on earth?* After all, Daed was lying in a hospital bed, and yet there they were, having themselves a good time. For pity's sake, he could hear their chatter clear over here!

Frowning, he stepped back, not wanting to be seen. He knew as well as anyone how bleak Daed's situation was—he'd never forget helping his father to the floor of the barn, nor performing CPR after Daed became unresponsive. It seemed wrong for Tilly, especially, to act this jolly, considering the rather tentative outlook for Daed.

Unless . . . does she know something new about Daed, perhaps? Oh, he hoped all would be well. He truly did. And he must not assume the worst but trust the Lord God for the outcome. There'd been far too much tragedy and loss in this family. Enough for a lifetime.

Ruth was content to let other relatives take turns visiting Daed, since she'd had some time with him already. And, too, she wanted to stay close to Mamm, who looked awfully peaked—the day wore heavily on her.

Ruth sat quietly in one corner of the family waiting room, now packed with bearded Amishmen and devout women wearing white organdy prayer coverings, all of them relatives. Most of the men were talking about the harvest, which made Ruth even more grateful for their sacrificial visit. Occasionally, a passing nurse would glance in and respond with momentary surprise, then quickly attempt to conceal her startled reaction, which Ruth found comical.

Even more amazing to Ruth was the appearance of Will Kauffman and his parents. She thought it wise to leave the room and go into the hall when Will called to her with his eyes. "Thanks for coming to see my father," she whispered as they took a short walk.

"I was sure surprised to hear 'bout this, Ruthie."

"We've been told he's going to be all right."

"Thank goodness," he said.

"And thank the Lord." She smiled, pleased he'd come.

"I made arrangements with my parents for us to ride back in the hired van with them, if you'd like. Then you and I can go for a spin in my carriage later. That is . . . if you're up to it." His face lit up when he talked; she'd nearly forgotten how well he expressed himself back when they were nearly an engaged couple.

She had little time left in Eden Valley—now that Daed was stable, it was all right with her to spend the evening with Will, and she told him so. "We can leave once you've seen Daed, if you'd like." She suspected he may have come mainly to see her, but he nodded, saying he'd like to go in and say hullo once the next two relatives departed the room.

"All right." Ruth still felt confused, even torn, when she was with Will. How much longer would she feel this way? Was it merely part of the process of getting better acquainted again?

"I'd like to stop off at the house before we go riding," she told him. "I have a surprise for you."

Instantly, he grinned. "I'm all for surprises, Ruthie."

She wondered how it would seem to ride with him in his courting carriage . . . the first time in years. Would being with Will bring happiness to her heart tonight? Or would she regret going?

The almost pumpkiny scent drifting through the atmosphere was not unfamiliar to Ruth. She recalled the sights, sounds, and smells of October and early November in Lancaster County from her childhood as she took Will's hand and stepped into his black courting carriage.

"You look almost like a regular Amish girl tonight," he said, smiling up at her and standing near as she sat to the left of where he would sit to hold the reins. "All ya need is a *Kapp*."

"Are you surprised, then?"

"To be honest, I kinda wondered if you might not put on Plain clothes for our date."

He's pleased I'm trying on my old life again. She watched him hurry around and climb in next to her.

"Let's go have some ice cream or pie at the Strasburg Creamery," he said, picking up the reins. "Sound *gut*?"

She agreed with a nod, a smile bubbling up. It was still light enough to see the smooth-washed stones in the brook running along the roadside. She remembered how cold the water had felt one springtime evening, when they'd stopped the buggy so she could follow a darling brown bunny rabbit. She and Will had both ended up wading in their bare feet, laughing and enjoying the moment like happy children.

"You're quiet tonight, Ruthie."

"Just thinking back to when you rolled up your pant legs and went splashing into that brook over yonder."

He chuckled. "Were ya?" He shook his head, as if quite amazed. "I was just thinkin' the same thing." Will slipped his arm around her. "So many *gut* memories before I messed everything up 'tween us." He paused. "But that's all over and done with."

"*Jah*, 'under the blood,' like some of my evangelical friends say." She'd heard the phrase at a revival meeting at her church last year.

"Do you remember takin' our scooters down Eden Road, too?" he asked. "We had a race, and I recall letting you win."

She rolled her eyes. "How can I forget? At the time, though, you insisted I won fair and square."

He smiled mischievously. "That I did. And I would let you win again, if you wanted to race me," he teased.

"Would you, now?" She was enjoying herself, though she felt strangely like she was stepping where angels might fear to tread.

"So." Will suddenly sounded tentative. "Have you decided what ya want to do yet?"

Her heart was in her throat. "I'm getting close to a decision."

Will inched back a bit, like he was bracing himself. "Like I said, I want you to take your time, so you'll know for *ausdricklich*—positive." His eyes shone in the growing twilight. "I mean that, Ruthie."

"*Denki*," she said gratefully, feeling more relaxed.

❧

After supper, Tilly took care to wash the countertops and table, and she swept the floor, as usual. When finished, she walked to the front room and stepped out the double doors to stand on the wide porch. As she recalled from her childhood, it wasn't used much at all. The front porch served as an overflow for funerals and weddings for most Amish families. But there hadn't been any weddings here . . . not yet anyway. The family activities had all taken place in the backyard.

It was hard to believe that she and Ruth had only been

back for five days. In that space of time, the radiant leaves had boasted their brilliance and begun to fall. Due to strong winds in the night, the leaves were nearly all underfoot now . . . on the ground in clumps around the bases of trees and caught in clusters beneath bushes.

There was a decided nip in the air, and she went back inside to get one of Mamm's older long shawls, noticing one was missing. Ruthie must have taken one, as well. *Out with her former beau,* Tilly thought, still getting used to the idea. She was worried Ruth might be swayed by Will tonight if he was to become romantic—the old tendrils of first love reaching from the past. Even so, it was her choice to make.

Wrapped now in Mamm's black woolen shawl, Tilly waited, leaning on the smooth porch banister, watching for her mother to return from the hospital. The English neighbor boy had stopped by on his motorbike over an hour ago to say that Mamm had called, hoping to spare Tilly yet another trip into town, though Tilly wouldn't have minded. And there she stood, hungry for the latest news about Daed and feeling a lack of enthusiasm toward winter's arrival in another month or so.

Winter will be less dreary for Mamm this year if Ruthie returns home. She frowned, her head spinning with the upcoming changes already decided—the move to the *Dawdi Haus* for her parents, and Sam and Josie taking over the original house. *Momentous.*

"If Ruthie succumbs to Will and returns, will she stay with Mamm and Daed in the *Dawdi Haus* or in her old room here?" Tilly whispered. She almost thought she saw her breath in the chilly air.

Thinking more of her sister's unexpected state of affairs,

she wondered suddenly why, if Will Kauffman was so eager to court Ruth, he hadn't pursued her by letter long before now. Had he actually needed Ruth to make the first move toward Eden Valley? If that were so, Tilly believed her sister deserved far better.

CHAPTER 37

*M*amm slowly inched out of the neighbors' blue Studebaker when she arrived at the house near dusk. Tilly hurried out to meet her, reaching to steady her. She offered to pay the neighbors for their time and trouble, which they graciously refused. She made further small talk, asking how they were doing, feeling a little strange about seeing the Eshlemans again now that she was an Englisher like them. Greg Eshleman hadn't changed a lot; he was still as stocky as she'd remembered, if not more so, and his blond hair had thinned in places on top. His wife, Jocelyn, had lost a significant amount of weight, and her light brown hair was peppered with gray. Greg had been one of the men who'd leapt into the river to try to save Anna that dreaded day, along with Chester and Melvin.

"We think of you and Ruthie so often," Jocelyn said, her voice sounding pinched as she regarded Tilly with her beagle-like eyes.

"Well, it's wonderful to see you both . . . and good to be home for a visit," Tilly said, glancing at Mamm.

"Call anytime, Tilly. It's good to stay in touch," Greg said before waving and then starting to back out the car.

"Such nice folk," Mamm said softly as they headed around the side of the house to the back door.

Indoors, after Mamm removed her best gray shawl, Tilly hurried to warm up the supper leftovers for her mother and sat her down at the table, lit up by the welcoming sight of the familiar gas lamp. "Have you eaten much today?"

"Oh, enough, I'm sure." Mamm mentioned that a number of Daed's relatives had brought food along, mostly fresh fruit and snacks, things to nibble on. "No one went hungry, that's for sure."

"Did a tray of food come for Daed after we left?"

Mamm said the nurses seemed to be taking good care of him, and that he would definitely be discharged in the morning. "The doctors want to observe him tonight, but he may not need a pacemaker after all . . . at least not for a while yet."

Tilly offered to drive her to the hospital in the morning, and Mamm seemed relieved. "As long as I'm here, you really don't have to call the neighbors, all right?" she said. "I'm happy to help."

"Well, but you've done so much runnin' today, I just thought . . ." Mamm's voice gave out.

"Don't worry, rest yourself . . . and enjoy Aunt Naomi's wonderful meal." She sat across from Mamm, where Ruthie had always sat growing up, getting up once to make some hot chamomile tea to calm her mother's nerves, and later for an ample dish of fruit cocktail. "Would ya like some ice cream with that?"

Mamm declined, which was a bit of a surprise, but Tilly just let it be.

Several times while they were quietly chatting—connecting so wonderfully as they had the past couple of days—Tilly was tempted to say that she and Daed had cleared the air . . . and that it was Daed's doing. But for whatever reason, Tilly held back.

Mamm glanced around. "Where's our Ruthie?"

"Out with her old beau, if I may be so bold. She was wearing her blue church dress and matching cape apron, too."

"Aw, I would so love to see that again." Mamm smiled sweetly. "She must look as perty as a bride."

Tilly worried that Ruthie might be just a little too excited for the evening, but she didn't say. She merely watched her mother take tiny spoonfuls of the fruit cocktail.

Some time later, when Mamm was finished, Tilly rose from the table and carried the paper plates to the trash under the sink. Her mother offered to help redd up, but Tilly wouldn't hear of it. "Go lie down, Mamm. I'll finish here. You've had a long day."

Standing in the doorway, Mamm leaned against the wood frame. "*Denki*, Tilly. I appreciate you. Can ya even begin to imagine how I've prayed for you . . . and for Ruthie?"

Tilly nodded, suddenly feeling clammy all over, like she'd fallen into deep water. How she wished her sister would return soon. *I can't bear to lose Ruthie to Will*, she thought desolately.

⌘

The Strasburg Creamery was homey and quiet on a Wednesday evening. "Prayer meeting night," Will told Ruth with a smile as they sat in the wooden booth. Many of the churches around Lancaster County held Bible study and prayer meetings that night.

"My church in Rockport has Wednesday meetings, too," she was happy to tell him.

"Well, there's none of that in Eden Valley," Will replied. "'Cept the occasional private ones, though I doubt Bishop Isaac knows about 'em."

She knew it wasn't customary for the People to study or discuss the Bible—the ministerial brethren had stated years ago that doing so had the dangerous potential to lead to stating opinions, or to taking verses out of context. Ruth had never felt strongly about that stance, however. She'd always assumed that if she read God's Word often enough, it would simply seep down into her spirit.

"Have you ever thought of visiting other churches?" she asked. "Just curious."

"Not sure how wise that is, since I've spent so much time talkin' with the brethren. They really helped me get my feet back on the ground after I went astray," he reminded her. "Why do you ask?"

She wasn't ready to delve into all of that, but she again thought fondly of her missions-minded church. "We can talk about it sometime, maybe."

This seemed to satisfy him. "Fine with me."

It was getting late, and she really hoped Mamm was home from the hospital by now. Was Daed still improving . . . and were some of his brothers and sisters still there with him? Many questions simmered in her mind, yet she tried to meet Will's eyes and engage herself in conversation. He seemed to yearn for it so.

Then, during the ride back toward Eden Valley, Will had romance on his mind. He sat closer to her once they were back on the unlit roads, away from town. He reached for her hand, adeptly holding the reins with his right hand.

Feeling surprisingly comfortable, Ruth enjoyed the distant sound of horses neighing and all the nighttime sounds as they turned off May Post Office Road. This special night—this moment—belonged to them. She breathed a silent prayer amidst her many emotions.

Will did most of the talking as they rode ever so slowly now. He encouraged her to snuggle next to him, both of them enjoying the peace of the evening.

He leaned down and kissed her forehead and paused, his breath so near. "I still feel like I must be dreaming. You're here again, Ruthie. You're actually here with me."

She'd missed him, too, or so she felt at that moment. *Maybe more than I realized . . .*

He ran his fingers across her cheek, along her chin. "Honey," he said dreamily.

She wondered if he was going to kiss her again.

He moved even closer. "Oh, Arie, I'm mighty glad you're . . ." He stopped right then, catching himself. "Wait, *ach* . . . I didn't mean—"

"Arie? I'm *Ruthie*," she said, bolting straight up. "Oh, Will . . . you kissed Arie Schlabach?" Her head and heart were whirling. "You said there was no romance between—"

"Ruthie, I—"

"Please stop the buggy." She fought back tears but was determined not to let him know. "I want out! This minute!"

"But it's dark and too late for you to go on foot," he argued. "Please, Ruthie—honey—don't leave like this. Let's talk."

"What's to talk about? Your answer is either yes or no. And I'm not your honey!"

"*Ach*, you're reading way too much into this."

"Am I?" She was furious, wanting him to simply refute the notion that he'd kissed the young woman from Ohio. "I asked you to please stop the horse."

When he pulled off the road and halted, he got down to help her, but she refused, tossing the lap robe aside. "I've just made my decision . . . I won't be moving back here, Will. You can be sure of that!" She lifted her skirt and began to run from him, running as fast as her legs could take her from her embarrassment and hurt.

Halfway home, she spied the shortcut Tilly had mentioned the other day and took off through the field between Chester's property and Daed's. She defied everything she'd heard from Daed and tore through the middle of the forbidden woodlot, sobbing and getting Mamm's shawl caught time and again on the low branches. She kept her eyes peeled for critters or whatever else might be so worrisome. But she saw nothing at all.

Back at the house, the lantern was lit in Tilly's room, creating a warm glow. Tilly was still up, as if waiting for her. Ruth plunked down on her sister's bed, not crying any longer—her tears had dried up on the way. "I'm certain now about what I want to do," she said, her words pouring out of her. "I want to stay English." She put her head down for a moment, then met Tilly's eyes. "It's over between Will and me."

"Oh, sister . . . what—"

"I was stupid to ever think of taking him back. *Dumm*—stupid!" With that, she covered her face with her hands again and more tears sprang forth.

"Ruthie . . ." Tilly sat next to her on the bed and tried to comfort her, but no amount of sisterly soothing could return the peace she'd known earlier tonight. Nothing Tilly could say or do would assure Ruth that Will hadn't cared deeply for Arie Schlabach. *He might care for her still,* she thought.

It took some time, but she managed to collect herself. Tilly had been right all along—entertaining thoughts of a life with

Will Kauffman was a mistake, indeed. His heart may have changed toward God and the church, but he sure didn't know himself when it came to women.

Ruth brushed away her tears and reached to hug her sister. Then, when they'd said good-night, she slipped away to her room and soundly closed the door. As fast as she could, Ruth began to unpin her cape apron. Her hands trembled and she couldn't get it off quickly enough. When all the pins were out, she flung it, uncaring, into the corner, then removed her best blue Amish dress, tossing it into a heap on the floor, as well.

CHAPTER 38

Tilly, Ruthie, and Mamm set right to work early Thursday morning, after a quick breakfast of cold cereal and bananas. They worked doubly hard to finish the very last of the packing before Tilly was to drive Mamm to the hospital later. Ruthie planned to stay behind to direct her brothers and others from the community when they came to move the furniture.

The day was exceptionally hectic and became even more so when one of the road horses got loose and Chester and Melvin dropped everything to run after the mare. A wind had kicked up out of the northeast, and heavy gray clouds loomed as Tilly drove Mamm to the hospital. "Looks like rain," Tilly mentioned, but Mamm was quiet, undoubtedly lost in a world of concern for Daed.

Once Tilly and her mother arrived at Lancaster General, they waited patiently for Daed to be discharged. Daed seemed almost perky while they sat in his room and waited for the final papers, including numerous instructions as to his care—primarily medication. He twiddled his thumbs, not grumbling but clearly eager to be let out of there. Every few minutes, he rose from his chair to look out the window, checking the sky in hopes of rain, talking in *Deitsch* about his livestock and the turkeys and the harvest. His thoughts were of home and the farm, and neither Tilly nor Mamm brought up the runaway horse.

By the time Tilly returned them to the *Dawdi Haus* after stopping off at a pharmacy to fill the prescriptions, Chester, Melvin, and the twins had located the runaway mare, as well as already moved in most of the heavy furniture. They'd immediately set up their parents' bed so Daed could rest upon his arrival. In an odd sort of way, Daed's being away for the move may have tempered the transition for him, Tilly thought as she led Mamm past the back steps of the main house, to the little porch and steps of their new home. "*Willkumm heemet,* Mamm!"

"It'll be awful nice to have less to dust and clean, *jah?*" Mamm quipped, her countenance lifted by bringing Daed home.

Tilly smiled and escorted her inside.

Not long after, Josie and her mother, Edie, along with Aunt Naomi and Mammi Lantz, arrived to help complete the unpacking. Tilly and Ruth were grateful and reminded again of the kindly way the People showed up to assist at the drop of a hat.

Once the main house was empty of all boxes and furnishings, except for the beds in Ruth's and Anna's former rooms, which Mamm and Daed would no longer be needing, the womenfolk converged over there and began washing down walls and windowsills, followed by sweeping and scrubbing the floors. They cleaned as thoroughly as if they were readying the house for worship. Even the ceiling.

Tilly was actually surprised that Ruthie didn't look any the worse for wear, considering she had shed so many tears the night before. *To think her happiness was so short-lived.* She did find it peculiar that Ruthie wasn't willing to talk in much detail about what had taken place, despite Tilly's attempts to reach out to her. *Maybe it's just too soon.*

Melvin finished stacking hay in the loft with his robust younger brother Allen while Sam and a few of their male cousins finished moving the last of the furniture into the *Dawdi Haus* amidst the threat of rain. Allen talked of nothing but Sam's taking over Daed's farm, saying he was glad it was Sam and not him. "Why's that?" Melvin had to know.

"For one thing, I'm mighty happy for Sam. Honestly, though, it'd be tremendous work to run this dairy farm, what with all the fowl, too."

"But a pretty *gut* living, you have to admit . . . 'specially for a young couple like Sam and Josie."

Allen scratched the back of his neck. "Well, if they have as many children as Daed's parents ended up with, that could all change."

Melvin felt he understood Allen's meaning to some extent. "That's up to the Lord, for sure. Thankfully, we parents start with just one and grow into our family."

Allen shot him a boyish grin and bobbed his blond head. "Ain't that the truth . . . and a mighty *gut* thing, too. Just think if we got married and then, *pow,* just like that, we were handed eight to ten youngsters to look after . . . and to feed. It'd take some doin', too, keepin' em all on the straight and narrow." He was chuckling as they headed down to the main area of the big barn. "Wouldn't that be something?"

"Can't imagine," Melvin said. He thought now of having run into Will Kauffman rather late last night. The young fellow's horse had acted up and stalled him in the middle of Eden Road, up a ways near the turnoff to the main road. Somehow the horse had managed to turn the carriage so it was at a right angle to the country road.

"I think I just lost ya," Allen said. He was waving his hand in front of Melvin's face.

"Sorry 'bout that. Deacon Kauffman's grandson Will came to mind, is all. He had some troubles with his horse last night." Melvin told Allen he'd been out making a call at the phone shanty and was walking home at the time. "It was a *gut* thing I came upon him when I did."

"Oh?" Allen raised his eyebrows.

"Let me tell ya, Will seemed flustered over more than his driving horse—he seemed downright upset. His voice sounded awful scratchy, too."

Allen frowned. "Maybe girl troubles again."

Melvin had heard tell of the breakup between Will and Ruthie some years ago. "Didn't ask what was the matter, but it sure looked like there was a lap blanket all rumpled up next to him, like his sweetheart-girl had just been out ridin' with him."

"Well, we don't really know 'bout these young fellas, ain't? 'Specially the ones who go wild for a time . . . then come crawlin' back to the church."

Melvin nodded. It wasn't any of his business, really. He'd done his best to help Will with the horse so the young man could get on his way. And he felt sure it was Providence that he'd stumbled on the situation when he had. It could have been a real tragedy had a car come by and not seen Will and his courting buggy, all turned like that.

Mercy's sake!

At noon, Tilly offered to take a tray of food to Daed, glad her mother had decided on the large downstairs bedroom. The southeast-facing room was presently cheery and light—the fast-moving storm had come and gone. The sunlight suited Daed. "The hospital just isn't my favorite place to be, no matter how hard they try to make ya feel comfortable."

"I understand," she said. "Nice to see you home again, Daed."

He looked around the room, undoubtedly noticing that things were laid out akin to how they had been in the other bedroom next door, theirs for so many years. "Things look a bit different here, but it's the same bed. I'm thankful for that." He chuckled a little.

"You'll be up and around in no time."

"I guess so, if I follow the doctor's instructions." He fretted over the several heart-related pills he had to take daily, one of which was to be taken twice a day.

"Mamm will help keep track. You'll be just fine."

He nodded contemplatively, looking out the window. "Your mother is one angelic woman, I have to say."

Thinking of Mamm and the terrible trial she'd endured all those years ago, Tilly wholeheartedly agreed.

"I did a lot of pondering while I was in the hospital," Daed said quietly, returning his gaze to her. "I realized my time could be short . . . and believe it's high time I told you the truth 'bout yourself, Tilly."

The room became so still she could hear her own heartbeat. "I already know," she said before even thinking.

He frowned, apparently confused. "What're ya sayin'?"

"It's okay, Daed," Tilly said. "I already know what happened to Mamm in the woodlot."

He folded his weathered hands, his expression grave now, even shocked.

"Mamm explained everything—confessed, if you will— after I stumbled across a letter she'd written. She'd meant for me to open it after she passed." Tilly paused to make herself breathe. "Daed, she revealed all because she thought it might help me . . . understand *you* better."

He sighed loudly and gazed at the quilt covering him, his work-roughened hands tan against the fabric. "I should've been the one to tell you . . . years ago. But I've been a coward, hushing up the facts and wanting to plow under the—"

"Daed, this is just too hard for you," she said, worried.

He ignored her. "Some things have to be said, Tilly. Life doesn't always make sense."

"*Nee*, Daed. And life here didn't always make sense to me, either. Not before I learned about this anyway."

He shook his head, then groaned, eyes watering.

"Even so . . ." She could hardly speak, considering how upset he looked. "You were always a good provider, Daed— took such good care of Mamm and the family. A God-fearing man."

He knotted up the quilt with both hands. "When you were an infant . . . all I could see was another man's child, Tilly. A brutal man, at that. Yet I watched your mother fussin' over you, lovin' you as if nothin' terrible had happened. You belonged to her, Tilly, no matter what we knew . . . but not to me."

"*Ach*, Daed . . ." As if a light had burst forth, she could sympathize with her father's reluctance toward her . . . and his enduring pain.

For the first time ever, she actually felt sorry for him.

"I wish I could roll back the years." He struggled to get the words out. "And, honestly, I don't know how you will, but I hope you'll forgive me for my sin of omission. Someday."

His hand shook as he reached for her.

She stared at this offering of reconciliation. Tilly clenched her teeth to hold back the tears. "You're forgiven, Daed. Of course you are."

Tears streamed down his flushed face. "I understand why you didn't want to stay here, not with your tough childhood . . . and my failings." He went on to explain how he'd wanted to do right by her, to raise her to be a good Amishwoman like Mamm. "Instead, I was much too harsh and overprotective," he admitted. "Always keepin' an eye on you—surely ya must have expected I was just waiting for you to make mistakes . . . and sometimes maybe I was. And Anna's drowning didn't help none." He raised his sorrowful eyes to her. "I feel certain you must blame yourself for that, daughter. You must think *I* blame you, too. That you disappointed me in not lookin' after your little sister that day . . ." His voice trailed off.

She bowed her head. "*Jah* . . . I do. Ever so much."

He drew a long breath. "You had nothin' at all to do with Anna's death. You must cast off that false blame and forgive yourself." He was weeping now. "Please, you must, Tilly-girl."

She choked back her own tears, disbelieving. "If only it were that easy."

He nodded thoughtfully. "*Ich verschteh*—I understand, Tilly. I do."

291

She took yet another bold step toward him. And trembled as she leaned to kiss his tear-stained cheek.

***

That evening, during family worship, Daed managed to walk to the small front room from the bedroom and sit in his favorite chair. He read from Psalm 51. "'Have mercy upon me, O God, according to thy lovingkindness: according unto the multitude of thy tender mercies blot out my transgressions.'" Tilly thought his tone was gentle and even somewhat expressive. It was as if their frankness earlier, their heartfelt exchange, had dispelled the sometimes humdrum feel of his reading. He articulated the Scriptures as though they meant everything to him, as if he was a man who wanted to live, and to live for a very long time.

Daed glanced at Tilly as he continued. "'Create in me a clean heart, O God; and renew a right spirit within me.'"

Tilly looked at Ruthie, worrying how Daed would take the news that there was no hope of his daughter's return to the People. Perhaps it was a good thing they were leaving for home tomorrow.

CHAPTER 39

*R*uth was aware of the barrenness of her former room that evening. Only the bed remained, and Anna's old room looked equally empty. It dawned on her that she and Tilly would be sleeping on this side of the house for the last time tonight. Saturday morning, Lord willing, Sam and Josie were planning to move in, and they and their children would occupy the house for their first night there as a family.

It felt unsettling to reflect on life's cycles—the comings and goings of people. *Including Will Kauffman.* "Good thing I found out about him before I made plans to move back here," she murmured, closing her suitcase. "Thank goodness."

Tiptoeing across to see if Tilly was still up, and pleased that she was, Ruth tapped on the door. "Did Melvin talk to you about going to the park tomorrow—to the Conestoga River?"

The lantern was lit on the small table next to the bed, and its light cast shadows on the far wall. Sitting there all cozy in bed, Tilly looked up from her book and shook her head. "Haven't heard from him, no. What time did Melvin say he wanted to go?"

"Well, he doesn't want to detain us, so right after breakfast makes sense."

Tilly nodded. "That should work." She indicated she wanted to try to be home in Rockport by midafternoon if possible. "I'm homesick . . . really miss Kris and the twins."

"Seems like we've been gone for weeks." Ruth took a seat on the bed when Tilly motioned for her to join her. Ruth got situated, facing her sister with her legs stretched out toward the headboard. "Does it to you?"

"Nearly a lifetime in some ways." Tilly encouraged her with a smile.

She'd noticed that Tilly and Daed had seemed uncommonly at ease with each other this evening, as if the old tension had drained away.

Not wanting to pry, she simply nodded. "And just so ya don't think I'm clamming up on you, I'm ready to tell you why Will's not for me."

"Only if you want to."

"Mamm always said if a fella is too interested in many girls before marriage, the chances of faithfulness afterward aren't so good."

Tilly's eyes were softer . . . gentler. "She's as wise as anyone we know, *jah?*"

Ruth agreed. "Come to think of it, seems like Mammi Lantz told me the same thing back when I first started going to Singings and other youth activities."

"If we're wise, we can learn from the people who love us," Tilly said. "Provided we pay attention."

Ruth contemplated that, glad to be here with Tilly, finally opening her heart. "But what if I never have youngsters so that I can pass on what I've learned?"

"Oh, sister . . . you will." Tilly reached to take her hand, smiling sweetly. "The Lord has someone special picked out for you. And you can rest in that."

"Well, it's not Will Kauffman." Even though it felt a bit like something in her had died—again—Ruth knew that for sure. "And I'm so glad I didn't tell Mamm and Daed anything definite about returning. What a mistake that would've been!"

"You spared them an emotional roller coaster, for sure."

"Still, we've had such a good time here with our family; I don't want to spoil a second more of it." Ruthie thought again of her father's shaky condition. "There's something else I've wanted to share with you," she continued. "I've met someone at church back in Rockport . . . someone you and Kris know well." For the first time, she told Tilly about going out with Jim Montgomery.

"Oh, Ruthie, he seems just wonderful! Jim's always one of the first ones to sign up to help, and he attends all the Saturday men's breakfasts with Kris."

Ruth couldn't contain her smile. "Has Kris considered him for me, maybe?"

Tilly's expression was suspicious. "Well, I'm not really sure about that, but I do know he speaks highly of Jim."

This was news to Ruth. "Maybe now that I know my feelings for Will are truly a thing of the past, I can give Jim's and my relationship a chance." She rose and blew a kiss to her sister. "Tomorrow will come quick, you know."

"Sleep tight."

Ruth smiled and paused in the doorway, lingering there. "I'm going to miss this big old house."

Tilly looked over at her and nodded slowly. "You know something? I am, too."

Ruth wiggled her fingers in farewell and left the room.

———

Tilly continued reading until she started to nod off. Somewhere in her haze, she heard footsteps in the hallway and wondered if Ruth was still restless and moving about.

When Tilly looked up from her warm spot, Mamm appeared in the doorway, wearing her heavy white bathrobe. She smiled timidly and came all the way in, closing the door behind her. "Mamm? Are you all right?"

"It's awful late, I know. But I just had to walk over and talk to you before tomorrow comes." Mamm sat on the edge of the bed, near where Ruthie had perched earlier. Her waist-length hair hung straight down her back, the beautiful thick locks glossy in the lantern light.

"I hope Daed's okay," Tilly said, her first concern for him.

Mamm drew a breath, then placed a hand on her bosom and pursed her lips. "My dear." She stopped as soon as she'd begun, seemingly unable to go on.

Does she know that it's all out in the open between Daed and me?

Tilly waited, then wondered if she ought to help this along. "Did Daed share something personal with you, perhaps?"

Mamm nodded and fixed her eyes on Tilly. "We talked for a long time before retiring for the night. And now, well, I can't sleep a wink. Ain't the best thing at this hour, hashin' out such a weighty topic, I'll say. Not sure we would've stayed up that late if things weren't so private for us next door, just the two of us."

Tilly felt she might split in half if she didn't speak. "Was I out of order, saying what I did? If so, I'm sorry."

A cloud fell over her mother's face. "Honestly, I'm relieved yous talked things through . . . but it ain't for just anyone to know, mind you." Mamm patted Tilly's hand. "And hearing Daed's made his peace with ya, well, that's worth everything."

Tilly reached for her. "Oh, Mamm, since you've told me, I've put myself in that woodlot, in my mind."

"But you were the result, Tilly. *You*, my precious girl."

It was hard for her to think that her mother had suffered so for Tilly's own life. "I love you, Mamm. I hope you know how very much."

"The Lord gave me beauty for ashes . . . and you must never doubt that, my dear."

And joy for mourning, thought Tilly.

She clung to her mother as the darkness of the past was swallowed up by the truth's radiant light. Oh, she wanted to purpose in her heart that no more harm befall this dearest of mothers. *Angelic*, Daed had described her.

Moments later, when Mamm was ready to head back to the *Dawdi Haus*, Tilly slipped on her own robe and went with her, the flashlight shining brightly. "Sweet dreams," Tilly said.

"You too, dear."

Tomorrow will soon be here. She thought of Ruthie's remark and hurried back around to the main house, recalling Anna's joy in scampering about that very area, calling for Tilly. *"Come an' play with me."*

"My little shadow follows me, even now," she whispered, heading inside. "In my heart."

After extinguishing the lantern, Tilly fell right to sleep, dreaming that Anna was still alive. And it was her very best dream in many years.

CHAPTER 40

As the crow of Daed's rooster pierced the golden dawn, Tilly awakened feeling more like herself. She welcomed the fact that her mother had shared so freely again last night, especially on the heels of Tilly's conversation with Daed. It made coming home all the more precious.

Buoyed by the memory of her father's gentle words yesterday, she slipped out of bed and went to push up the shades. Standing at the window, she tried to memorize what she saw up and down Eden Road. Field work was in full swing, and she relished the view from north to east and back again. Oh, the many times she'd dug her fingers into the rich black soil, helping Mamm plant her colorful annuals—finding plump earthworms just below the surface.

She raised her face to the sky, nearly indescribable with a luminous sunrise. Elongated wisps of rose-pink clouds provided the perfect mirror to reflect the golden shades.

Tilly was ever so thankful for this new day—a day when she looked forward to seeing her darling Kris and their sweet girls again. She could just imagine being wrapped in her husband's strong arms. *Tonight!*

Josie arrived right on time, after Tilly and Ruth came back to the main house from having breakfast with Daed and Mamm in their cozy new kitchen.

She joked that this was her "biggest and best fall cleaning ever" and seemed excited to get settled into the house. "My sisters and a few cousins are comin' to help finish up the scrubbing," she said, her pretty face aglow.

"You're going to love living here and raising your family," Tilly told her while they stood in Mamm's former kitchen, surrounded by sunbeams.

Josie glanced about the large, empty room. "I can't tell ya how happy Sam is."

"And you'll be close to Daed and Mamm, too."

"It's an honor to keep an eye out for them." Josie smiled. "I really mean that."

Thanking her, Tilly reached to clasp her hand. "I hope you've forgiven me for going silent all those years."

"Oh *jah* . . . don't worry yourself. Really."

Don't worry yourself. . . .

Tilly smiled; her dearest friend sounded like her.

Forgiveness is a matter of the heart, she thought and thanked the dear Lord above.

Sammy and Johanna were sitting quietly on the floor in the opposite corner, building a block tower together, chattering in *Deitsch*. Johanna kept her little hands out, waiting to knock down the blocks without warning. "Your children resemble each of you," Tilly commented. "They really do."

"We're thankful for such healthy little ones."

Their talk eventually turned to a few larger pieces of furniture

Mamm had pegged earlier for auction. Josie mentioned that Daed said she and Sam might have first dibs on those. "Ain't that nice?"

"So good to hear. That way, the house can continue to remind all of us how it looked when my parents lived here."

Josie's face burst into a smile, and she reached to hug Tilly, clasping her arms. "Does that mean you'll come back and see us? Will ya stay with us, too, just maybe, with your husband and children?"

"Would you mind?"

"Are ya kidding?" Her sister-in-law gave a merry laugh. "Sam and I would really like that." Josie glanced at her children. "So would Sammy and Johanna."

"I'm sure my parents would enjoy it, too."

"Drop me a note now and then, all right?" Josie went to get her purse and pulled out a small tablet. "Won't ya jot down your address for me? I know your Mamm has it, but I don't want to trouble her for it."

Tilly obliged, finding Josie's enthusiasm to be very sweet, even contagious. She wrote her mailing address and gave her another hug.

Josie seemed reluctant to say good-bye and went along with Tilly out to the car, where Ruthie was loading the suitcases into the trunk. Ruth also had a box of things from her hope chest she was trying to squeeze in.

"I'm glad you'll be living in Daed and Mamm's house," Ruthie said, giving Josie a quick embrace. "Have a happy life here. . . . I know you will."

Tilly waved again, and at that moment, she wished she and Ruthie were heading straight out to the old Lincoln Highway, and then east toward home. But their brother Melvin was waiting, and so was the river.

CHAPTER 41

"I've just spotted my sisters a-comin'," Melvin told Susannah as she pounded down her bread dough at the kitchen counter. "I'll see you in a little while."

"Do ya expect to be gone long?"

He shook his head. "The girls have to get on the road if they want to make it home by sundown."

His dear wife gave a gentle wave, and he reached for his jacket and pushed his black felt hat down on his head. Outdoors, he waited for Ruthie to move from the front seat to the back when she insisted he ride up front with Tilly. "Ain't necessary," he protested, but Ruthie had her way. A right spunky one, she was.

He didn't have to wonder why Tilly was quiet during the drive. *Just as well,* he thought, taking in the sights as they swiftly moved farther from his home and familiar surroundings. It was strange to see other farmers' fields zipping past so quick-like. Goodness, he didn't think he'd ever get used to riding in a car, or, for that matter, a rented van.

When they arrived at the park, he saw that the area hadn't changed much in nine years, with the exception of the trees and the undergrowth along the riverbank. But of course it was deep autumn now. As he recalled, the place had been greener than green that long-ago Sunday in July when he and his family met up with Daed and Mamm and the rest for the picnic.

He'd never forgotten the crest of the river that fateful day. The swiftness of the water, too. *Little Anna never had a chance*, he thought, wishing he'd been standing closer to where she'd fallen in. *I might've saved her.*

The thing that got Melvin through the worst times—and surely his parents, too—was the hope of seeing Anna again in Glory. He needed to just set his mind on that and not let it fade away.

"What do you recall most about that day?" Tilly asked, falling in step with him while Ruthie wandered off on her own.

He'd come for this very reason—to remember. "Well, it was Ruthie, Josie, and little Anna—the three of them—moseying toward the river, if I'm not fuzzy on that. The older girls were laughing and talking, but Anna was smirking, looking back at me. Hard to forget that." Melvin coughed a little, nearly overcome. "I thought she was daring me, wanting me to do again what I'd just done ten minutes before."

"Oh? What was that?"

He led Tilly slowly to the river's edge, close to the actual spot on the embankment where Anna had tried to mimic Melvin's stunt that terrible day. "Poor little girl, she saw me and must've thought it was easy to balance herself—and right there, of all places." He pointed to the exceptionally narrow ridge where he'd last seen Anna, her tiny wavering arms stretched wide. "She tried to walk as though on a tightrope, hovering frighteningly near the roaring river." He shook his head. "It was my blunder . . . I'm to blame for it. Shoulda been more responsible." He mopped his eyes with his kerchief now, unable to continue.

Tilly looked stunned. "But I was the one who turned my back—I thought she was safe with Ruthie and Josie." Her voice cracked. "She must've toppled. It happened so fast!"

Solemnly, he nodded. "I shoulda known better."

Tilly pushed her hand through the crook of his arm. "Oh, Melvin, and you've lived with this for so awful long. I'm so sorry . . . so very sorry." She paused. "I, too, have carried guilt for her death. I've never told a soul, but Anna bickered with me that morning—and a few days earlier, as well." Tilly began to share the things their little sister had said. "At the time, I tried to overlook it as mere childishness, but I was tired of her feisty attitude and insisted she obey me—demanded it. She did not seem very receptive to what I'd said . . . not right away."

"Well, to your credit, she could be a handful. Susannah had to reprimand her for bein' lippy nearly every time we baby-sat her."

Tilly looked shocked. "And here I thought it was just me she got sassy with."

"She was just a little tyke, still learnin' to obey an' all." Melvin shook his head. "Wasn't her fault she fell in, though."

"No . . . not at all." Tilly sounded like she was crying. "Nor was it yours, dear brother."

Arm in arm, they stood watching the river flow past them. Melvin said he hadn't been able to return there after that summer. "I'm glad I could come here with you today, close a ya always were to her. I hope ya know how Anna looked u to you. She loved ya so."

"And I loved her. If I could go back and live that day ov I would never have let her out of my sight. Never," Tilly gripping his arm, her hand trembling. "Anna would be fourteen if she'd lived . . . ever think of that?"

"*Jah*, I do. And often. Daed would soon have his work cut out for him, fending off would-be beaus. Doubt any of 'em would have met his expectations." Melvin gave a chuckle. "Ya know, when I contacted you and Ruthie to come for the anniversary party, I never dreamed I'd be standing here spillin' my guts like this."

"Maybe it was time." Tilly smiled at him. "For both of us."

Melvin heard Ruthie calling to them from up a ways. She waved at them dramatically as she sat on an enormous tree limb, high over the river. "You're givin' me the heebie-jeebies up there," he called to her. "Be careful, won't ya?"

Tilly groaned. "I think she must be feeling her oats."

"Freedom does that, I 'spect."

Tilly turned to face him, frowning. "What do you mean?"

"I just think she's better off in Massachusetts near you and your family."

"You honestly believe that?"

"In Ruthie's case, I do." He wasn't going to say what he knew about Will Kauffman's inability to follow through with much of anything, not to mention the lad's clumsiness with road horses. Will had good intentions, but he still needed to grow up, and then some.

"*Denki, Bruder* . . . means a lot."

Melvin led her back to the car, away from the river. He heard Ruthie running up behind them, calling to them, sounding like a young girl again. "I'm glad you both came to Eden Valley to see us," he said as they all got back into Tilly's car to head to his place.

"We are, too," Ruthie piped up from the backseat. "Aren't we, sister?"

Tilly started the car and smiled at him. "I wouldn't have missed it for anything, Melvin. Not for the world." She laughed at what she'd said. "Well, you know."

They exchanged glances, and he was laughing now, too.

"Will you keep us posted on Daed's health?" Tilly asked before they arrived back at his farm.

"I intend to, *jah*."

"You have my address," Tilly said.

"And you . . . why don't ya send Susannah and me a note from time to time, if ya don't mind."

Tilly leaned over and squeezed his hand. "So good to hear your side of things today. At long last. You have no idea how much it meant to me."

"Almost said the same." He cleared his throat as tears threatened. "Next time, don't wait so long to visit."

Ruthie got out of the car when he did and wrapped her arms around his neck, warming his heart down to his toes. "I never, ever expected to return to Eden Valley," she said, eyes blinking up at him. "But I'm so happy I did."

He stood there, watching them go, back to the outside world. And now that he'd spent some time with Tilly and Ruth, he wouldn't say that it was a terrible thing they lived fancy. No, he couldn't say that at all.

When he no longer could see Tilly's red dot of a car, Melvin turned and headed for the barn, then changed his mind and walked toward the house instead. He went in and kissed Susannah soundly, catching her off guard, sniffing to see if her delicious rolls were ready to sample.

"Well, ain't you somethin'," his wife said, surprising him with a kiss right on his lips.

"When's dinner?"

"When do ya think?" she joked. "Same time as always."

He chuckled, cheered by the sameness of his life, a regularity he embraced, and thankful for his daily routine around the farm, the fertile soil entrusted to him as a gift from the Lord God above. Mighty glad, too, for things like a creaking windmill, his holey work boots, and the warm knit sweater Susannah had recently made for him. *I'm just plain grateful for life.*

Sunset was not far off, and the evening sun shone in a spectacular way on the Rockport harbor this time of year, making for golden views. Tilly wondered if Kris's mother might have supper waiting.

"Are you all right?" she asked her sister, who'd joined her up front for the long drive home.

"How's it possible to experience heartbreak and relief at the same time?"

Tilly nodded. "I'm sorry you had to relive that old pain."

"It's okay, really." Ruth explained how she'd privately worried if she could even cut it as an Amishwoman anymore. "Especially being as submissive as expected . . . and the whole mindset in the Plain community. And oh, the hard work! Many things would've been difficult for me, as you can imagine." She talked about how she'd struggled with the idea of joining church there, after enjoying such a different type of worship in Rockport. "I guess, if things had worked out between Will and me, I might've been able to compromise somehow . . . if he had been willing. Somehow I doubt he would have." She shrugged. "Who knows now."

Tilly listened, aware that Ruth sounded much more composed today. *More sure of herself.*

"But, to tell you the truth, I'm not sure I wasn't looking for an excuse."

The thought had crossed Tilly's mind, too. "I think you made a good choice," she encouraged her. "No looking back."

"Sometimes, I guess you just have to get the past out of your system. Maybe I was trying to live out what might've been."

"Hmm . . ." She nodded.

They pulled into a gas station at the top of a hill, overlooking their postcard-worthy little town, and Tilly asked if Ruth wanted to join her and the family for supper.

"That would be nice. And I'd like to see the twins . . . seems like eons."

Tilly laughed. "You're not sounding very Amish anymore."

"Eden Valley almost feels like a dream to me now. Were we really there?"

Tilly realized she, too, felt nearly the same.

"Hey . . . we forgot to stop by the cemetery before we left," Ruthie said, getting out of the car to stretch her legs while Tilly pumped gas.

"I thought of it after we dropped off Melvin but decided I'd had enough gloom for one day," Tilly said.

"You didn't look miserable, though, walking along the river with our brother."

"It was a blessing, really." She wouldn't go into the things Melvin had shared, and regarding precious Anna, there was really nothing more to say. Their little sister had been taken early—their heavenly Father's supreme will, whether Tilly or

Melvin thought they had been responsible or not. Tilly had to let herself step out in faith, wholly trusting in the sovereignty of God, knowing that the sufferings of life didn't have to crush her but could instead draw her closer to the Savior.

Tilly realized, while overlooking the radiant harbor, that sometime in the past week, she had also forgiven herself. Somewhere on Amish soil, where heaven touched earth in Eden Valley.

EPILOGUE

*K*ris's kitchen chair scraped back against the floor when Ruthie and I walked into the kitchen that first evening home. The twins came running from the family room—oh, did they ever! So much love, and I was wrapped in it times three as my husband and Jenya and Tavani squeezed me into their happy circle. *"Mommy's home!"* There'd even been a few hugs to spare for Ruthie, as well.

Weeks later, close to Thanksgiving, when things had settled down for Ruthie, she confided in me that her young man from church wanted to court her—the English way, of course. I was delighted to see the quiet joy in my sister's eyes, to know she was valued by someone who truly seemed to know the path God had set before him. Ruthie feels sure a marriage proposal is in her near future, and this time, she'll have no hesitations!

Since our trip, letters have been coming from both Mamm and Melvin, and one from Josie, too—she's expecting another baby, come next summer. It's really wonderful, knowing the love of family continues to blossom there in our first home.

While at Ruthie's recently, a letter arrived from Daed addressed to her—unheard of. As we sat, rather shocked, in her comfortable living room with its contemporary trappings, I told my sister I doubted he'd ever written a letter in his life.

"*My dear Ruthie,*" it began. And then, quite unexpectedly, she handed the letter to me to read.

"Are you sure?" I glanced at the scrawled handwriting. She said she was, and I saw why—her eyes were already filling with tears. "Aw, sister . . ."

"I'm nervous—no telling what he's written."

Words can hurt. I knew this.

She motioned for me to read it silently. "Please, Tilly," she pleaded, and I knew then she must be worried it related somehow to Will Kauffman.

I'm feeling some better, and I wanted you and Tilly to know. I've even started a woodworking project—making rocking horses for our Kinner—starting with Sammy and Johanna next door. How about that?

Something else, I've agreed to have pacemaker surgery in a few weeks, and I'm asking for your prayers. Jah, I'm uneasy, even though the doctor says it's routine and he's done hundreds of these implants.

Your brother Melvin paid me a visit here lately. I was mighty surprised to hear that Deacon Kauffman's grandson is planning to move out to Ohio—Mount Hope, to be exact. I'm glad he'll be on his way. You were a wise young woman to cut things off right quick, Ruthie—both times. I'm proud of you for having such good sense.

By the way, Josie's holding her breath for another reunion, this one at Christmas. Will you and Tilly think about coming? And if ya do, bring Tilly's Kris and my grand-twins with the interesting names. It would do this old heart mighty good.

Well, it's been a long time coming, but I honestly believe you and Tilly are better off living out there amongst the Englischers—together, like sisters should be.

I hope you'll write back. Either way, you'll be hearing from me. I need to practice my penmanship, for one thing!

Oh, and give my first daughter a greeting, will ya? Tilly's one very special young woman, for sure.

> *Your Daed,*
> *Lester Lantz*

"What is it?" Ruthie asked, seeing me brush back tears.

"Who would have thought he could write like this?" I handed the letter to her. "There's nothing to fret about, and every reason to smile."

"Truly?"

"Read it and rejoice." I got up and walked to her kitchen, where the teapot was simmering, and I went to stand below the beautiful wall hanging Ruthie had made years before. I stared at it and thought of Daed—yes, my father. So very grateful for Ruthie's urging us home.

Tilly's one very special young woman, Daed had written. Something I'd never expected to hear from his lips, nor see in print.

"Thank you, Lord," I whispered. "Thanks for the trials that make me stronger."

∞

On Thanksgiving Day afternoon, once Kris's parents said their loving good-byes, Kris, the girls, and I began making plans to go to Lancaster County for Christmas.

"Can we milk the cows?" Tavani asked, big-eyed.

"*I* don't want to do that . . . I want to swing on the rope in the hayloft!" Jenya declared.

Kris chuckled at his girls' cheer. "Since we're naming off our wishes, I'll admit that I'm looking forward to having my first taste of mincemeat pie." He was grinning.

"You don't have to leave home for that, hon," I said, promising to make the delicious dessert soon.

Tavani babbled about learning to talk Pennsylvania Dutch "chust maybe." The twins giggled and decided which stuffed animals to take along.

"Are you sure about this?" I asked, studying Kris.

"Isn't it about time we blended with your Plain family?" He winked. "But I might need a pair of suspenders before we go—and I could sprout a beard, too. I'd like to fit in."

I tossed the dish towel at him . . . then, laughing, found my way into his loving embrace.

AUTHOR'S NOTE

The Conestoga River captured my attention one October afternoon two years ago—it seemed to call to my heart. I was preparing for the final shoot of the long day, the last segment of my documentary, "Glimpses of Lancaster County with Beverly Lewis" (available via my website, www.beverlylewis.com, or on YouTube). We were set up right near the historic Hunsecker's Mill Bridge, and I had walked down the grassy slope to review what I'd planned to say, inching my way toward the wide river. There, as I stared at the rushing water, Tilly's story presented itself to me, as did little Anna's drowning. In that moment, I knew I had to write *The River*, with all of its heartrending yet redemptive threads.

I will long remember the surge of emotions, the power of the story. And the way the river seemed to demand top billing in my lineup of Eden Valley characters.

There were many wonderful people who assisted me during the development of this novel, including my own dear father, who, as he always did, prayed daily for its themes to touch readers' hearts. Then, in the wee hours of January 9, 2014, he slipped peacefully away to join the Church Triumphant.

Even though it may not be theologically correct, I like to think of Dad, my great encourager, looking over my shoulder as I wrote *The River*.

I also wish to offer my enduring gratitude to David Horton and Rochelle Glöege, for their expert editorial work and friendship; Dave Lewis, for reading the first manuscript, for making dinner when I was on deadline, and for fully understanding the challenging life of a writer; Martha Nelson, for listening to the story lines with cheerful support; Barbara Birch and Julie Garcia, for early chapter readings; Jenya and Tavani, for lending their beautiful names; Roswell and Sandra Flower, Alice Henderson, Donna DeFor, Jim and Ann Parrish, Dave and Janet Buchwalter, Aleta Hirschberg, Iris Jones, Judy Verhage; Dale, Barbara, and Elizabeth Birch, and many other prayer partners, including Facebook friends, for answering the call of intercession; Hank and Ruth Hershberger, for accurate translation and spelling of *Deitsch*; Barbara Birch, for final proofreading; Don Kraybill, for his proficient exploration into Old Order Amish culture; and last but never least, my anonymous Amish and Mennonite research assistants, for their joyful willingness to be "on call."

And finally, a couple of notes in closing: Abner Mast's jovial personality is modeled after my own cheerful uncle Fred Jones, though the beard is all Abner's! Lastly, the Strasburg Creamery was not in existence in the early 1970s, when Ruth was being courted by Will Kauffman; however, because I am so very fond of this quaint little country store, I've chosen to take a slight liberty for this story and include it.

Soli Deo Gloria!

Beverly Lewis, born in the heart of Pennsylvania Dutch country, is the *New York Times* bestselling author of more than ninety books. Her stories have been published in eleven languages worldwide. A keen interest in her mother's Plain heritage has inspired Beverly to write many Amish-related novels, beginning with *The Shunning,* which has sold more than one million copies and was made into an Original Hallmark Channel movie. In 2007 *The Brethren* was honored with a Christy Award.

Beverly has been interviewed by both national and international media, including *Time* magazine, the Associated Press, and the BBC. She lives with her husband, David, in Colorado.

Visit her website at www.beverlylewis.com or www.facebook.com/officialbeverlylewis for more information.

More From Bestselling Author
Beverly Lewis

To find out more about Beverly and her books, visit beverlylewis.com or find her on Facebook!

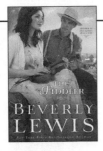

Journey home to Hickory Hollow, the setting where Beverly's celebrated Amish novels began in *The Shunning*! With her trademark style, this series of independent books features unforgettable heroines and the gentle romances her readers have come to love.

HOME TO HICKORY HOLLOW: *The Fiddler, The Bridesmaid, The Guardian, The Secret Keeper, The Last Bride*

Desperate to find her long-lost daughter, Kelly Maines is thrilled when her private investigator finds a local girl who fits the profile. She arranges a "chance" meeting with the girl's guardian, Jack Livingston, and it goes well—so well, in fact, that he asks her out on a date. But when she starts falling for Jack, can Kelly come clean about her motives and risk losing everything?

Child of Mine (with David Lewis)

BETHANYHOUSE

More From Bestselling Author
Beverly Lewis

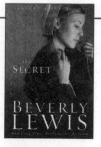

When her mother's secret threatens to destroy their peaceful Amish family, will Grace's search for the truth lead to more heartache or the love she longs for?

SEASONS OF GRACE: *The Secret, The Missing, The Telling*

Their Amish community has been pushed to the breaking point, and Nellie and Caleb find themselves on opposing sides of an impossible divide. Can their love survive when their beliefs threaten to tear them apart?

THE COURTSHIP OF NELLIE FISHER: *The Parting, The Forbidden, The Longing*